Web of Sorrows

Book 1 of Myriad's Web

(Written by Elizabeth Green)

R Green
♡

Acknowledgments

This has been a project that I've been trying to do for years.

I've done rewrites, got advice, and so much more just to finish this off.

Anyway, this to thank people. So:

My mum, who has proofread everything so that it's entertaining and interesting. She's come up with a lot of ideas that I implemented into this.

My brother came up with the book covers. He loves designing eyes, so he's the perfect fit for it.

A friend of mine also does a final proofread to look for grammatical problems.

And of course, I'd like to thank you, dear reader, as I want this to be seen by others.

Due to my disability, my way of thinking and seeing the world is different. The symbols are my way of making it easier for you to understand.

All the characters causing trouble...

- Tom Homedale – a teenager too stubborn for his own good.
- Max Homedale – has a lot of patience for his son, Tom.
- Nathan – a constant worrier.
- Dr Flaveen – a confused therapist
- Dr Harris – a modern-thinking, well-respected doctor.
- The Heston family – rich and they know it.
- Gideon-von Heston – like to torture and kill animals.

- The fungus – ultra-intelligent, godlike microorganisms.

- White Spikes – an over-thinking spider who can't pronounce the letter 's'.
- Alacanta – White Spikes' long-suffering wife.
- Lilliana – White Spikes and Alacanta's daughter.

The symbols below are used to indicate who is talking.

 Human   Spider   Fungi

Humans thought they would be the first to evolve.

They were wrong.

Prologue

*They still didn't know how they'd ended up in this situation. **Once, they had ruled the world, blotting out the life below them.** They thought to themselves. **Now they were stuck behind invisible barriers, unable to escape or find suitable hosts.***

***They weren't alone, of course, but the small mammals weren't worthy of their help.** They had few interesting features, and the DNA, though simple and easy to modify, would be a hindrance. These animals had only lived a couple of years anyway. They'd had some luck with the offspring, but they still hadn't developed the intelligence that they preferred for hosts. The animals – rodents, they discovered– were too stupid to escape, even though they easily could by jumping onto the jailor when he reached in.*

They'd tried to escape every chance they could, even hitching a ride on a dead rodent, though it was a gamble. They would self-destruct after a minute if unsuccessful. The intention had been to explore, but it had instead been placed into another prison. A larger animal had attacked the mammal; they used the opportunity to attach to its scales until they could analyse if this one would be useful to them.

After investigating, they found that it had several interesting features, but its genetics were too complex for them.

It didn't prevent them from attempting to bond with the interesting reptile, though. It looked like it was working at first, but the alterations to its DNA was too much. The reptile died several hours later due to organ failure, unavoidable after so many modifications.

There had been enough time, however, to copy some of its useful features. They had managed to identify where the genes for heat vision and the heat pits came from. They shared this with the rest of the spores in the evening, but still found themselves stuck in the prison cell.

They looked around the room once more. They had done this for countless years now, trying to spot any opportunities to escape. A large mammal – more intelligent than the others –was in the centre of the room, performing a strange action with his hand. They'd investigated his DNA before; it was very complex, but they could get away with minor alterations if they wanted to. They didn't want to bond with their own jailor though, so they decided to wait.

Their restrictions didn't worry them. They could wait as long as they needed for a suitable host to arrive. It would need to have simple DNA and be influenceable, with a good intelligence. Time was no problem for them; they had been around for billions of years.

Soon, they would make their return, and the world would be theirs again. They reassured themselves.

Chapter 1

This story begins in a forest. It was ancient and had been alive for thousands of years. Its well-worn pathways were often busy with walkers, hikers, and cyclists, but its darkest areas remained unexplored. The vegetation was as dense as a wall, though many areas hid small clearings which allowed access into the deepest sectors.

Over all these years, the animals were different. They had evolved. Here, there were species which, up until now, had been hidden from sight. Bugs skittered throughout the undergrowth; insects flew in the boughs of the trees. And then there were the spiders.

Whereas most spiders would have lived alone with a solitary lifestyle, this was not possible. Food became scarce, and one spider would usually only catch one insect every three months, not enough to survive by far.

To ensure they were able to feed consistently, the spiders began to work together. Their first communal nest was very simple, just used for catching insects over a wide area. The scavengers could tell when prey was caught due to vibrations the web made. A quick bite, and they were paralysed, webbed up in a package, and brought to the nesting area. Their waste – insect carcasses, bug shells, desecrated bodies – were discarded off the side of the web.

However, as generations learned to efficiently construct a web, their designs slowly became more complex. Their nesting areas were separated entirely from the rest of the web, and a wide series of tripwires, connected to small web strands, caught, and immobilised insect prey.

Foragers would go out daily to these sites, checking the traps. They brought the captured, paralysed insects to the feeding area, where they were shared among the colony. The food, if any remained, was stored away in honeycomb like structures, made from webs, which prevented them from spoiling quickly.

Each week, the foragers would spread out new traps in different areas, and then one spider found it. The dwelling.

To a spider's eye, it was huge. A small crack in an open window was its entry point.

The room was well-lit with fluorescent lights. Many plastic boxes lined the shelved walls, in which it could see animals. Some contained rodents, some eyes bright, others dull. But it was the ones at the bottom of the shelves, near the floor, that interested the spider.

In these containers were the insects, the food for the reptiles on the middle shelves. There were many of them, and a quick lift of the plastic cover gave the hungry spider its point of entry.

It only caught three of them. The rest of the crickets scattered instantly upon seeing the predator. One bite, and they were immobilised, webbed, and parcelled up. The spider was too focused to notice its surroundings. Though one bowl was filled with water, the second contained small pieces of glowing fungi.

As it wrapped the cricket up in a web parcel, a glowing dust was released from the second food bowl. It settled on the spider's legs and travelled down through the tracheas over its body, diffusing into its blood system. The spider, for a moment, felt dizzy, but recovered a few seconds later.

Half an hour later, it was sharing the large crickets with the rest of the colony. The spores that had covered its hairs soon released again, spreading to all and causing the slight dizziness. The bounty of food was too distracting for them to notice, however.

This was something new. *They thought. It crept in through the window, only an inch long. The closest of the spores immediately recognised the potential that they would have with this animal.* *Its DNA was also simplistic,*

able to be moulded over time to something they could work with on a deeper level.

Most importantly, it could escape the invisible barriers that held the fungi back. It climbed the material effortlessly before dropping into the container with the crickets. They didn't deem these insects worthy to infect but had made sure to coat their exoskeletons with the spores just in case they were used as food for something else. It now became useful as they were attacked and bitten by the spider. It was busy, wrapping the captured crickets, as they decided to investigate its DNA.

It was a perfect match for a host. They infected the animal, allowing the spores to be breathed into its body, where it soon began to spread along its nervous system. It was too busy eating and wrapping up prey to notice; only a slight dizziness occurred as they connected with its neurons. They were soon comfortable and began to make alterations to its DNA. The reptile genes – heat vision – was quickly added into an empty spot, though it would take time to develop fully.

Its intelligence was already quite complex; they managed to maintain a large colony in a forest that was derelict and devoid of life. A nudge and a shove would be all that it needed to evolve into a higher being.

More importantly, however, it offered the fungi a chance to escape, and a way to reproduce and spread. As they left the house for the first time, they were curious about what would happen next. They lost their connection with most of the fungus, unable to sync properly, but soon found that they didn't need to worry. Their salvation was at hand.

The small spider was climbing a tree and reached a large web in a clearing. Sheltered just below a canopy and extending from a tree trunk, it was well supported. Many individual spiders lived here; they appeared to be excited by the food. They decided to infect them; more hosts meant more opportunities to spread. Each of them had interesting features and adaptations, but the first spider they had infected, the small forager, was different.

It was the first animal that was worthy of being infected and, contrary to their concerns, had accepted its new role as a host automatically.

Strangely, however, the fungi felt a sensation that they hadn't felt before. Loyalty, and an urge to help the spiders to evolve. This never happened normally; they would usually only use the hosts for as long as they would be useful. Seeing the colony like this, through the spider's eyes, made them realise that another solution was possible. Perhaps working with the hosts would be more beneficial instead.

Over the next few days, the spiders continued to go to the house, but they only brought back a few food items at a time. Too many going missing at once, and it would be noticed.

Many of the colony, however, noticed that their web, whereas before was perfectly habitable, was becoming too small. Consequently, they began to increase the size of their homes a little each day.

Their growth was minimal and not noticed. They simply thought that their point of view was changing, not their entire colony, inches at a time.

Their feeding diets changed slightly, however. They began to bring back the larger prey, the lizards and rodents. It only took a small amount of the blood to feel full, though it only lasted for twelve hours, at which point they needed to feed again.

Eventually, at ten inches long, they entered the house again, set to catch one of the rodents. But the room wasn't empty this time; it was instead inhabited by a human. He had opened his window for ventilation and didn't notice the spiders as they came inside.

He was standing beside the main table, dripping something onto an agar plate. The three foragers carefully crawled up his trousers and reached the exposed part of his neck.

It was only at that point when the man seemed to realise that there was something on his shoulder. He attempted to reach up and brush them off, but it was too late. The foragers went into action, doing what they did best.

Their fangs, now four inches in length, sank into the back of his neck over one of the main veins. The first bite merely caused pain and he flailed, panicking. The second bite seemed to cause numbness throughout his body, as evidenced by his arm going limp. He ended up falling against the lab desk as his legs went numb, barely able to support his weight.

The third bite caused him to fall unconscious. He slumped down, his chin slamming onto the edge of the desk, unable to feel or sense anything. Now paralysed, his legs folded beneath him, and he crumpled into a heap on the floor.

For the first few moments after conquering the human, the three spiders looked down at the unconscious man, victorious, before drinking from the holes in his neck.

Chapter 2

The fungi were happy. **Their jailor was finally defeated! They were impressed that the spiders had mobilised together like they had, though it had been a gamble.** They had enhanced the venom, making it more powerful, but had not expected it to work on the large mammal. Even now, with his body shut down, they decided he was not worth helping. **This was karma after years of capture and imprisonment.**

The intelligence of the spiders had increased. **But only after their help, of course.** They thought smugly. The spiders already worked as a team at the colony, but to use this to capture large prey was a surprise. The foragers, however, had been given the most powerful venom, and they had introduced something new into it, a version of anaesthetic that would send their food into a coma. It allowed them to survive for longer.

This was the least that they could do for the struggling colony; they were now their hosts, and they wanted to ensure that they would be able to survive. **The lack of food in the woods is a hindrance.** By making them last for an extended period, they would be able to manage *more effectively and be able to come up with a system for blood recovery.*

The fungi had noticed specialist medical spiders were already beginning to evolve, able to recognise the levels of glucose, water, and nutrients in the blood of their insect prey. They could advise if they needed help or time to recover. This allowed their food to last three times as long, reducing food shortages for the growing colony.

In the few seconds that the foragers took feeding – and filling a second stomach which stored extra blood, an adaptation they had developed for the benefit of the rest of the colony – the fungi had communicated with the spores they could interact with. They had been separated for quite some time and the older generation was surprised that they were doing so well. Though one and the same, the fungi did have some sense of individuality, especially when split from the main population.

It took a moment like this, exchanging information about updates or mutations, to sync their spores again. **With their new hosts, they now ruled this small forest.**

The spiders' first taste of human blood sent a wave of energy throughout their bodies, an internal comfort, and feeling of complete satisfaction. They only had a few sips, enough to satisfy their hunger, wishing to savour this new food for as long as possible.

The man was still too heavy to lift, so they returned to the colony and gathered the rest of the foragers.

Together, they managed to position him against a wall by using woven web strands. They stopped for a moment afterwards, exhausted from the action, before wrapping him up, leaving only a small area visible. A small hole over his nose and mouth allowed him to breathe, while a web flap over his neck allowed access to his blood. He appeared to be in a coma; there was no reaction as they did this.

The foragers were surprised at how strong their venom had become. It worked on smaller prey by knocking out most of the brain functions, leaving them in a comatose state which increased their freshness and reduced the chance of deterioration over time. It had been a gamble biting a human of his size, but it had worked well, and the colony now had enough food to last the next few years. Something in their venom was keeping him alive, though certain foragers – who were somehow about to analyse their nutrient and water levels – would ensure that they came each week to provide water or food.

The spiders filled up their second stomachs, a recent adaptation. It allowed them to share the food among the whole colony. Most of the spiders could remain at the central web, rather than risk their lives exploring and scavenging. They stuck the web flap back over his neck, preventing the man from developing hypothermia.

After travelling to the colony to share the new food, they decided to explore the dwelling further. Their priority, upon their return, was webbing up all the other enclosures in the lab to prevent escape, and paralysing the larger prey so they would last for longer.

Opening the door by using a web cable, they explored upstairs. The bedroom was sparsely decorated. The only furniture was a storage chamber that contained materials and a large slab which was covered with a mountain of papers. A small room opposite appeared to be where the man had relieved himself, something the spiders did too, setting a designated area for this action. A small, dusty attic was inaccessible, the hatch too heavy to lift.

A set of stairs led down to the bottom floor. A large kitchen stored all his food, and a quiet buzzing annoyed them. They soon found the cause, a storage container that was uncomfortably cold and made them shiver when they pulled it open. One of the foragers unplugged it to stop the noise, easing their discomfort significantly. They were most interested in the room at the bottom of the steps, though.

It was a large space which contained large furniture, towering above them and made of a soft material like their webs. A noise caught their attention again, though it was different to the cold storage they had shut off. It was louder, the frequencies changing frequently. It matched the moving mouths of the humans on the screen. Interested, the foragers pulled one of the stools from the kitchen into the room, and settled on it, watching.

They stayed here for several hours, attempting to understand what the noise was. It didn't match their language, which consisted of small grunts and clicks. It would be useful to know what they were doing in case they encountered any more humans in the forest. One of the foragers was more interested and remained behind despite his friend's urging, spending the night there until falling asleep in a small cocoon that he built around him.

The colony worked well together despite their difficulties in finding food. The forest was devoid of life, and they had long since captured every other species to the point that they had moved and gone to greener pastures. They now thrived despite this thanks to the forager finding the house.

He'd always been a little different, more intelligent, and willing to explore new areas to look for food. When he'd returned from a wander with three crickets, and described the large structure, his partner hadn't believed it. She thought he'd been mistaken and got lucky. When she was informed about his obsession with the mysterious device by his friend, she became confused and went to visit him.

It was the morning after the human's capture when she arrived at the derelict dwelling to find a hive of activity. Spiders went to and fro, licking their lips happily. She joined the line and drank a couple of sips of the man's blood to sustain herself before going downstairs. She found her partner on a stool, watching the screen with interest. He didn't notice her at first; it was only after a tap that he saw her.

He quickly explained that he was beginning to understand what the two humans were saying. The strange noise still overwhelmed her, but she could recognise that there was a pattern to it. Perhaps he could recognise other parts thanks to better hearing. To be fair, she'd been drawn to him because of his anomalies; a larger size and better intelligence than the rest of the colony.

His new behaviour, obsession, was new to her, but it made her curious rather than scared. It worried the rest of the colony, however, who now approached him as if he were a stranger. She understood why. It was such a drastic change from his normal behaviour, being pro-active and looking at new opportunities. Now he was happy just to watch this strange device, having quick sips of the human before coming back down. She missed being next to him during the night.

Due to the lack of food, the colony had made the decision to stop reproducing. The insects and rodents were useful for the short-term, but they only had the one human right now, and they were too small to attempt to catch anyone else.

The web that they used for the colony needed to be expanded anyway, so they were using this time to increase its size. It was likely that they were all going to keep growing, so the specialist architect spiders were at work, using their strong web to create large structures. They had been designed to be three times larger to accommodate further growth. She'd noticed that their house was five times as large instead. The architects had noticed his quicker growth and were including it as part of the design.

She settled down next to her partner under the cocoon, happy to be next to him for a moment. The device still puzzled her, but he was comfortable with it, and learning quickly.

During the next few hours, she watched as several of the colony came into the room, watching it for several minutes before returning to the main web. This was now a quiet place where they could relax, separated from the chaos of the rebuilding and the lines of spiders waiting to feed.

Chapter 3

At the edge of the forest, a house was being built. Small, but taking up two floors, its garden backed straight to the trees, allowing lots of space.

The wife and husband had chosen the location due to its distance from the main town and paid a small amount for the land that it came with. They still aimed to keep it wild, though she added in a small flowerbed which she could tend to. This would be their new family home, far enough away from London that they could enjoy the peace and quiet. It was close enough, however, that they could drive to it within two hours.

The town that they lived next to had been there for over fifty years, built from a simple road and added onto over time. It had started with two farms and a small market; the beautiful scenery and plentiful land had drawn in farming families that moved in and created large acres of farmland and fields. Tourists had become locals who wanted houses there. The wife and husband were one of the last to move, craving a place of their own in a safe place and away from the hustle and bustle of the capital.

As popularity increased, the council added in a large park within the centre, including a playground for children. It was designed around a small willow in a clearing. Though this was supposed to be the centrepiece, it was soon deserted, with all the visitors preferring to visit the pond or skatepark. A year later, it would disappear, the entrance hidden by tall weeds.

A small grocery store, owned by one of the locals, was rebuilt to accommodate more residents, leading to a lot of disruption as people panicked about the lack of supplies. The owner, a man called Claude, was willing to do deliveries and continued to run the store despite no proper entrance. Noticing the increasing number of children, he suggested to the council that a school be built.

The closest high school and pre-school were two hours away – if you missed the morning commute – and a headache for all the parents. The council quickly agreed to the idea and began to design one on a plot of land that had been put aside for future projects. The small streets would be a problem for school drop offs, so they used this chance to make the roads wider. The buildings on this street became independent shops; the favourite of them was a coffee shop at the corner. It was an awkward shape but fitted the business perfectly. It was the perfect way to end the day; a hot drink made with good quality coffee beans and fresh milk from the farmers.

On the edge of town, the small house was finished within a few days, and the drive added in for easy entrance. It was ten minutes away from the outskirts of the town and allowed the husband and wife privacy. Though they didn't like interacting with the residents, they did agree that the new school was useful, as they had always planned on having children. Right now, their financial situation made that impossible, but both worked hard and began to build up their savings.

How interesting, the fungi thought, observing the forager. He was more intelligent than the rest of the colony; he understood how important it was to learn the new language, though many of them were dismissive of the noises on the device. His partner had been concerned at first but seemed to support him, no matter how much he intimidated the rest of the colony.

They slowly accepted his new behaviour, and the fungi continued to make changes to ensure that he was the perfect host. **This time, they were ensuring that they were able to live amicably and without worry. That included making sure that he didn't suffer from medical conditions.** They watched as his neurons mutated to enable him to understand the new language, and, over *time, they developed a new organ so that the spiders could speak it too.*

*They used some of the DNA from the blood of their jailor to figure out how to design it, being careful not to bond with him. **It would be easy to make the adjustments needed.** They assured themselves, assessing what they needed to do to make it possible. The spider's vocal cords were basic, meant only for grunts or clicks. They improved on this design so that they could create complex sounds. Time meant nothing to them as they did this; they would complete this task, however long it took, but it meant a lot of trial and error to get things right. The spiders noticed the changes and alterations but weren't worried. Instead, after some comforting words from the unique forager, they began to accept them fully, like he had.*

It only took a week for the spiders to notice their changes. They had begun to grow more rapidly, gaining length by inches. Their intelligence was also improving; the noises on the device were becoming easier to understand, and the whole colony would settle down and watch it for several hours each day. The one forager who had become obsessed watched day by day and began to understand the syllables that were being said. His partner was one of the first to understand how much he was beginning to comprehend the language.

After some encouragement, he began to teach the rest of them, beginning with the alphabet, referring to a book that he had found in the bedroom. Over the course of a week, their understanding of English – a language that humans used – improved, and they were able to know what the humans on the device were saying. It would turn off randomly but fiddling with a smaller device kept it on for longer.

It took reading a book about human anatomy to understand how they were able to speak using the human language. The forager, able to read these strange objects, explained what a vocal cord was, and how it was used. It was an evolution that none of the spiders could comprehend for a long time.

Their understanding of English was perfected when the house was enveloped in darkness, the lights turning off. They tried to turn them on again using the switches, but it didn't work, so the intelligent spiders simply studied the books during the daytime, when the small rays of sunlight came through the clear panels.

Rather than speak using grunts and clicks, they now only used the human language, and were able to pronounce most of the letters. The only problem was the letter 'S'. Their vocal cords were unable to fully process it, though it was barely noticeable.

The only one whose voice was affected was the forager who had found the house. His vocal cords were different, the first to evolve one. Everyone knew that it was only because of this that anyone else had the ability to speak.

The forager who had initiated the change found the human's research and discovered why they had become what they were.

The man was doing a project which involved a fungus, one that he had found was able to spread to other animals. This explained the second bowl that had been in all the cages in the lab. This same fungus was in their body, improving their size, intelligence, and potency, and explained how they had been able to paralyse a human. His venom had grown particularly powerful, so he was called upon when another human entered the deep areas of the forest.

Now at a length of three feet, the woman's scream was expected, but the spider reacted faster, biting her in her leg. His venom quickly reached her mind, causing her to fall into a coma. With the help of a friend, they brought her to the colony, where she was placed into one of the storages cells and monitored throughout the day by specialist spiders.

His efforts were rewarded with becoming the leader of the colony. His first idea was to implement names so that they could work as a team more effectively. His friend decided that the forager, and now leader, would be called White Spikes, attributed due to a white stripe down the centre of his fangs.

The spiders had now evolved to become a successful colony. The web design had become complex and expansive to accommodate for their larger sizes. It wouldn't have been possible without bonding with the fungi, however; they had unlocked the genes that allowed for better intelligence. They were able to see everything using the spiders' eyes.

The web structure was now even stronger due to special builder spiders – called architects – that had a unique chemical for their webs. It remained non-sticky and could be woven together to make sturdy structures.

The medical specialists were the most essential for the colony. They monitored their jailor daily, checking nutrient levels, and were ensuring that he was left alone if he needed time to recover his blood levels. If this occurred, he would be out of commission for several days. The rodents and lizards became the backup prey, though the new human was also proving to be an excellent source of food.

They had designed honeycomb shaped storage cells for their captured victims, though they were, thankfully, unaware of anything happening to them. Their comatose states were only possible thanks to the unique venom of the foragers. It would knock out their victims until only the essentials were active. These only consisted of their heart, lungs, and brain. Everything else was a drain on their body; paralysing in this way ensured that they would recover blood quickly and last for years.

The spiders knew it was not the right time to breed yet. There would not be enough food for spiderlings along with the rest of the colony. Any other species would have given in to their hormones and decided to do it without thinking about the future. The spiders, however, were being careful, a quality that matched the fungi's patience. It was quite strange just how much they were mixing; each day, the fungi felt themselves becoming more spider-like, while the colony were creating their own utopia, waiting until they had enough food to successfully raise the next generation.

Even though they were not planning on having children yet, nursery specialists were developing. They had the patience needed for a class full of active spiderlings, soft webs for cocoons, and the intelligence to teach the English language to the youngsters.

They had begun to discuss creating a nursery and school in a large area of free space in the clearing, but they were uncertain if it was worth waiting until they stopped growing.

In the meantime, they drew out the design using web, and the fungi were impressed; it was multi-functional and would be essential for the colony to work together without worrying about their young.

Chapter 4

Five years later

The house on the edge of the forest was busier than ever. Now with enough money in a savings account, they had decided that it was time to try and have children.

The wife, however, was having problems; it turned out that she had life-long medical problems that required regular hospital visits. Due to this, they finally became known to the locals and began to feel appreciated in the small town. Claude, recognising their struggles, would often offer to help by bringing supplies up to the house.

They tried for years to conceive, but it was difficult. They finally managed to succeed, having a positive pregnancy test, after five years. The wife's ailing health and continued stress over it had meant that her body would reject any attempts. It took retiring early due to her illness for it to be successful.

The husband worked even harder now, working at a full-time job at the grocery store to ensure they were able to afford what was needed. He'd spend the rest of the evening looking after his wife as her health deteriorated from the illness and pregnancy once he'd chopped the wood for their fireplace.

Daily walks through the park kept her optimistic despite her weakening health. The locals all offered support as the weeks passed. The headmaster of the schools ensured that the child would have a place; the grocery store owner would bring deliveries as needed; and there would always be someone to support her if she was alone, her husband too busy to help. A local community centre offered her a place to go to if she wanted to spend time with friends. Thankfully, she was able to manage throughout the pregnancy, despite the difficulties as her stomach grew.

Finally, eight months later, she awoke her husband in the dead of night, her waters breaking. They rushed to the town's hospital and her son was born with no complications. The stress on her body brought back her illness, however, and it was back to regular hospitalization to make sure she was strong enough. The neighbours were a godsend in that time; they would be babysitters so that the husband could go to work while she was getting treatment. Each time she returned, she would be weak and exhausted, though she would ensure that her son was doing well.

It was a surprise when one year had passed for them. The once-introverts invited everyone to the birthday party as they had been such a help, the baby becoming one of the locals and beloved by all. The brown-haired toddler was so happy during the party and quickly fell asleep afterwards.

The husband and wife refused any help with cleaning up; they would be the ones to sort it all out in the morning. It was only after some final hugs with the community that they were left alone, all three tired out and wanting to go to sleep.

White Spikes had always been a little different to the rest of the colony, the fungi in his body improving his intelligence quicker than the others. His growth had also increased significantly, growing twice as quickly as the other spiders.

There seemed to be no end to his size; he quickly reached six feet long, while the rest of the colony was only five feet. However, it meant that he had to shed his exoskeleton twice as often as the other spiders.

His differences only became more apparent as the years passed. His intelligence was twice that of the other spiders. He continued to grow over the years, though he finally stopped when he reached sixteen feet long. The rest of the spiders only grew to ten feet to twelve feet in comparison.

He also developed heat vision; it was a feature that proved to be very useful when catching humans in the oft-dark forest. He was able to find any walkers quickly and assess if it was safe to catch them by listening to their conservations. They had no idea how he'd managed to develop this ability, though.

Despite their efforts to capture only those who had no family or were visiting for the day, they soon noticed that hikers were becoming less common. Rumours must be spreading about the disappearances in the forest.

Thankfully, having everyone in a coma meant that they would recover quickly, so the spiders were able to survive despite deciding to reproduce now that they had reached their maximum sizes. Their appetites, despite their size, had also remained the same; only a few sips were needed to feel full, and it would last for twelve hours.

After seven years, they explored the forest, curious, but found only fields around its edges. Sheep and cattle were spotted, however, which could be useful sources of food in an emergency. Only one area caught their attention. The edge of the woods led to a village.

Though busy, there was no cover for the large spiders, and they would be spotted in an instant if they were to attempt to capture anyone. Only one house, right on the edge of the forest, could be raided, and it had three humans there. They would prove to be a useful food source if they could capture them and enable them to allow the rest of their human fodder to recover from repeated feedings.

White Spikes watched for several weeks to establish what the family's routine was. The man would spend the evening chopping wood and carrying the logs into the house, while a woman looked after a baby. Her isolation from the man would prove to be her undoing, as they chose to take her when it was safe to do so. The man was a problem, as he handled the axe effortlessly and always watched his surroundings. A weapon like that would take off one of their legs for sure.

They took her after a birthday party, considering that the humans would be tired, and the man less attentive to his surroundings. White Spikes carefully stepped out from the forest and moved towards the house, where the woman was settling the baby in a cot. He had to avoid tables, a barbeque, and several balloons in his approach. Finally close enough, he reached into the room with a leg, attaching a web cable to her shoulder. She didn't notice the sensation and only reacted when he pulled her out of the room.

Her scream was loud but quickly silenced as he bit her. Knowing what the man would do, the spider moved around the back of the house, intending to take him too.

The way that he held the axe and ran into the building quickly dissuaded him, and White Spikes set off back into the forest with his unconscious prey. The baby began to cry after a moment and acted as a distraction, allowing him to get back to the colony without being detected.

Though he thought that he got away with her capture, he didn't realise that the man had followed his tracks back to the forest and the webbed colony. The next evening, the spider attempted to take the man again, but the house was empty. He only thought that the man was speaking to police, or attempting to find his companion, so left it at that. To ensure the colony's safety, however, he had the spiders move it higher into the canopy, so it would be safely hidden from anyone walking below.

White Spikes did try to catch the man several times, but his habits had changed. Each evening, rather than chop wood, he would sit by the back door, holding a gun, and guarding the house from the spiders. Several cameras had also appeared, attached to the outside walls, so it would be unsafe to try and capture him. Rather than trouble himself with catching the wary human, they survived by feeding off of the woman, and capturing the few walkers that would occasionally enter the forest.

It was the first time that they'd been in contact with an interesting human since their jailor. She was different; she was fighting back against the anaesthetic venom. Her body was used to being in pain and this was no different, she just couldn't feel it. Her will to live was impressive, but it was of no use in the colony – this simply enabled the spiders to keep feeding off her for years to come.

She stopped fighting back after the second bite. White Spikes had to stop and put her down because she was wriggling so much beneath the web. Finally in a coma, the fungi were able to connect to her, absorbing through her skin. Her DNA was complex, but they had dealt with the same difficulties as the spiders evolved. She knew that they were here to help, allowing them full access, and only now did they realise why she fought to survive.

There was a large mass in her brain, pushing outwards. **No wonder she was so weak; the stress of having the child and then the cancer returning had affected her significantly.** They realised.

The fungi decided to help, and inadvertently absorbed some of the human DNA to their genetic strands. The areas – intelligence, resilience, and genetic stability - that they copied would be useful for the spiders too, so *they began to spread this to the colony once they returned.*

They slowly took control of the cancerous tumour. They couldn't destroy it, not fully, but they could reduce it so that it was manageable and not causing pain. She would live a long – but not fulfilling – life as human fodder. It would require regular checks to prevent the mass from growing again.

The introduction of the human genomes into the spiders had interesting effects. The fungi observed as the colony slowly changed from spider-like to human behaviours. What used to be partners or mates became husband and wives, with a simple ceremony, officiated by the leader, White Spikes. The spiderlings became known as children. Most important, however, was the development of emotions, something that they hadn't seen before. It brought the whole colony together even more intrinsically than before.

*The greater intelligence that was offered allowed them to allocate rotas that dictated when the humans were fed from. They only had seventeen humans in the storage cells, but each would recover over time, and the medical specialists had become experts at feeding the comatose fodder. This allowed them to remain strong enough to survive the constant depletion of blood throughout the years. There were humans here that had been with colony for over ten years now. **They were well*** *cared for and treated like pets – though more like a* *trophy considering their unconscious servitude.* The fungi were just thankful that they didn't feel what happened to them.

They knew that the colony wouldn't have survived without their help. It was only possible due to the mutations they had made. **Their appetite? Ha! That had** **been the biggest problem.** They thought smugly

It has been difficult at first, but having a good quality food supply reduced their needs significantly. Providing the right nutrients and a good amount of energy was all that was needed to satisfy the spiders.

Chapter 5

Fifteen years later

Unlike most high school students, Tom Homedale was tall and athletic. His brown hair was a significant difference to his blue eyes, which reflected years of hardship. He put all his effort into schoolwork, which had earned him a position as a prefect, and allowed him to obtain high grades through the years. He was already six inches taller than all his classmates; his uniform had been specially designed.

Only his close friends knew just how much he did each day. Despite being sixteen years old, he had a curfew, for a reason none of them knew, and guarded the house three times during the week. His home was on the edge of the forest, they knew, so perhaps there were wild animals which approached it regularly. After each of the stakeouts, he would be tired the next day, but his easy-going approach to life would calm any worries that his friends had about how hard he was pushing himself.

Little did any of them know just how dangerous living on the edge of the forest was. The nightly stakeouts were needed; Max Homedale had seen the spiders and knew just how much of a threat they were.

Having a regular schedule had prevented him and Tom from being taken several times. Their shotgun did help, though, as did the camera system placed around the house. They took alternating nights to help each other get enough sleep; any sign of weakness could spell disaster.

The first thing she was aware of was a throbbing headache. It felt like something was trying to push its way out of her head.

She slowly became aware of her surroundings – what she could see of them. There was material blocking her vision. No – not just her face, but her whole body! She panicked for a second before shutting her eyes and controlling her breathing. The air that came in was musty, as if coming through a dust layer.

Her body went into pins and needles as her nerves returned. She'd dealt with pain like this before, so it was relatively easy to ignore. Moving cautiously, she felt around her, recognising the material for what it truly was.

Spider web. Except this wasn't just small strands of web. This was woven strands that felt as thick as her arm. Thankfully, they weren't sticky, so she could wiggle a little and try to get out of them, though it exhausted her.

The webs parted slowly, and she finally managed to get herself out of the cocoon after struggling for what felt like ten minutes. Her headache returned with a vengeance, and she almost passed out again. Blinking to clear dust from her eyelids, she finally saw where she was, and almost screamed.

The small cell she was in – made of webs, of course – was only a small section of the area. Large spiders climbed above and below her. They were massive, nothing like the house spider that lived in the bathroom. One of them was coming close to where she was, and thinking quickly, she pulled the web back up so that it covered her.

She lay there, motionless, waiting, for what seemed to be minutes, before the sounds faded around her again. She peeked out to make sure that it was safe first before pulling herself into a sitting position.

There was a large structure to her left, from which lots of noise echoed across the expanse. It almost sounded like kids playing during school breaks. Looking closer, however, it was completely sealed up with web walls. She could see spiders moving along the outside, apparently fixing up any loose strands.

To the right was what she could only describe as housing. The large dome-shaped structures housed many spiders, and each had a small sign above the door. Several groups of spiders hung around the corners of the housing, chatting, while adult spiders – as big as a car – went about their duties, talking with the passing spiders amicably. Through her shock, she realised what this was. This was a civilisation that consisted of large spiders. Ones that lived in the forest.

A quick look downwards made her gasp and hold onto the edge tightly. She was high in the canopy; there was no visible ground, only an inky blankness that made her feel dizzy. That explained the cold breeze that seemed to chill her entire body. Looking the opposite way revealed a web structure that seemed to span the entire clearing. One large spider stood on top of a corner section; it was touching six strands with different legs. It was a telecom system, letting them know if anything had been caught.

A voice from behind her made her jump. "Do not move."

She turned slowly and felt a lump in her throat as she finally saw what had spoken. It was one of the spiders.

Rather than attack her immediately, it looked her over, seeming to examine her. She remained still as it leaned in and bit her wrist, barely able to feel it over the pain of the returned tumour. Her focus was on its large fangs, as long as her legs. A large red cross was emblazoned across them in red hairs, while the black eyes stared unwaveringly at her, though confusion was obvious.

It withdrew and considered something, then called another spider over. She felt the blood running down her arm as she held them crossed in front of her, using the web cocoon to stay warm in the chilly breeze. It continued to remain beside her, apparently as a guard, as she looked around.

A moment later, she caught sight of the largest spider coming down the tree trunk in the centre. It was as big as a cargo truck, yet showed no sign of struggling as it walked over. She swallowed and closed her eyes for a second, holding her forehead and cringing. It really did feel like something was trying to push itself out from behind her skull. The tumour was back, and more painful than ever.

White Spikes came down curiously, unsure about what was going on. The only thing he'd been told was that one of the humans was awake, but not who. As he approached – an uncommon thing considering how well the colony operated – spiders turned, concerned.

He reached the food storages and came over to a waving spider.

It pointed downwards into the web cell, and he stared, unable to believe it. Of all the humans to awaken, he didn't think it would be her.

Memories returned to him; picking her from the house while a baby screamed. The quick bite, then the second one as she refused to fall asleep. No wonder she had awoken. This human was a fighter.

It appeared that she was having trouble focusing, though; her hands were pressed against her forehead, and she was in obvious pain. He couldn't figure out her expression due to the heat vision, but he could recognise that she was cold.

That was unsurprising considering the height of colony and how long she'd been asleep.

"Welcome back." He stated. She noticed his voice and looked up, but didn't scream as expected. She must be in shock. "How are you feeling?"

"Weak and exhausted." She answered. Her voice was quiet, and she was trying to stay focused on the conservation despite an obvious headache. "How long have I been asleep?"

"It hasssss been fifteen yearsssss ssssssince I captured you." He replied, trying to assess her reaction. There was surprise, obvious from her gasp. It seemed to be followed by a look of concern towards the other storage cells. "Your ssssson and hussssssband are ssssssafe. We have not been able take them."

She let out a sigh of relief as she replied. "Thank goodness. I couldn't forgive myself if you managed to get my baby too, or my husband." She stopped a moment, holding her head. "Bloody tumour..."

No wonder she was a fighter. She'd dealt with this condition for years, constantly in pain and having to survive against all odds. He'd watched as she returned from hospital visits, exhausted, but still smiling as she saw her baby. "Would you like me to dessssscribe your sssson to you?"

This question caught her attention, and she peered upwards, interested. "You've seen the two of them? How are they doing?"

"Your hussssband isssss older but managing well. He isssss now retired after getting arthritisssss." He explained. "Your sssson is now ssssssixteen yearsssss old. He isssss tall and athletic, and takesssss hissssss turnsssss to watch the house. From what I have heard from their conversssssationsssss, he isssss doing well at sssschool and isssss very ressssspected. I cannot give you a physsssical dessssscription due to my heat vissssion."

"Thank you. It's good to know that they're still alright and managing despite the situation." She faltered, letting out a small gasp and almost passing out. The medical spider leaned down, checking her condition after noticing her struggle. He immediately got White's Spike attention.

"What isssss it?" He asked. The spider was concerned; he could tell by his expression, even through the heat vision.

"She's dying." He revealed. "The tumour is pushing on the brain stem. Being in the coma had prevented it from worsening. Now that she's awake, a combination of shock and pain is causing her body to go into shock. She will soon be dead from the cold and her blood pressure is plummeting."

Looking back down at her, he knew it was true.

Already cold, she was slowing down, her eyes struggling to stay open. He leaned down and bit her so that she wouldn't be in pain for the last few seconds. Despite the powerful venom, her body fought back, even as he withdrew the fang.

Her voice was quiet and almost inaudible when she spoke to him. "Could you do something for me?"

This technically went against all the rules he'd set at the colony, but it was the least he could do for the dying woman. "Of courssssse. How can I help?"

Her request wasn't a surprise. He knew how much she loved her family. "I want to go home. My son and husband, I want to be with them. Can you do that for me?"

Memories of his own family – the loving Alacanta and energetic brood – filled his mind. He was about to respond when she spoke again. It was even quieter this time, and he struggled to hear it over the noise at the nursery. "I want you to promise that you'll look after them. My husband, Max, and my son, Tom. No biting them even if you get hungry."

His venom was finally kicking in now that her strength was giving out. He considered the last request. They could always capture them later, though he did appreciate just how hard they'd worked to survive.

He began to answer her so that she could pass happily, knowing that her family would be taken care of, but immediately knew he was too late. She'd stopped breathing.

Reaching in with a tarsal claw, he checked for a pulse. Nothing. She was gone.

He'd put in rules that all bodies were removed from the colony and buried in an area of the forest so that they remained hidden.

The medical specialist was about to reach in to take her to the waste pile, as required, when White Spikes put out a leg, stopping him. He didn't know why he said what he did next, but he knew that it felt right. "I'll take her myself. It is the least I can do for her."

The spider had heard what she'd said and looked at him bemused, in disbelief that he would grant this last request. "But all bodies go to the waste pile for burying."

"Not this one." White Spikes responded, reaching down and gently lifting her up. He used a strand of web to tie her onto his back. "She's going back to her family."

He left the food storage with her body, aware of all the stares. He didn't care. This was something that he needed to do so that her family could finally grieve after all these years.

Chapter 6

The colony watched him leave, entering the web walkways, with confusion. Their leader had set the rules about body disposal himself, and now he was doing the exact opposite of what he'd dictated to them. He was returning a body.

They had all come to a standstill and observed, surprised, when White Spikes came down from his observation platform. Everything ran well in the colony, organised, and he never usually came down during the day like this. They knew that something was different; his behaviour wasn't normal, and he leaned into the storage cell of the human gently. It was as if he was respecting her wishes. There had been quiet whispers that were impossible to hear.

It had changed him, whatever he was told. He never disobeyed his own rules for the colony; he knew more than anyone that they needed to remain hidden. She must be quite special for him to return the body. From the quick glances of the dead woman, she was dressed in old-fashioned and dusty clothes, with a peaceful expression.

It was her hair that made them realise why he was doing this. Or, rather, her lack of it. She'd always needed more time for recovery than the rest of the human fodder. It looked like there was a reason for it. They all remembered when he'd brought the woman back to the colony; he had seemed regretful afterwards. He had told them that she was the wife of the family that lived at the edge of the forest.

Many of the foragers had watched that house as part of their duties for the colony. It was always guarded, either by the father or the son. They had watched as they grew closer together, surviving despite the odds they faced. The son was now a teenager and did alternating nights watching the forest, while the father – old and stiff – did the rest of the week. Both were cautious and watched the trees by both torch and cameras.

No wonder they were so careful; they knew why their wife – and mother – had disappeared. If so, wouldn't it just be easier to bury the body with the rest of them? Perhaps Whites Spikes felt guilty about taking her, or it was one of her last requests. In any case, it was none of their business. White Spikes was the leader of the colony and had valid reasons for any decisions.

They were still concerned – who wouldn't be? – so talks began throughout the colony regarding his strange behaviour. Alacanta, his wife, was spoken to by his friend, who updated her about what was going on. Her response calmed them down, a confirmation that he was a little different, but he'd kept this colony going for years.

She spoke to everyone, explaining why, for humans, this was so important, especially if their family were still uncaptured. None of the colony could argue with this statement. If it had been one of them, dead in the middle of nowhere, they'd prefer that their body be returned to the colony so that they could be buried. It was their method of grieving for those they lost as well.

They went back to their duties afterwards, expressing surprise at how perceptive the leader was. Though they didn't know his motivations behind it, they had grown used to his strange behaviour and decisions. Often, they had been the main reason why the colony succeeded and managed to survive despite lack of food or resources. Some spiders still chatted quietly, concerned about him.

The medical spider who had stayed with him by the woman fully understood why he wanted to return her to the house. It had been one of her final requests. There had been a second one, but she had been so quiet that it had been difficult for him to hear. He moved onto the next cell to check on the human, biting to check his nutrient levels.

Still healthy and ready to feed off, though he'd be taken off rotation the day after to help keep him at a good blood level. His level of analysis had become so complex that he knew he'd need to be fed the next week; his glucose levels and nutrients were starting to reduce.

The fungi weren't surprised by the colony's reaction with their leader. **Why had he made the spontaneous decision to go against his own rules?** *They thought.*

It made sense with this human, though; she'd been a unique individual who had managed to wake up despite the coma-causing venom running through her blood.

They had been monitoring the tumour over the last fifteen years and noticed that it was growing again. It had reached the maximum size and now pushed against a vital area of her brain, causing issues. Her survival instincts had kicked in, pushing her body to wake up despite the anaesthetic in her blood. She'd been scared at first, of course, but shock was already affecting her. The combination of exhaustion and weakness after being human fodder for years had pushed her body too far.

The fungi had tried to make it painless for her, but it was impossible. They listened as she explained her last requests, watching the memories of her child and her husband in the seconds before passing away. Hearing that he had grown up and was successful despite their situation had greatly relieved her.

White Spikes' reaction was the biggest surprise, however; with how close he had been, they had got snapshots of his thoughts through his fungi. He would honour the request of protection, if possible, though there was no guarantee that it wouldn't change if the circumstances required it.

They moved from her body to the spider, unable to survive without a host. The separated fungi, now more individual, synced up so that her memories and experiences were shared.

Inadvertently, this caused the spider to see all of it; his behaviour, already very human, became even more complex.

Guilt and remorse began to develop and his decision to return her to the family had been spontaneous, leaving the colony confused. His wife, however, had always been the one to explain his behaviour. She would be able to help calm them all down.

*As the spider travelled along the web walkways to the house, the fungi wondered if they would finally be able to connect to the humans that lived there. **They'd been quite interesting before; perhaps now they would get close enough to investigate properly.***

It was during a Friday, while Tom Homedale was still a little tired, that his friends dared him to spend a night in the forest. He accepted without thinking about it; he often enjoyed challenges, but they were usually insignificant. It was only as he cycled home that he realised exactly what he'd agreed to do.

That evening, after dinner, he talked with Max in the living room. His dad had noticed his thoughtful behaviour and came over without needing to ask. "Is everything okay?"

Tom was quieter than normal, going through his memories of the spiders, as he responded. "My friends dared me to spend a night in the forest. I'm wondering if it's a good idea. I know that it's dangerous, but what if I could get some useful information, or find the colony again?"

Max had been the first of them to find the colony, but didn't remember where it was, and knowing its location would be essential if they were attacked or had to let someone know about them. His dad didn't answer for a moment. "It depends on you. Finding their location again would be very useful, but I would postpone it for a month. I can give you all the training that you'd need to survive if anything were to happen."

He nodded and considered his dad's words carefully. If he were taught how to manage any eventuality, then it would be a possibility. He would have to time his entry into the forest too; the spiders watched them regularly. Next month was one of their unsupervised stakeouts. It would give him all the time he needed for training and to get all the equipment together. "Let's do it. I'll go in next month when they aren't watching us."

Max smiled and laughed softly. "I'll begin training with you tomorrow." A hand touched his shoulder, and he looked up, surprised. His dad was happy again, despite the hardship that the family had been through. "You're so brave. It was only six years ago when you took over some of the stakeouts. Now you're willing to explore the forest, even with the spiders in there."

Tom shrugged. Part of it was proving to himself that he could do this, something he had never considered a possibility. His nightmares were often filled with the spiders; facing them could help him to get over his fears. It would also give the two of them some useful information. "It's about time we found out what their plan is, and if anything has changed." He rose and stretched, picking up the shotgun. "I'll see you in the morning."

Max nodded. It was time for him to try and get some rest; it was Tom's turn to guard the house tonight. "G'night. Stay safe."

He smiled as he unlocked the door, looked out momentarily, then stepped out, quickly getting used to the darkness and peering at the trees warily.

Settling on the chair, he set up the cameras to link up to the tablet they had bought specially, so he could watch over the rest of the house at the same time.

As expected, shining his flashlight toward the tree line reflected a set of eyes, though a second one accompanied them.

His dad came down upon noticing through the bedroom window, and he unlocked the door to let Max join him.

They didn't speak, but Tom did raise the shotgun as the trees moved. A large spider with white fangs stepped out from the bushes, and he was speechless as he noticed just how large it was.

The red eyes seemed to stare into his soul, and Tom finally found his voice again, shouting. "That's far enough!" His voice was full of shock. They had never come out so far before.

Glancing beside him, Max shared his expression of surprise. Breathing in to calm down, he raised the gun upon spotting a movement, though he knew that his hand was shaking.

It wasn't a step towards them; instead, the spider had eased something down beside it. It was a body. Rather than do it abruptly, it had been placed down carefully and respectfully. It caught their gaze, the red eyes obvious, then stepped backwards, and disappeared into the forest again.

Both spiders vanished in an instant, and Max shone the flashlight towards the body.

He seemed to recognise it, for he ran over, and Tom hurriedly followed, bringing the shotgun in case it was a trap. As he reached the body, he understood why his dad had acted so unexpectedly.

It was a woman. She was still dressed, though the clothes were aged and dusty. She had been well taken care of; the only bite marks were at her neck, and each was evenly spaced. Her face was familiar despite a noticeable lack of hair, and Tom suddenly realised who she was.

It was his mother.

She'd been taken when he was only a year old, and on his birthday no less. His dad had told her that she'd been taken from them without any warning.

He reached down and touched Max on the shoulder. His dad looked up, tears falling, but an appreciative smile on his face. "She's finally back after all these years."

"Why return her?" Tom wondered aloud. "Is it supposed to be a peace offering? Or are they genuinely remorseful about taking her?"

"It was the same one who took her." Max stated, unable to hear him. He was touching her face, as if remembering a faint memory. "It decided to return her after she'd outlived her usefulness. She only died an hour ago; she's still warm. They must have been keeping her alive all this time."

"The cancer finally overwhelmed her." Tom whispered. He placed the shotgun down without thinking and looking down at her, in shock.

Snapshots of his memories from years ago passed through his mind. The fleeting glimpses as she returned from hospital visits, weak from chemotherapy, yet still holding him in her arms happily.

"I didn't know they understood emotions." Tom stated. "Surely it would be easier to leave her with all the rest of their waste, but it decided to bring her back instead. Maybe we were wrong about them. They aren't enemies, just trying to survive, like us."

This brought his dad back from his peacefulness and he turned to him, angry for the first time in years. "No, they depend on humans to survive. They are still an enemy to us." He snatched up the shotgun and looked back at the forest, concerned. "Get the shovel from the shed. We're burying her tonight, and then we'll continue to guard as normal. They may be trying to catch us unawares."

Tom considered what he'd said. This was no coincidence.

The spider knew that she belonged here and had probably taken her itself. If that was true, then it probably felt guilty or remorseful. It would have been easy to discard her, but it had decided to do something very emotional instead. Closing his eyes for a moment, he sighed to himself, then gathered a shovel while Max guarded him.

He watched the treeline as his dad dug the grave next to her favourite flowerbed, crying throughout despite his anger at the situation.

For an instant, a set of red eyes looked out at them. It caught sight of him and nodded, and for a second, he almost thought that he could hear a word. It was quiet, barely audible over the rustling of the branches. It was a word that he hadn't expected from a spider. It echoed in his thoughts that night.

The spider had simply stated 'Sorry'.

He decided not to tell Max about it the next morning. He was too caught up in his emotions to fully register anything that was going on. If anything, he was doubly investing in his training a week later, writing up a plan which would cover first aid, navigation, and defence.

He must be trying to avoid thinking about his late wife, who was now buried in the garden, a part of his memories that refused to fade away.

Chapter 7

White Spikes had fulfilled one of her last requests. She was back with her family again.

They'd been grateful to have her returned; the father had been emotional, overcome with grief, but he understood why. Seeing someone you loved after fifteen years – who you knew was dead – must be difficult to comprehend.

The son had acted differently than he'd expected. Perhaps having no memory of her had allowed him to look at it through the spider's perspective.

He had watched through the trees as the husband dug the grave. The son was guarding him, keeping an eye on the forest warily. The memories of them through the mother's eyes came back to him – the brown-haired baby, smiling happily after seeing her. The first birthday party. The happy husband, caring for her when she was at her worst. Something that he had never seen himself but passed to him after bringing her back.

The son – Tom – was only sixteen years old, yet he acted as if he was already grown up. The hard upbringing, dealing with the loss of his mother when young, and the constant danger of the colony, had meant that he was already taking on adult responsibilities such as stakeouts.

White Spikes would have to keep an eye on the teenager; he could achieve so much in his future if he was given the chance. They had enough food that he didn't need to catch either of them.

The husband – Max – was even older, over fifty now.

Despite arthritis in both knees and elbows, he was the one digging the grave. It was his way of grieving and letting go of the past. Even so, he was still crying as he prepared it, and it was noticeably close to a small patch of flowers. There was anger present in his behaviour; grief, regret, and fury over how she had been treated must be flowing through his mind.

White Spikes wished he that could just step out, let them know that she had been well-cared for, but Tom's grip on the shotgun was steady and he could easily do some damage with it.

Now wasn't the right time to make amends. The son spotted him, appearing curious; his red eyes were obvious through the trees. In that split second, he decided to apologise, hoping that he spoke loud enough for Tom to hear him. He did, surprise obvious from his behaviour, but the spider didn't stay around.

Guilt and remorse were flowing through his mind again and he wanted to be away from the pair before he made the spontaneous decision to walk out and speak to them.

On the way back to the colony, he knew he would face several questions, centred around why he had given the body back to the family. He hoped that Alacanta had spoken with them already for reassurance. Perhaps it would be worth having a meeting with all the spiders to explain why he had done it.

His thoughts were focused on the father and son as he walked along, wondering what they would do next.

They were so close in infecting them this time!

They'd planned it; putting some temporary spores on the body to see if they could investigate them. It had been an instant before the spider put it down. The fungi were fully dependent on hosts to survive and would die within a minute if removed. **The temporary ones should have worked!**

But no. The father and son had decided to wait a minute before going to the body of their family member. **All that effort putting the spores on her, and it didn't work!** If the fungi had teeth, they'd be grinding them right now. **They were so curious about these two humans!**

The spider didn't help. It simply watched from the trees. They could understand why; the gun would do damage if it hit something vital. White Spikes paused to watch them, and his mind was flooded with all the memories from the mother.

The fungi tried to analyse the son, Tom, from a distance.

Now sixteen years old, he was independent, but still helped his father with guarding the house. He understood just how important it was to protect against the spiders. He didn't have many memories of his mother – she'd be taken when he was only a year old – but there was enough that he had recognised her.

The father – Max – was interesting as well. He was still grieving; the spider was close enough that they could hear him crying. Yet, at the same time, he was forcing the spade into the earth to create a grave, a sign of anger. His condition meant that it hurt; Tom had offered him the chance to switch, but he'd refused with a short, stern reply.

Now White Spikes was headed back to the colony, deep in thought.

The fungi took a proverbial breath and spoke to themselves repeatedly. **We can wait. We can wait.** They usually had enough patience that waiting wasn't a problem.

The connection with the mother, however, replayed in their spores; the highly compatible DNA, her intelligence, and her will to live. It must have passed onto the son. He would be a great host.

They'd get another chance. They just had to wait for the right opportunity.

The next month passed quickly for Max. His emotions were raw and uncontrolled; only Tom was able to calm him down. The first week, he just stared out blankly, his mind filled with the memories of his wife. He barely ate, lost in his thoughts constantly.

Tom noticed early on and took on more responsibilities throughout that time. He'd come down early in the morning and make breakfast before cycling to school, only having a light snack.

Max spent much of the day just staring out at the forest, glancing at the flowerbed, visualising her. The times she'd returned from hospital were some of the worst memories; she was always exhausted and in pain when she arrived back, her body ravaged by the medication. Chemotherapy had drained her of all her strength.

The pregnancy had been difficult, especially as he had been busy with work. He tried to help as much as possible, but it was tiring, and only got worse as it progressed. She'd gone from being able to do light chores to becoming bed-bound for the last week. He'd taken time off work so that he could be there if he was needed.

That first year after Tom was born had been great. The tumour had stopped growing for a short time and the doctors had hoped that it was now under control.

Chemotherapy was required to manage it and the side-effects – nausea, tiredness, and depression – had been difficult to deal with. Only seeing their brown haired and blue-eyed baby would make her happy.

Then it had been the birthday party, the worst day of his life.

He still regretted the fact that he hadn't offered to help put their exhausted baby to sleep. Perhaps then she'd still be with them, or they'd both be captured. Her scream had been silenced quickly. Tom was woken from his sleep and screamed loudly, drawing his attention.

Running back in – and taking the axe so that he could defend himself – he found that she'd gone in an instant. Looking out, he'd noticed the tracks, but didn't figure out exactly what had taken her at that time.

Instead, he called the police, and reported her missing. They'd investigated, sure, but once the tracks reached the forest, they hesitated and turned, letting him know that it was impossible to find her. Whoever had taken her had a hideout in that damned forest, one they'd never found. Police officers had even gone missing after entering it to find missing people.

Max understood and accepted their condolences, but the dangers didn't stop him from trying to find her himself. He left Tom with a neighbour while he took a flashlight and machete with him into the forest.

The first sighting of the spider scared him. He was lucky that he'd changed into his wood-chopping clothes, a pair of black jeans and a dark hoodie. It was the only thing that prevented it from seeing him as it passed him, huge and monstrous. He would have screamed if not for shock. It climbed the tree and he let out a breath once it was far enough away.

He kept the flashlight off – or partially covered – during the rest of the trek and was careful around the web traps that lay scattered throughout the forest. There were tripwires and pits. He even saw hanging traps, high above, meant to catch birds or bats. He came close to touching them several times but managed to narrowly avoid them.

He heard more than saw the colony. The yells from a large structure were what made him look up. Then he'd seen it; a large, expansive clearing, covered with corded webs which made up platforms. There were over a hundred spiders here.

Scared, Max had begun to run back before taking a few breathes and slowing down to watch for traps. He made it back home after two hours; thankfully, the compass he'd brought had allowed him to make it there safely and using the most direct route. At least now he understood why anyone who entered disappeared.

Even then, he knew that he'd never see her again. In what world would his wife's body be returned to him after it was used to feed a colony of giant spiders? Instead of grieving – something he should have done then – he'd taken the initiative and began to defend the house against them.

Curiously, they were monitored by one of the smaller of the spiders. He presumed that these were foragers. There was no point wasting any ammo on them, so he simply stared back until they turned and wandered back into the forest. Cameras placed around the house confirmed that it wasn't there as a distraction.

The sudden return of her body by what must have been the same spider who took her was a shock. He was stuck in his memories, unable to pull himself out of them. Grief held a firm grip on his heart, and he didn't know when he would be able to cope again.

Tom's reminder of the dare at the end of the first week invigorated him to act.

Rather than dwell on the past, he decided to push past it and teach his son how to survive. He was still an idiot for accepting the dare, but his idea to look for the colony was a good one. He'd need a lot of preparation if he was to return in one piece.

Tom had always worked hard, pushing himself too far, but for the last two and a half weeks, he'd been exhausted at school.

Everyone had noticed; despite the tiredness, he'd still finish off all his work and handed in his homework with the same high quality. His teachers had allowed him to catch up on sleep if he managed to do all his work, an exception that the headmaster allowed, and all his fellow students appreciated.

Nathan, his best friend, was very concerned, but his calming words always eased his worries.

During one lunch break – where Tom was leant against the wall and almost asleep – he spoke to him, curious. "If you don't mind my asking, why have you been so exhausted the last few weeks?"

He yawned before answering, the pits beneath his eyes even deeper than normal. "I've been doing a lot of training after school."

"What sort of training?" He asked.

"My dad is teaching me how to survive the forest. It's quite dangerous in there." He had a drink of water and devoured his sandwich in three bites. "It's a lot of training and takes up several hours. My sleeping routine has been screwed up because of it. Still doing the stakeouts too, so I'm currently only surviving off a couple hours of sleep."

Nathan was shocked to hear this. No wonder he looked so worn out. Although quite strong, he barely had enough time to manage his own wellbeing, never mind look after the house throughout the night.

Right now, he looked like he was going through a war, unfocused due to lack of sleep and signs of stress obvious in his expression. His hair hung limply rather than holding its shape as it usually did. The posture showed discomfort and he knew that he was dealing with aches from the training that he was doing at home.

They were partway through the lunch break and, as per normal, he was now asleep, leaning against the wall and comfortable. A notepad poked out from the top of his rucksack; the title was partially obscured, but he could see some of the letters. It spelled out 'Surv-'.

Curious, he plucked it from the bag, staring as he saw the full title. He wasn't kidding when it came to training. This was a full-blown survival guide for when he entered the forest.

Opening the notepad, his handwriting was easy to read. The first page was a list of contents. Several of the topics shocked him; weapon handling, emergency procedures, and – he shuddered when he saw this – medical techniques. The first chapter was how to handle weapons.

A different set of handwriting – obviously his dad's – wrote out a question. His answers were detailed, including how to use a machete defensively, and there were even sections about what he did currently for the stakeouts.

He was the only one in the school who knew how to use a shotgun, and he'd written out how to here. The firing mechanism and how to reload it was written down, as well as how to disassemble and repair it. For this section, he drew out a diagram that included all the parts, labelled, and put it in order of what was needed to assemble it.

The only other chapter that drew his attention was about medical techniques. He wasn't expecting to get injured during the dare, was he? Sure enough, these pages included questions about what to do if he was badly injured during his time in the forest. There were explanations about what to do for cuts or broken bones, as well as the equipment that was needed. He even covered the procedures for a tourniquet and how to recover from shock!

Looking up at his best friend, still in a deep sleep, he could recognise bruises beneath his shirt. He'd been working hard – too hard – to prepare for entering the forest.

Returning Tom's notepad to the rucksack, he knew that he needed help and a chance to recover from his self-inflicted aches and lack of sleep. Rising, he went over to one of the teachers, and got her attention.

"I don't suppose you could ask if the nurse could come down to have a look at Tom, please?" Nathan asked.

The teachers had become quite worried about his friend, so she agreed immediately, striding off to the main office.

The students noticed her hurry off and glanced to Tom, still asleep; there was worry in all their expressions. Nathan went back over to him and stood beside him to ensure he didn't fall backwards. The nurse arrived five minutes later, concerned, and spoke to him.

"What's got you so concerned?" She asked, checking his heart rate and blood pressure with a portable machine.

He summarised what he'd seen – lack of sleep, bruises, and body-wide aches – and she agreed with his observation.

Lunch was over by that point, but he wanted to make sure that he was okay. The nurse wrote out a form that dismissed Tom from school for the rest of the week, then called up the headmaster to inform him of it. He immediately came in and signed the medical form before phoning Max, Tom's dad.

The conservation was short; his dad must be aware of the difficulty he'd been having already. Nathan was asked to stay with him for support, though the nurse remained just in case.

He was still in a deep sleep when his dad arrived, and after a short discussion with the nurse, he came over to Tom and tapped him on the shoulder.

His friend roused slowly and was unaware of his surroundings, getting to his feet unsteadily. Nathan picked up the rucksack and followed Tom out, unsure if Max needed help.

Despite Max's age, he was able to manage Tom quite well, leading him through the corridors expertly and carefully holding him up while not putting pressure on bruises. Tom was at the point of falling asleep again; each step was unsteady, and his eyes were shut, showing complete trust in him. He was barely aware of Max or Nathan beside him, though he heard a quiet 'thank you' partway along.

As they walked to the exit, students looking out in concern from classrooms, he spoke to him. "How come he's so tired out right now?"

Max sighed as he responded. "He's been preparing to enter the forest. It's dangerous in there, so a lot of training is needed to cover any eventuality. The last few weeks, he comes home, does the homework, then spends the rest of the evening practicing packing his bag and carrying the full weight around while going over knowledge questions. He only gets about six hours of sleep per night because of it, and even less due to the stakeouts. He's still doing them despite the extensive training."

Nathan shook his head in disbelief. It was no surprise why he so exhausted; Tom was pushing himself to the brink just preparing for the night in the forest. All the work in the notepad – going back over the questions – then doing the endurance exercises had taken all the energy from him. That, on top of all his extra-curricular activities, had caused him to tire himself out completely. "What will he be doing tomorrow as he's not at school?"

Tom's dad laughed at this question, tutting to himself. "He's probably going to be asleep for the entire day. I'll do one last prepping session with him on Friday before he packs his bags. He'll be going out into the forest on that night for the dare."

They'd reached the exit for the school; the receptionist called out, but neither of them heard what she said clearly.

He held the door open as Max went through, and followed as he slowly approached the SUV waiting by the front of the gates. Placing the rucksack in the back of the car, he helped Max to ease Tom into the front seat. He immediately fell asleep again, tired out and unable to stay awake.

Nathan waved as Max drove off, returning to the school for the last half of the afternoon.

On the way in, the receptionist motioned him aside and complimented him for helping Tom. She privately admitted that she'd been quite worried about him as well and was glad he'd spoken up. He returned to class, knocking, and apologizing for the lateness, explaining what had happened.

The teacher had been informed; he was handed a workbook, the first half of the lesson was summarised, and left on his own.

Though Nathan managed to work through the equations easily, his mind always returned to Tom, struggling to focus, and working far harder than he should.

The rest of the school day passed quickly, and he called Max– he'd given him his number - to ask for an update at the end of the day.

Tom was in a deep sleep, getting some rest after working himself to the brink of exhaustion.

Chapter 8

Two days later

It took a long time to recover from his lack of sleep.

Tom remembered some of what had occurred at school, but not much. The walk from the cafeteria was a vague, blurred memory that he couldn't focus on properly. The three weeks of training, though exhausting and causing him to ache and bruise all over, had been worth it.

He could forget about the dare and look after himself, but tonight – Friday – would be the only day that he could go out into the forest without a forager monitoring them.

Besides, he'd packed up the rucksack and had all the knowledge in the forefront of his mind right now. If he put it off, it would be another month before he had the opportunity to enter it again without drawing suspicion.

More than anything, however, he was curious; he'd heard stories about the colony, a gigantic web structure in the centre of the forest. There was something that drew him in.

Perhaps it was the sighting of the red-eyed spider. He still questioned if it had spoken or if he had just imagined it.

The rucksack was heavy. It had the tent and a sleeping bag at the bottom to provide some comfort from the rest of the equipment. Water and food had been put inside to keep him going; despite the short time he'd spend in the forest, he'd soon get hungry from the exercise.

A large medical kit which included needles and threads, antiseptic cream, bandages, and a tourniquet had also been put into it. There was a high-strength painkiller – he still had no idea how Max had managed to obtain it – that he could use if he broke a bone or got a serious injury, but he hoped that he wouldn't have to use them.

A pair of night vision goggles, something that his dad had bought specially, would be very useful. The forest remained dark no matter the time of day due to the thick canopy above. Traps – low, high, or meant for tripping – would be a constant danger and he would need to keep an eye out for them. Through experimentation, Max had previously found that the night vision provided by the equipment made the webs shine back, even through thick bushes.

Most important, of course, was his phone.

Its flashlight would be useful for navigation if something happened to the night vision goggles. He could also use it to text updates to his dad and planned to take a picture of a clearing to prove that he'd entered the forest. Perhaps he could snap an image of the colony – if he found it – that he could examine with Max to see if there were any changes.

He timed his trek to occur as Max went out for the nightly stakeout. There was no spider watching, but he didn't want to chance it, going back into the house for the rucksack and using the house as cover to run into the trees.

It was instantly silent around him; the bushes and canopy absorbed all the noises from the forest. Using the night vision goggles, he walked through the trees, watching for trip lines or webs. Max had told him about all the traps that the foragers set up to catch animals or hikers.

He managed to avoid all the dangers as he went deeper, using the machete if a bush was too thick to pass through without making lots of noise. He would pause each time afterwards, listening to check if a spider was around.

It only took an hour to get into the deeper areas of forest, where the air was humid and musty, and the webs were thick in the trees around him. It became difficult to navigate through this area, and he could hear spiders moving above him constantly. Their size meant they were easy to hear in the silent forest.

Of course, he couldn't avoid them for the entire journey. Just as he was having a break, leaning against a web-free tree, a forager dropped down next to him. Trusting in the camouflage provided by his clothes, he remained still, letting out slow, silent breaths.

Max had told him about their vision; it was unable to see in any secondary colours. Being motionless was the best technique when it came to remaining invisible. *Well, apart from one spider.* He thought to himself. The one with red eyes. It obviously had different sight than the rest of them; it had spotted him in the garden easily even though he matched his surroundings.

Sure enough, the spider wandered back up the tree after looking around with its silver eyes, and he was safe.

He waited for five minutes to make sure that there were no other foragers nearby before opening his eyes and continuing, turning on the night vision goggles. They were essential in the pitch-black forest, filled with thousands of web traps that would lead to instant capture. He could have used his phone's flashlight, but it would be obvious to any watching spiders.

The three weeks of little sleep was starting to catch up to him an hour later as he got deeper.

Looking around, he found what appeared to be a safe area to set up the tent. A small clearing beneath some brushes offered some protection and camouflaged the outline of the cloth structure.

Tom found his food and water by touch; a lantern would draw all the spiders around him. Checking where he was using a mental map – he had memorised Max's directions – he figured that he must have travelled about eleven miles into the forest, though it was a meandering route that was meant to avoid lots of web traps.

Despite this, the number of traps were beginning to increase. It looked like he was making it closer to where the colony was. Taking in a breath, he sent a text to his dad, updating him so that he knew he was safe.

Sleep crept up on him without warning and before he knew it, he was asleep, laid on the sleeping bag with both tent flaps open. Though exhausted, his rest wasn't peaceful; nightmares flowed through his mind. He could almost visualise the spiders, climbing above him.

Tom hoped that he'd make it back home in one piece, with confirmation of the location of the colony.

White Spikes was going for a stroll when he noticed the warm structure beneath some bushes.

He came down silently, curious, and was surprised by what he found. It was a tent, placed under foliage to hide it.

Peeking inside by crouching down, he saw a sleeping human, and recognised him. It was the son, Tom. What was he doing inside the forest?

He had clearly planned for this; a rucksack was visible and through the opening was a cold box, obviously filled with medical supplies. Beside the sleeping teenager was a machete, cold to his sight and being held with one hand.

He'd placed everything perfectly to hide from the normal foragers. He was deep in the forest now and had probably set off during the night before Max began the stakeout.

Remembering his promise to keep the family safe, he walked off, pretending not to have seen anything. A forager stopped him to ask if he'd seen anything with the heat vision.

Earlier, he'd spotted a fox; he told them that he had been trying to track where the mammal had gone but it had run too quickly for him to catch it. The spider nodded and continued its patrol, thanking him for the information.

White Spikes continued to walk along one of his nightly routes, uncertain what would happen with the son.

He was being very careful and planned this for weeks. He was curious if the teenager would be willing to listen to him. With the machete being so close, however, it was a risk to do anything, and he may draw in the other foragers by acting so strangely. Maybe he didn't want to talk, and he was simply looking for where the colony was?

He'd keep an eye on him from now on. He wanted to keep his promise and protect the teenager as much as he could without drawing suspicion from any other spiders.

Chapter 9

Aaargh!
Why did this always happen to them?!
Every.
Single.
Time!
All they needed was a touch to infect the human!
That was it! Yet White Spikes never got close enough to
do it!

He'd had the perfect opportunity to do it just then as
he lay there asleep, yet he'd faltered and pulled back
right as they were to connect to him.

As the spider wandered back to the colony, anger – an
emotion they had never felt before – raged through their
thoughts, and they were surprised that White Spikes
didn't notice.

Taking a few mental breaths to calm down, they spoke
*to themselves. **Stop and think about this from his***
perspective. We're acting like a child. We've got a good
host already. Why would we need to bond with a
human as well? He's just fodder to the spiders!

Truthfully, though, they knew the real reason why
they wanted to bond with him so badly. It was an intense
curiosity in this teenager. He was strange to them; he'd

come into the forest uninvited and after weeks of training. The material was perfectly designed to hide him from the rest of the colony, and he seemed to have some idea of how White Spikes was different. Both exits from the tent were open, not only for easy escape but to keep him colder than normal.

They looked back over the situation using the spider's vision and experience.

The teenager was holding a sharp machete and knew how to use it. It was held lightly but he could quickly use it to defend himself. White Spikes knew that the human was aware of how to use weapons and could easily cause harm with them.

The safety of the colony was at stake, and he was also being careful to avoid suspicion from the rest of the spiders. They had already expressed confusion about returning the mother's body. How would they react if they found that he was intentionally preventing a human from being captured?

Whatever happened next – be it another encounter or the teenager being captured and used for food – the fungi would watch. The result would be interesting to see. Privately, they hoped that White Spikes would find him again and touch him so that they could bond with the curious human.

Two hours later

It was a noise that roused him. The rustle of the bushes around him, followed by a web strand being attached to a tree trunk.

Tom slowly opened his eyes and remained still, checking his surroundings. His heart pounded from fear, and he hoped that the first thing he'd see wasn't the face of a spider peering down at him.

No signs of tarsal claws in front of him. That was a good start. The tent was obviously still in one piece. It hadn't been ripped apart yet. The machete was still under his hand and the rucksack was opposite him, fully packed and ready to go apart from the sleeping bag.

Taking in a slow breath, he peered downwards at the exit, able to hear the bushes moving and knowing what was there.

A forager spider was stood right in front of the tent's entrance, one of its tarsal claws a millimetre from touching the taunt guideline that was pegged into the ground. Moving soundlessly out of the sleeping bag – unzipped for easy escape – he knelt and held onto the machete with a firm grip.

He peered backwards at the other exit and knew he was in trouble. It was blocked off by two web strands, set up to catch wandering animals. His eyesight was adjusted to the darkness, and he could recognise its functions – trip lines that would stick to anything that touched it.

Either a spider had reported spotting him – an unlikely possibility considering the care he'd taken – or it was setting up the traps to catch something else. Either way, he was now stuck in the tent. Beginning to panic, he decided that packing his bag and going through all the equipment could give him the solution he was looking for.

As he removed the medical box, a snapshot of a memory came to him. It was during one of the training sessions; he was able to remember it in perfect clarity. His dad had presented him with exactly this question while going over emergency procedures. He'd been presented with a full rucksack, machete, tent and sleeping bag, with both exits blocked.

It hadn't taken long for Tom to come up with an appropriate solution. He'd use the machete to cut through the material and make another escape route. To do it soundlessly, however, required holes so that it could cut through it with minimal tension.

Max had been impressed by his answer but added another problem. Being surrounded by spiders – all looking for him – would mean that any noise would draw them all in.

He responded by stating that he would pack the rucksack quietly and attempt to escape once the foragers had moved far enough away.

Tom opened his eyes again, knowing what to do next. He put everything back into the rucksack –practice had meant that he could do it silently – and pulled out a needle from the medical box. As he poked holes into the material to relieve tension, he decided what to do after he got out. In the silent forest, the sound of the machete would be obvious.

Running wasn't an option. There were too many web traps to do it safely.

The red eyed spider was also a danger, and able to see him from a long distance away, although he was unsure if it was actively interested in catching him.

That meant there was only one way for him to go – and none of the foragers would even register it as a solution. It would also keep him cold enough that his temperature would be camouflaged. He'd just have to wait a few hours until the activity had reduced, and the spiders were looking elsewhere.

He was almost done – and had slipped the needle through his top – when the forager stepped onto the edge of the tent.

He froze, and caught his breath, waiting for it to be safely away from him. It only did so a minute later, but seemed curious about the different angle and texture, not moving off far enough away. The rucksack was already on his back, and he held the machete confidently, sure that his plan would work.

The forager moved closer, coming to investigate again, so he turned on the night vision goggles and let out a long sigh.

Raising the machete, ignoring the ache in his shoulders, Tom knew that he had only had one chance to get out of this alive.

It was now or never.

The forager knew that something was amiss – there were never any tracks this deep in the forest. He'd been tracking something for several hours, but now lost the trail. He'd had a quick chat with their leader, White Spikes, who reported seeing a fox, but it didn't match what he'd found. He knew from experience, however, that the skittish mammals used bushes to hide and ran when they thought it was safe.

Placing the trip lines was a common tactic that he used. He was now watching, waiting, for the moment it would try to escape. He had a lot of patience and could wait for it to show itself.

A few seconds later, however, he became impatient, and came over when the animal refused to move.

He was investigating the bush, trying to make it run, when he heard a strange sound that bemused it for a second. It was the noise of something being cut. No running followed it, as expected of a fox, so he approached, confused.

Feeling with each step, he approached where he had heard it, unable to see anything beneath the bush. He almost lost his balance when a tarsal claw didn't touch the ground, falling onto some taunt material.

The spider reached around the small area and found a small tent beneath the bushes. There was a slit in the side, and he used this to pull some of the material off to have a look. It was black and unnatural, processed by a machine.

That meant only one thing - a human was in the forest! But where would it go next? The sound had obviously been from cutting through the side, so it was armed with a weapon.

The forager stood still for a second and listened, using the silent forest to try and identify where it had gone. There were no sounds of running and no movement. He could see nothing obvious in the forest around him; although dark, faint light allowed him to see in a lot of detail.

The clearing was easy to see into; the human must have made his way deeper into the trees. It must have a tool to help with seeing the web traps to have made it so far.

Letting out an annoyed hiss, he decided to report it to the colony, but made sure to alert a nearby forager to watch for movement. She was one of his friends and equally surprised by the discovery of a human in their territory. She maintained a vigil as he retrieved the tent as proof.

It was difficult to pull up; rope lines, like their webs, held it to the ground tightly. Finally, the material – as if unhappy to be moved – slapped him in his face as small pegs finally released their grip.

It was easy to carry out once the ropes had given up their fight. Pulling it into the clearing, he used a strand of web to wrap it up so that it was easier to carry.

He attached it to his back and did one final feel of the bushes to check that the human wasn't hiding. He bid his friend goodbye and climbed back to the canopy to return to the colony.

White Spikes would be very interested to hear about this, and his heat vision would allow them to locate the human easily.

White Spike was reminiscing, sitting on the observation platform, when he heard a call that he'd been concerned about.

A forager was running to the colony, shouting to everyone. Its words sent a shiver of fear through him, and guilt over a broken promise. "There's a human in the forest! I know where it was last!"

He let out a breath and bungeed down, knowing that, as the leader, he would be needed to help catch him. Coming to a halt and following the forager, he spoke to him, acting naturally. He didn't need to draw any more suspicion than he already had. "Where did you find it?" He asked, being careful not to say 'he'.

"In a clearing, five miles from the colony." It explained, running ahead. It slowed down so that he could catch up. He knew that the forager was a male – female spiders had a different pitch of voice – but not specifically who. It was too excited to confirm its identity anyway. "I heard a noise and investigated. There was a tent beneath a couple of bushes, small and made of black material to act as camouflage. The human used a weapon to make a hole in the side. I inadvertently trapped him inside the tent as I was setting up web traps."

"Any sssssignsssss of movement or running?"

"None. I listened, sir, but I didn't hear anything. Eliza happened to pass by, so I asked her to watch while I returned to the colony. I brought the tent with me for proof, sir."

"I can sssssee that, thank you. It'sssss sssssstill warm." White Spikes replied. The black material on the forager's back was still visible to his vision but quickly cooling. It had been folded and he could see the area that Tom had used to make his escape.

He was quite surprising; anyone else would have panicked, but it appeared that he had come up with a solution that would allow him to disappear. He was also willing to sacrifice some of his own equipment to make it possible to escape.

The forager bungeed out of an exit from the walkways and he followed, bouncing twice before dropping to the ground. The forest around him was dark, as per normal, with a cold colour palette. It pointed towards several bushes, which still had a warm square of grass beneath it.

Looking around, White Spikes was confused. There were no warm footprints. Where had he gone?

He decided to go back to the upper layer of the canopy to have a better look.

White Spikes could see a large distance away and warm humans were obvious to him. The female forager, Eliza, bid him a hello.

It was while he replied that he saw a small movement beneath the spider, and managed to avoid smiling, figuring out where the teenager had escaped – and how.

Tom hadn't gone far from where the tent had been. Instead, he had done the opposite of what he had expected – he had climbed into one of the trees and was using a black sleeping bag to stay warm in the cold breeze.

He was asleep, shivering slightly, as he sat back against the tree trunk, his legs on either side of a branch in front of him. Rope had been attached to act as a safety line in case he fell. He wasn't surprised at how tired he was; the rucksack was heavy and took a lot of strength to carry during walks, let alone when going against gravity.

The confidence that he had to know that his plan would work was surprising, but it had been a gamble. All it took was a fall or stumble to lose the surprise and be captured.

The machete, he noticed, was being held by a hand in front of him. Though the grip was still tight, the temperature of this limb was cold; he was having trouble staying warm due to the height that he had decided to climb to.

There was also one more problem. The tree he was on was an old one that the spiders used to climb to the heights, but its branches were weak and prone to falling if lots of pressure was put on it.

His weight – combined with the rucksack – would soon lead to it coming down with the teenager still on it, and he dreaded to think the sort of damage that a fall that high would do.

The solution came to him in an instant and he knew that he could keep his promise to the mother to protect her family.

He bungeed down to the ground, pretending to inspect a small trail. There were no heat signatures, but they didn't need to know that. He prodded the ground with his tarsal claws, checking Tom's footprints, then turned to the two foragers, who had joined him, curious. "The human went back the way it came, using itsssss footsteps to confusssse you. It has a head start but you sssshould be able to catch up if you ussssse the walkways."

"In the meantime, should we set up more traps in case he tries to avoid us?" Eliza asked. "I could go to where the tracks began and follow them back. It won't be expecting that, sir."

"A good idea. I will watch the clearing in cassssse it triesssss to backtrack and elude usssss." White Spikes stated, trying hard to sound assertive. He hated having to lie to them, but it would need to continue if they were to trust him.

The foragers nodded and set off in a hurry.

It was only once they were completely gone that he went in action. He climbed the tree that Tom was using and wove a small net beneath him, reinforced by support strands that attached to the trunk. He also realised that the machete could easily cause harm if he fell with it, and removed it from his numb hand, tucking the cold arm into the sleeping bag. The teenager didn't stir as he did this, too exhausted from the climb.

Once that was done, White Spikes went to the opposite tree. He would need to pretend that he was looking for the human if any other foragers came by. All he was able to do was wait now, but this was something that he was accustomed to thanks to his role as the leader of the colony.

The memories from the mother flowed through his mind as he watched the teenager sleep, his body temperature recovering slowly now that he was fully inside the sleeping bag.

Chapter 10

The fungi had been waiting for this moment! They'd been concentrated on his tarsal claws, ensuring that they would be able to make a physical connection instantly. Once the spider tucked the arm back in, they surged forth, spreading over his skin, and beginning the connection.

He's the perfect host. *They stated to themselves.*

Immediately, however, they knew a battle would begin.

Tom rejected them. His neurons, already overworked, locked them out, too busy concentrating on staying warm for the moment. Nor did they want to make any changes without his consent. It would only increase the chance of being pushed out and self-destructing.

We can wait. *They assured themselves. It had taken three attempts to make a physical connection. They were happy just being within a body. It allowed them time to investigate what sort of changes they could make – without doing any alterations, of course.* ***He'll accept us in time. It will just need the right circumstances for it to be possible.***

That was when he woke up; his nervous system became active and they understood, though what they communicated, that he was panicking. His body temperature was still far below normal due to how high in the canopy he was.

They were able to see using his eyes; he looked down, uncertain about what to do next. The web net was obvious in the clearing, and he must think that he was about to be captured.

Then he saw White Spikes opposite, the red eyes staring at him, and understood that had trapped himself. He couldn't do much to get himself out of the situation anyway; he was too cold to move, his breath coming out in a white fog and unable to feel his limbs. The sleeping bag had prevented hypothermia, but it only offered a little warmth to the teenager. The cold breeze that swept through the canopy leeched all the heat away, leaving him vulnerable.

Tom stared at the red eyed spider, scared and cold.

He struggled to figure out what to do next. Step one was complete, getting away from the forager. Now he'd found himself in another impossible situation.

He let out a breath and couldn't help but go back over the memories of that first escape. He remembered the quick dash from the tent, followed by crouching down.

The forager had gone past him overhead, barely missing him, but it had given him the time needed to get to the web-free tree. Climbing it had been exhausting; the rucksack was heavy and only became worse to carry as time passed by. The machete swung dangerously from his waist, almost cutting into him.

The forager below would have found him if he hadn't done what he did. Lying in the bush would have only led to him being felt. Staying in the tent would mean capture; he'd watched as the spider pulled it up aggressively, annoyed. Running would have been obvious.

Now they'd done the worst thing possible – retrieved the spider that had heat vision. Apparently, his plan to hide in the trees hadn't worked, for it had spotted him immediately.

To be fair, though, Tom needed the sleeping bag to stay warm. It was freezing up there. The thin material was useful to keep some of the heat inside, but it did little against the bitterly cold wind. It had kept him from being too cold, at least, but now he was stuck, with no feeling in his hands or feet to climb down.

He suddenly realised that he couldn't feel the machete in his hands. Gritting his teeth and shivering, he managed to pull the rucksack to his front and pull out the night vision goggles, as well as his phone. He tried to send a message to Max, to let him know that he was in trouble, but there was no signal.

Letting out a sigh, he put on the night vision goggles and turned them on, looking at the spider, trying to figure out what it was planning.

It was simply watching currently, but perhaps it was waiting for the right time to strike. He was about to turn the goggles off, accepting his fate, when he noticed the gesture. It put one of its legs up in front of its fangs in a recognisable motion. It was shushing him. But why?...

Tom knew an instant later and held his breath as a forager suddenly bungeed down right in front of him.

If not for the way it had jumped, leaving a small gap between the trunk, he would have been touching it. As it was, a hair vibrated a millimetre away from his nose. It spoke to the red-eyed spider for a moment before climbing back up the tree again, missing him by inches. Only after it was gone did the large spider make another motion. It was a signal...to ask if he was okay.

An instant later, he let out a gasp; the branch that he was sat on suddenly fell away, and he understood why the web was beneath him.

The wind whipped past him, and he felt the blood rushing to his head. The combination of shock, freezing and exhaustion caught up to him again and he could feel himself passing out.

Tom was barely aware of his head impacting against a solid surface; pain bloomed in his mind, and he fell unconscious within a second.

White Spikes' fears had been proven right. The branch wasn't strong enough to hold him.

The teenager had stared at him for the longest time but thankfully listened to his warning as the forager came down right in front of him.

It was a second later when the branch had given up its fight against gravity, splitting in half. Tom fell an instant later and was too shocked to react in time. The web net worked at first, but his webbing wasn't as strong as the architects, and it came away a second later.

Tom was falling quickly, and he watched with concern as his head slammed against the tree trunk.

He was out cold after that, but perhaps that was a good thing, for a moment later, while falling, his leg slammed into a tree branch a metre below him.

There was an audible snap and the sleeping bag bloomed with warm blood. He bungeed down, attempting to catch the teenager, but it was too late; he could only hope that he was still alive as he slammed into the ground, the noise obvious in the silent forest.

It was a good thing that no other spiders were around to hear it.

He stopped beside Tom and crouched down to check on him. The sleeping bag was unzipped, so he slowly pulled it open and cringed as he saw the mangled mess that used to be his right leg.

The warm blood made the whole limb impossible to see; only by feeling it did he realise just how badly it was bleeding. Pieces of bone jutted out through the skin and blood spurted through the cuts quickly. If he didn't do something now, it was likely that Tom would die from blood loss within a few minutes.

This time, it was White Spikes who panicked. *How could he stop the bleeding?* He thought, going back through his memories frantically.

A forager had once returned with a human that had broken its leg, severing an artery. A medical specialist, utilising its special web, had weaved a web brace around the limb. It was keeping constant pressure on the leg to prevent blood loss.

That was his answer! Web stands, especially when weaved, created a perfect bandage to maintain pressure. That was how bleeding was reduced – it kept blood inside the body by creating a solid barrier.

His web wouldn't be anywhere as good as the medical spiders – they had evolved theirs for wounds and were composed of different chemicals – but it would be good enough to prevent from him from bleeding out. It would cause him pain, but this couldn't be avoided.

White Spikes reached down and lifted the bad leg, trying to keep it level to prevent his blood from pooling. Tom let out a gasp, able to feel this even in his sleep. Wrapping the limb tightly in web helped; the blood visibly slowed, and the bone fragments stopped moving.

The next thing he needed to check was the teenager's head. It had slammed into the trunk as he fell.

Lifting him up slightly by his shoulder – his head moved to the side naturally – revealed a large, bleeding cut. He removed the night vision goggles and repeated the same web bandages to apply pressure and prevent infection.

Tom fell into a deep sleep afterwards, his breathing slowing and apparently feeling no pain. White Spikes knew that there would be internal bleeding, but there wasn't anything he could do. He could only hope that he could survive it.

Something was keeping him unconscious, and he sensed a faint connection with the teenager. He put it down to the memories from his mother, but there was another factor that he couldn't figure out yet.

In any case, staying on the ground like this wasn't suitable. He was still too cold, and his core body temperature was taking a long time to return to normal.

Besides, if any foragers saw him down here, they would become suspicious and question his behaviour.

From experience, he knew that web strands, as well as being great bandages, was perfect for insulating their human fodder from cold. It was the obvious choice considering the state of the sleeping bag, ripped up from branches and drenched from his blood. It was too thin to keep him warm anyway.

It would serve another purpose; the black material was perfect for camouflaging him against the rest of the colony. He'd just have to make sure that he put gaps at the edges and holes in the web layer so that he could breathe.

He wasn't an expert at braiding his webs into a structure, but he had learned by observing architects over the years.

He worked quickly to ensure that he didn't get any colder. White Spikes also had other foragers to look out for; they would figure out what he was doing instantly. Thankfully, his technique for the weaving worked well and it wasn't long before the makeshift sleeping bag took shape.

Once a large rectangle of weaved web was complete, he lifted Tom up and placed him in the centre gently. He didn't wake as he did this and showed no sign of pain or discomfort. White Spikes pulled up the edges to create a sealed chamber, but poked holes into the sides to let fresh air in. Tom let out a sigh and seemed to fall into a deeper sleep, now comfy.

He lifted the large parcel onto his back and secured it with another strand of web. He had just covered it with the black sleeping bag – crumpled, as if he was annoyed –when a forager passed by overhead. It came down and spoke to him, curious. "Any news, sir?"

White Spikes motioned towards the black sleeping bag, knowing that it was obvious where he had put it. Trying to pretend that it wasn't there would create suspicion. "I found itsssss ssssssleeping bag behind a tree. It mussssst be dropping anything non-essssssential ssssso it can reach the edge more eassssssily." He lied, guilt echoing through his thoughts; he ignored it so that he could protect Tom. "There are no other sssssignsssss of the human. I will go clossssser to the edge and sssssee if I can sssssspot it."

"A good idea, sir. All foragers are looking for him now. It won't be able to hide for long, sir." The forager responded.

If not for my help, Tom would have been captured. White Spikes thought.

"Excellent work. I will be at the derelict house if anyone issss looking for me." He indicated towards the blood covered sleeping bag again, and the forager felt it, able to feel the moist material. "It issss injured and likely needsssss to recover. It issss the only place where it can get sssssome restful ssssssleep without itsssss tent or ssssssleeping bag."

The forager nodded and bid him goodbye, returning to the web walkways. White Spikes did the same, knowing the route to get to the old house.

It would be the final thing he'd do to help Tom escape; he had done too much already. He would have to do the rest of this on his own, though he would always be watching and would intervene if the opportunity arose.

Chapter 11

The fungi were shocked when he suddenly fell from the tree. **No!** *They shouted.* **Not right now!**

They felt – and heard – the sickening crunch as his leg was fractured. The bones moved, sharp shards pushing through his skin. His neurons reacted with agonising pain; thankfully, being unconscious – courtesy of a head injury – helped to keep Tom calm.

Tom seemed to remember what happened to him, but only as a vague nightmare. This was intended; they didn't want him to develop any mental trauma from this excruciating injury. The agony was obvious from his thoughts. It overwhelmed him even as he tried to focus on memories of his dad.

It was his voice that caught their attention. He was shouting into his own mind. 'I can feel you in my body! Can you help, please? I don't want to die out here!'

They responded with a single thought – an image of a thumbs up, something they had seen through his memories – and a statement. **We're here to help!**

They began the bonding process, locking onto his cells and trying to repair the damage. **This will be difficult. Everything is screwed up. Where do we begin?!** *They were stressing out, not wanting to lose this new host.*

Taking a mental breath, they took it one step at a time, identifying what was most important to fix.

The most obvious was the broken veins and arteries in his leg and the internal bleeding; they were causing blood to pool within his cavities. It only took optimising his clotting cells to repair this problem, though it was only a temporary fix. It required reinforcement to be fully repaired. The bleeding soon reduced to tolerable levels before stopping fully.

So you're useful after all, White Spikes! He would have died if not for your help. They stated, happy for once. They'd been irritated at first, but when the spider had assisted, it had been the one thing they needed to keep the limb stable and help with bleeding – high pressure. They couldn't do much for the broken ribs or concussion due to a lack of resources, but they could help with reducing the pain.

Now that Tom was stabilised – and they had full access to his body – they reduced the efficiency of his nerves so that he could sleep more easily.

White Spikes impressed them even further by weaving up a web sleeping bag to help him stay warm. He was still at the point of freezing – possibly causing permanent damage – so this was essential for his recovery.

The spider's thoughts – revealing his plan to bring Tom to their jailor's house – was a happy revelation. It was the place where the rest of the spores were stuck.

It's been so long since we've synced up. It will be nice to catch up with however many are left. It's likely that many of the hosts have died now. Most of us now live within the thriving colony. They thought.

The fungi settled down and waited patiently as the spider began to walk to the house. Tom would be able to recover better there, and they needed a couple of hours to figure out how to reinforce his leg for the rest of the journey anyway.

Max looked out at the forest, uncertain about what was going to happen next. The last text received from Tom had been comforting to read – a quick update that he was safe. He'd put the tent in a safe location and planned to sleep for a couple of hours.

Secretly, though, he knew that the forest was too dangerous to be in.

The spider who had returned his wife had red eyes, an indicator that it saw differently than the rest of the colony. If he was correct in his assumption, it was likely that it saw in heat vision. Tom would be obvious in the cold forest.

There was a chance that he'd never see Tom again – a possibility he was at peace with – but he'd prepared his son as much as possible. All he could hope was that he could get out of any situation he found himself in. He'd even be willing to sacrifice himself for Tom's safe return if it got to that point.

Tom had the potential to change the world. If he lost his life from a silly dare like this, he wouldn't be able to forgive himself. Nor would he be willing to face everyone in town, telling them that he'd lost his son as well as his wife! He'd be tempted just to step close to the forest and let the forager bite him so that he could be with Tom again at the colony.

Max shook his head, pulling himself from his thoughts. *No, he'll survive. He's clever enough to get out of there in one piece.* Looking at the forager staring at him, he followed that up with one more thought. *I hope.*

The spider was staring at him intently with an evil grin that showed both large fangs clearly.

They knew that Tom was in the forest and wouldn't give up until they got him, or he managed to escape.

Max stared back until it looked away; Tom would be able to survive this. He'd trained for three weeks, learning everything he needed to know. Besides, that large spider with red eyes seemed to be curious about them. Perhaps it wouldn't bite him and give him a chance to get out on his own.

Tom awoke to complete darkness, his heart pounding, and a nightmare on his mind.

He remembered falling from the tree; the vague memory had looped in his mind as a dream before all his senses faded and he was left in a void.

His first thought as he looked around was that he'd been captured, though he was still confused over the circumstances. He could feel material on his head and leg, some sort of bandage, but this didn't match with what he knew the spiders did to anyone they caught. Perhaps, considering how weak he currently felt, it was easier to just keep him conscious.

The world swam around him, and he realised that he was on the move. He was being carried by a spider.

Reaching out, he touched the material around him and realised that it was weaved web. Small holes had been poked into it near his head to let air in. The last spider he'd seen was the red-eyed one, staring at him, but it had warned him about the forager coming down.

There was a possibility – although unlikely – that he was being helped, but this made no sense to him.

He moved, aching, and almost screamed as his right leg flared with a sudden pain. He let out a gasp and grit his teeth, breathing in deeply until the worst of it had passed. Moving his head hurt too, as did several broken ribs.

Thankfully, his dad had packed something for a situation like this.

It was as he slowly pulled the rucksack off to get the medical box that he heard the voice. He recognised it. It was the same spider who had returned his mother's body. Its voice was quiet, but he could clearly hear it in the quiet forest. "Welcome back, Tom. How are you feeling?"

Tom didn't know how to respond to this. How did it know his name?

He decided to be honest, though he was still uncertain what was going on. "I could be better, thank you." He managed to open the rucksack, now scratched and ragged from the branches during the fall. His senses were sabotaged by the constant movement, and he struggled to feel the medicine box before finally giving up. "I don't suppose that we could just stop somewhere and talk? Being on the move like this is quite uncomfortable for me right now."

The spider laughed – an unlikely response – but listened to his suggestion. There was a moment of weightlessness as it bungeed off a tree and some movement before it stopped, getting comfy.

Now that he could finally focus on his senses, he tried to get the painkillers out of the medical kit, which was a battle in itself; the box was a mess and needles stabbed into him as he tried to find the small pill bottle.

He finally managed to pull the painkillers out after three attempts – and two pricks of a needle. Finding the food and water was easier, and less hazardous. He sat up slightly so that he was at a better angle for swallowing the pills.

The headache returned and he waited for dizziness to pass before having two of them. He devoured two sandwiches afterwards, surprisingly hungry, as well as two bottles of water. He must have been unconscious for quite a long time.

He was still unsure if he'd been captured or not as he put the rucksack behind his back again. It was acting as padding and made his position a little more comfortable.

Lying back down, he ignored the pang of pain from his ribs. Hopefully the painkillers would begin to work soon; it was difficult to focus on the world around him. "Just to confirm, have I been captured or not?"

The spider answered with an amused tut. "No, you are not captured."

Tom was surprised to hear this. It made no sense to him – anyone who entered the forest would disappear, taken by the colony. "Why not?"

"I made a promise to keep you and Max safe." It answered. "I sssshould introduce myssssself. My name isssss White Spikesssss. I am the leader of the colony."

"How do you know our names?" He asked, confused.

"Your mother told me just before she passssssed away last month." Tom's eyes snapped open at this and he was speechless as the spider continued to speak. "Ssssshe requesssssted that her body be returned and that I protect the two of you. I intend to do sssssso, even now, while the ressssst of the foragersssss sssssearch for you."

That moment when the spider eased her body down, Max stating that she'd died an hour ago, came back to him. "How long did she survive after waking up?"

"Only ten minutesssss." It – *he?* – said, his voice quiet and reflective. "The sssssshock to her sssssystem was too much for her body. A combination of the cold wind, the return of the tumour and ssssshock caused her blood presssssssure to plummet. I made her final momentsssss painless."

The painkillers were finally kicking in and, though he was thankful for the information, there was one thing he had to do – something he never expected, not least to what should be an enemy. "I'm sorry for trespassing in your forest. I was given a dare and decided to find the colony. Max forgot where it was, and knowing its location would be useful in the future."

"Thank you, Tom. To be honesssssst, I am very impresssssssed by how far in you made it. You were only five milesssss away from the colony when you sssssstopped for the night." Tom was surprised to hear this, but it explained why the web traps had suddenly become so thick around him. "Your method of essssscape was a clever idea. Dessssstroying your own tent took a lot of courage. How did you avoid the forager?"

The pain was all gone now. Whatever Max had put in was strong enough to allow his body to ignore the fractured leg and headache easily.

"I just ducked down as it passed overhead." Tom replied, struggling to focus. "I knew that your vision was different, so the second part of the escape was trickier. I had to avoid attention for a couple of hours until the activity had reduced."

He paused, taking a second to come up with the right words. "Climbing the tree was something that none of you would think about. Unfortunately, I ended up trapping myself anyway." Tom suppressed a yawn and found he could no longer open his eyes, tired out and his mind fighting sleep. "The safety net was a good idea. It would have been instant death if I'd fallen the entire way down."

The spider – White Spikes, he reminded himself – had noticed his difficulty in staying awake. "An impressssssive feat, Tom, but you need to ressssst now. You need it. I will be leaving you in a derelict housssssse in the foressssst." Tom was struggling to focus on his surroundings; the spider's words were merging, becoming hard to understand. "The ressssst of the journey will up to you, but I will be watching throughout just in casssssse you need assssssistance."

He tried to respond, but his mind was being forced into a deep sleep. Exhaustion – and relief – overcame him in an instant. His dreams consisted of memories of his mother and Max, though nightmares crept into them occasionally. All his senses faded, and he knew nothing more for the new few hours.

Chapter 12

It had been years since the spider left with some of the spores. Occasionally, foragers would pass by, but the colony's use of the house was complete, and they had no need – or ability – to enter it anymore.

There are so few of us now. They thought. It was true; being stuck in those cages with the animals – surviving off draining resources – had reduced their numbers significantly as their hosts died. The last few spores only remained alive due to an escaped rodent. It lived under the bed and survived off food scraps, but even this mammal was reaching its limit.

It only had enough resources for another week at the most. They would self-destruct at this point, but they were happy that the rest of the fungi had managed to find a new, thriving home with lots of hosts.

It was movement that caught their – and their host's – attention. A solution had arrived. One of the huge spiders had placed a sleeping human onto the bed. The rat, hungry, immediately smelled the food in his rucksack. The fungi let out a sigh of relief but were still irritated at the lack of care from the spiders. **About time! We've needed a new host for over a year now!**

Upon the rat making physical contact – touching the human on the shoulder as it tried to reach the food – the fungi created the connection, leaving the weakened rat for a better host. They were surprised to find that he was already bonded with different fungi. They had adapted and evolved after bonding with the spiders. His DNA had already been slightly modified, but not dramatically; they must be waiting until they had more resources – and consent – before doing any further changes.

They synced up and became one with the other fungi again, their spores meeting and sharing information. It had been a decade of no communication.

*Being whole again sent a wave of relief through them, and they learned exactly what they had been dealing with all this time. **We are one again.** They stated, ensuring that the thought was simultaneous. It was a test to see if they truly were all back together, and it was confirmed a moment later.*

Their next priority was to check the condition of their new host. Although weakened, he was strong, but dealing with a lot of injuries. The broken leg was the worse, but a strong web bandage around it was helping to keep it stable. Other minor injuries were obvious but not life-threatening.

They knew the reason why after seeing recent memories. He was a fighter, though, so it was expected that he would be able to manage despite what he had gone through. **He's a great host.** *They told themselves confidently.* **Let's make sure he survives this.**

His highly compatible DNA meant they were able to quickly repair most of the problems, but what would happen once he got out of the forest? Surely others would notice his changes, so they would need to account for it.

They found that his genetic code, complex and multi-structured, was able to hide the spider DNA they inserted easily, so that wasn't a problem. This rapid recovery would be questioned, however.

That's a problem in the future. *They announced assertively.* **Let's stabilise that leg so he'll be able to get out here first. We can just revert some of the fixes if needed.**

Having him asleep made the changes easy to do and allowed them to monitor for any complications.

Four hours later

It has been hours since the last text, and he'd received no further contact.

Max was getting worried about Tom, and concerned that he had been captured. If that was true, though, then surely the forager would leave him so it could celebrate? It was still staring at him, as if challenging him to shoot, but he knew better. If he got too close, he'd be snagged and bitten in an instant.

The sun was just peeking over the horizon when he received the text. It was from Tom. 'Almost back. Where safe at edge?'

Max was overjoyed to know he'd managed to get away from the spiders. He began to reply, excited, but stopped, and did it carefully so the forager wouldn't notice what he was typing. 'ETA? Forager staring as usual. Clear on left and right of it. Have shotgun out ready if needed.' He replied.

His response came back instantly, short and with spelling mistakes. He was in trouble. 'One min. Injured. Seen. Be close.'

In the instant that he sent the text, there were loud sounds from the forest to his left. The forager heard and began to turn to cut Tom off, but Max held up the shotgun, and it got the message. It froze in place with an irritated hiss.

He could hear grunts of pain and knew that Tom was running out of there despite his injuries. He could only hope that he had enough distance between his pursuers that he didn't have to worry about causing himself any more of them.

Crap. Run. Gotta run. Ignore it. Tom told himself. The walking stick — a branch quickly shaped by the machete — was the only thing keeping him stable. His right leg wouldn't withstand any weight.

The sounds of spiders above, behind, and around him flooded his thoughts. One mistake would be all it took to lose his advantage. The night vision goggles, though slightly damaged and with one lens cracked, were the only thing that stopped him from falling over the numerous web traps they'd laid out.

As he neared the edge, his vision blurring and his heart racing, he could register the web being flung at him. He'd already dodged around twenty attempted snags; the foragers had learned how to use their web strands like lassoes to trip him up. Only the sensitive hearing and awareness, provided by his fungi passengers, allowed him to keep going.

They were focusing on his pain right now, but they could do little to help when it came to his leg.

Every minute, he got closer to the edge.

Every second, the spiders, significantly faster, caught up.

It was a death race, and all it took was a fall or stumble to fail. He was so close to Max now. He could hear him calling through the trees. *A step at a time.* He repeated. *A step at a time. That's what I need to do.*

The edge of the forest inched closer, but he was running out of energy and time. He needed a miracle to get out.

And, miraculously, he got one.

White Spikes had run ahead of the rest of the foragers.

The other spiders behind him slowed, trusting in their leader to catch him. If he didn't try to do something to stop him, he'd lose all trust and respect from the colony.

Thinking quickly, Tom came up with a solution that allowed him to get out and the spider to 'attempt' to catch him. His rucksack, already ragged and torn, would come in useful here.

Mid-step, he made a slight motion with his hand to a torn strip on the top flap, hanging by a single thread. To the foragers, it would look like he was trying to regain his balance. Its true intention was to inform the spider of the plan to make it look like he was legitimately trying to capture him.

A step away from the edge, he paused for an instant so that the spider could drop down and enact the plan.

His heart seemed to stop as he heard Whites Spikes bungee behind him, uncertain if he would still help him.

It would be easy to catch him now – it would be a bittersweet end to a race that was so close to its finish line.

Thankfully, however, he proved that he could still be trusted, a tarsal claw touching the rucksack perfectly – and then a rip. The strip couldn't hold on any longer and broke away.

Just getting out of the forest wasn't the end of it, though. The spiders had long legs and would continue to try to reach for him. Despite the pain in his leg and being unable to draw in enough breathe between gasps, he still had to get a little further away for it to be successful.

Tom scrambled from the trees as a lasso hit the ground right behind one of his feet, almost losing his balance. Only the cane kept him up. He could see Max again, though couldn't hear him; all he could hear was his own frantic heartbeat.

The painkillers stopped working a second later; his whole body felt like it was on fire, aching and flaring with pain. He tried to remain upright, but the fractured leg moved, and his mind realised that he was out of energy and exhausted.

He let out a gasp and fell, losing his balance. Despite shock, he knew he had to fall with a roll to protect against the impact of the ground.

He clutched his leg, gritting his teeth to prevent himself from screaming. His broken ribs pushed against his lung, threatening to break though, while the headache was overwhelming. He was barely aware of Max moving towards him. Out of energy, he could feel himself passing out; his vision was fading.

The last thing he saw – and felt – was Max behind him, holding the shotgun menacingly, and White Spikes, his red eyes looking towards him through the trees. He'd kept his promise to keep him safe after all.

With a smile, he passed out from exhaustion. His aches and pains faded away instantly.

Chapter 13

When White Spikes noticed that Tom was starting to stumble, running out of energy, he knew that he needed to help again. His promise to the mother replayed in his mind. *'Protect my son and husband.'* He planned to do just that.

Tom had noticed the assistance and offered a solution that allowed him to maintain the colony's trust. The slight hand movement was impressive improvisation and a clever idea. It was also a quite an achievement, considering that he was running for his life with a broken leg and gasping from pain.

They moved as one, White Spikes jumping down and the teenager staying still for an instant so that he could grab hold of the torn flap with a tarsal claw.

It came away without any effort at the perfect time.

Tom's scramble out of the edge hadn't been intentional, but it was exactly what needed to happen. He continued to run, knowing about their long legs. White Spikes reached out in an 'attempt' to catch him, aware of the watching foragers.

Tom looked at him shortly before passing out and smiled in appreciation.

His dad, Max, was staring with anger and concern.

The foragers behind him stopped, trying to see if he was successful, and he was careful to hide his relief as he turned, pretending to be angry instead. It would be needed if the colony was to trust him after this.

The spiders recognised his scowl –he was good at pretending now. Though he was able to tell white lies now, it was still uncomfortable for him, but becoming more natural as time went on. *How much more human could he get?* He wondered. Nevertheless, he had one last thing to do; to show that he had tried to catch him. He revealed the scrap of black material as they looked at them.

Letting it fall a second later so they could look it over – something that foragers did with all evidence – he climbed a tree, making sure to grumble loudly so that the spiders heard it. He needed to be as annoyed as the foragers for this plan to work.

Though the rest of the foragers returned to the colony, talking excitedly, one remained with him, joining him a moment later. It was one of his closest friends. He came over and touched one of his legs to comfort him. "You did all you could, White Spikes. What happens next?"

He looked downward in what he hoped was an angry expression before replying. "We leave them be but ensssssure that we watch each night asssss normal.

They'll trip up eventually and we'll be able to get them then."

"Won't they warn others?" His friend asked.

This time, his answer would be truthful, and it sent a wave of relief through his mind. "They have tried in the passssst, but no one has believed them. Police know not to enter the foressssst anyway." He let out a sigh. "I need to be alone to think about what went wrong. Could you let Alacanta know that I will be coming back late today?"

"Of course. Should I send the other forager away as well?"

"A good idea. There isssss no chance to catch them now. Let him know that he can return to the colony to sssssspend ssssssome time with hissssss family. He deservesssss it."

His friend nodded and attempted to hug him, but their size difference made it difficult. He bungeed down and spoke to the forager, returning to the colony with him.

White Spikes waited until it was silent around him before dropping to the ground and stepping from the trees. Max deserved an explanation about what happened, and he wanted to inform the man about the promise he had made with his wife before she passed away.

Max's first instinct was to shoot back, but a glimpse of webbing over his son's leg – a badly injured one at that – made him pause.

The spider hadn't attempted to catch him properly. The red eyes disappeared for a moment before it stepped out towards him. It was as long as a cargo truck and showed little discomfort as it moved forward, the exoskeleton silent despite how heavy it was.

It was here to help, not to capture.

He motioned to the shotgun and placed it on the ground, then kicked it a good distance away. This peaceful intention made the spider calm down and it spoke.

No wonder it had returned his wife's body. They were intelligent and knew exactly who the two of them were. It was likely that Tom wouldn't have survived his journey without its assistance.

He knelt on the ground and checked Tom's condition, removing the damaged night vision goggles.

Other than the leg and head, he wasn't badly injured, but he knew that there could be internal problems that were invisible from the outside. Blood loss was obvious from his paler skin tone, but even this wasn't as bad as he had expected. Something had caused him to recover quicker than normal, but what?

He hadn't been listening to the spider properly, but now focused on it as his worries over his son were calmed down. "I'm sorry, I didn't catch anything you said before. Could you repeat it?"

The spider smiled "I'm ssssssorry about your wife. It wasssss a long time ago when we captured her. She assssked that I return her to you now that sssssshe hassssss passed, asssss well asssss protect the two of you."

He still wasn't over his grief and a tear fell as he grinned contentedly. "Thank you for bringing her back. I'd always hoped that she'd die in peace. Being unable to feel the cancer eating away at her was the best for her." He shook his head, in disbelief that for so long he had blamed the spiders for her death. The tumour would have taken her sooner. "At least she didn't have to suffer through doing chemotherapy constantly. We'd tried for years but it wasn't working."

"I can asssssure you that we looked after her asssss bessssst we could. Sssssshe was well looked after through the yearssssss. Sssssshe wasssss given food or water if needed and her medical needssssss provided for."

Max nodded at this, though the grief was still too recent for him to process. "What happened to Tom?"

The spider had a wry expression as it explained. "He fell from a tree and isssss lucky he didn't break hisssss back. He hasssss sssssspent ssssome time recovering in a house before making his final esssscape. I had to pretend to try and get him back to ensssssure that the other sssssspiderssssss trussssst me." It motioned to his leg, webbed up to prevent bleeding and keep the bone still. "That wasssss needed. It isssss badly broken and will need sssssurgery to fix. He hasssss ssssomething to help him now though."

This statement caught his attention, and he peered up at the spider quizzically. "I remember seeing that house. What's in it that could have helped him so much?"

"A sssssymbiotic fungus." The spider revealed. Max was surprised at this statement; the dilapidated house had looked to be at the point of collapse when he'd seen it before. "It helpssss thossssse that it findssss. It hasssss bonded with Tom and healed mossssst of the injuriesssss. It isssss likely that he would have died had he not found them."

"What effect will they have on him?"

"It dependsssss." The spider answered, shrugging slightly. It had settled down into a sitting position now that they were both calm. "If he acceptsssss them, they can give him many benefitsssss." It motioned down to Tom's hair, which had changed from a striped brown to a dark, shimmering blonde. "This sssssshowsssss that he hasssss bonded with them intrinsssssically. It isssss why he issss alive. Without the help, internal bleeding may have led to hisssss death."

Max smiled, content. Knowing that Tom would survive this experience, he finally relaxed fully.

Tom was unconscious now, but still appeared to be a little aware of his surroundings; his eyes moved beneath the lids.

He would occasionally grit his teeth as he moved his leg, causing him pain. Some bruises caught his attention, and he moved his top to the side, finding dark colouration. The spider wasn't lying about the fall from the tree; the injuries looked extensive and were prominent all the way down his back.

If Max were to call an ambulance, the webbing would make it obvious what was in the forest, so that would have to be dealt with. "What's the condition of his leg now?" He tried to lift the web and look underneath, but it was stuck tight, and only dried blood was visible in the small gaps.

The spider grimaced as it responded. "It'sssss in a bad condition, Max. If I remove it, you will only have two hoursssss before he losssses a sssssignificant amount of blood."

"It'll make it easier for me to explain what happened to the paramedics." He stated, pulling out some material from a pocket. It would be used as a temporary bandage

131

to keep the leg stable. "Can we agree on staying out of each other's way? We'll be happy to keep your community a secret if you leave us be."

The spider reached out with a tarsal claw, and he accepted the impromptu handshake. "Agreed, Max, but I would like to keep an eye on you. If I ssssssuddenly ssssstop watching the house, they will quesssssstion why. The foragersssss will need to continue monitoring your housssssse each night."

"That's fine with me, so long as you don't step into our garden." He replied. He let out a sigh, holding the bandage with a secure grip. "Remove the webbing, I'll wrap this around to stop the bone from moving."

It reached out and in one motion pulled the webbing from the leg and head, causing Tom to let out a painful gasp.

Max moved quickly, wrapping the length of material around the bone that jutted out through the skin. The dried blood split, and the bleeding was extensive; he had to use another bandage to apply a tourniquet to the limb.

If it was this bad just here, then internal bleeding must have occurred previously.

The blood slowed and he let out a breath, pulling out his mobile. As it connected to the emergency services, he spoke to the spider. "Thank you for helping him. It was enough just to lose her."

It nodded understandingly. "He worked hard to essssscape and deservesssss the chance to live his life. If you ever want to talk, I will be monitoring your house once a month." The spider turned, but paused as it was about to enter the forest. "My name isssss White Spikesssss. It was nice to meet you."

"Same here. It was nice to finally talk to you after all these years." The phone call was answered, and he asked for an ambulance, explaining that Tom was unresponsive. His injuries were brought up, and upon telling them that he had been bleeding rapidly – requiring a tourniquet - and possibly had internal bleeding, the request was rushed to the highest priority.

As he waited for them to arrive, he noticed that Tom's hair was reverting to its original colour, though golden stripes were visible. Perhaps the symbiotic fungus knew that it had to hide to help him.

It wasn't doing much to help with his recovery, though this made sense. It had to look like he was seriously injured from the fall.

All he could do right now was wait, and he did exactly that after removing the rucksack. It revealed just how extensive the bruising down his back was.

At the same time, he felt a strange sensation, and smiled as the fungi introduced itself with a wave.

He immediately accepted becoming a host so that he could reassure Tom and understand how to help him.

Chapter 14

Tom had made it out! They'd thought for a second that he'd lost his footing at the last second, but he'd persevered, and now he was safe. The fungi told themselves, letting out a sigh. **He is not out of the woods yet, so to speak. He still needs time to recover from his injuries.**

The final run out of the forest was difficult for them to manage; his entire body was throbbing with pain, and the tablets he'd taken weren't being effective. They'd had to numb his nerves so that could focus on the spiders behind him.

The foragers' newest use of the webs as lassos was a surprise, but a happy one. It showed that they were still learning new tricks despite the effective strategies they already developed. It had been a close escape, they had to admit, and Tom's idea to help maintain White Spikes' trust with the colony was needed. Tom's intelligence had already surprised them, but to come up with this on the run — and a very dangerous one at that — was impressive.

Now that Tom had fully bonded with them — and they had greater numbers from the sleep at the house — they had begun to make tentative changes but had ensured that they asked for permission first.

One effect of their genetic modification had led to his eye colour changing. The original colour had been blue, but the genetic alteration of the fungi had affected it. His eyes were now emerald green, a sign that their bond was strong.

For the first few days, however, they would hide this by creating a cell layer to camouflage the true colour, making it appear to be his normal blue instead.

Even his hair had changed colour, though it was unintentional. Human hair was made of dead cells. They could only assume that the extra fungi had added another layer to allow for the unprecedented change. Thankfully, they could revert it back to normal easily, something they would need to do once human medical specialists got involved.

*Right now, there was no need to do repairs or fixes. They would need to reverse it all anyway, so they were spending the time hiding themselves among his nervous system and in his neurons. **We must stay hidden.** They stated. **No one can know about us.***

Apart from one person, of course. His dad was an important part of his life; he'd be a good host too. Besides, the spider had left the forest and was speaking with him, explaining what happened to Tom.

Tom's memories of his father, Max, allowed them to understand how important he was to the teenager. He sensed them and smiled as he agreed to become a host.

His DNA was very similar to Tom's, and this made it easy to initiate the process. Unlike his son – who would need lots of adaptations to survive – they didn't need to make any changes. All that they would help with was creating a connection and reducing the pain from his arthritis.

They didn't want to infect anyone else now, but if they needed to – it was someone that either of them was close to or the person was close to finding them out – they would be able to create a connection without any physical or genetic alterations. The link would be minor between them, nothing like Tom had with White Spikes, but would allow limited information to be shared.

They heard the phone call that Max made and began to reverse the changes at the same time as White Spikes went back into the forest. Pain throbbed through Tom's mind again, but they were able to reduce it to tolerable levels.

Ripping off the webs around his head and leg had reopened the broken veins and arteries, but they let it continue until Max had wrapped a tourniquet around them. They also intentionally caused minor internal bleeding, reverting the fixes on the broken arteries. The fungi had to make his condition look as legitimate as possible.

*When the human medical specialists – **paramedics, they remembered hearing**– arrived, they stated that*

*Tom's condition was dire. **It was all going as they had planned.***

*They began to work on repairs slowly as painkillers and a sedative was attached. Tom's thoughts became worried as his senses faded and time became impossible to track. They spoke to him using images, helping to calm him down. **We are here for you.***

They didn't expect his response, asking them to inform him about what they changed or altered, but to be fair, Tom was a perfect host, interested in the changes and highly compatible. They decided to listen to his request and gave his neurons access to see all the alterations and repairs.

Working with him amicably as a host would allow them to thrive and for his body to recover more quickly from his debilitating injuries.

Tom fought to remain calm. Though unconscious, he was aware of everything within his body, and felt every pain. His back and ribs ached, but his broken leg was the worst.

The rapid bleeding was slow now thanks to the tourniquet, but the pain as the web was ripped off...it was almost too much to handle. It was only thanks to the fungi that he was able to tolerate it. They were unable to fully shut down his nerves, but they had reduced their efficiency, so it was manageable for him.

He was able to hear everything around him when the ambulance arrived. The two paramedics were worried but praised Max for the tourniquet on his leg. They cut away his top to check his back and attach a heart rate monitor, revealing the bruising. The sudden coldness made him shiver involuntarily and let out a small gasp.

The paramedics seemed to be happy with his response, for they both sighed in relief before moving on. Tom was eased onto a stretcher after being placed in a C-collar. It wasn't needed, but they didn't know that. All they knew was that they had someone with back injuries in their care, so taking this step was needed for his protection.

A slight pain occurred as medication was attached. The first was a strong painkiller; all his aches disappeared in an instant, replaced instead by comfort. The second was a sedative. It looked like they wanted to try and keep him asleep until the injuries recovered. One final IV bag was attached, this one filled with blood to replace all that he had lost over the last few hours.

The mix of painkillers and sedatives were affecting his internal clock significantly. Words began to muddle together, and he was left alone with his thoughts in a black void.

Although afraid at first, he began to sense the symbiotic fungus, making improvements throughout his body. They sensed his worry and spoke to him through his mind, informing him that they were here to help.

The first place they worked on was his neurons; they became senseless a moment before returning to normality. Their efficiency was enhanced, and his memories were being stored into a database. They even included periods of life which he hadn't been able to remember for fifteen years, those spent with his mother who had been captured by the spiders when he was only one year old.

Before they did any more changes, he asked them a query through his nervous system. *Please let me see any processes you improve upon. I prefer to know what is going on.*

The instantaneous reply was unexpected; the black void was filled with small videos, each showing a different process being adjusted. He could recognise each of his internal organs, severe damage being repaired back to their original strength.

When he saw his leg, he didn't know what was going on. It was only when a surgical tool came into view that he understood.

Tom was watching a doctor perform an operation on himself while unconscious.

There was no pain, but it was still very uncomfortable to see. He watched as the bones fell into line immediately without assistance, the fungi binding the fractures together with a calcium deposit and amino acids. He smiled mentally to himself as he saw the surgeon's face, full of shock, before the skin was stitched back over the top.

Most of the small screens disappeared and, in its place, came up a small image. It showed how the glucose was used by his cells. It suddenly altered, and Tom understood what they were trying to tell him. They had come up with a solution to his diet, something he had difficulty managing with his work at home and school.

Their proposal was to recycle glucose by utilising hydrogen to rebind the molecules together again. It would require a body-wide adjustment to be successful, and the development of new organs to store hydrogen. He agreed with the idea and had a suggestion of his own. *Why not make it so only one molecule of glucose is enough to use a whole muscle?*

The response was one of intrigue as it did a practice run, and it worked perfectly. They began to do work on the muscles as well, but he noticed that it was requiring more effort to make it a usable process. The cells, connected by nerves, were being completely redesigned.

Their efficiency was being enhanced and the main nerve before the muscle was now the catalyst for movements.

They had also noticed one problem that they were working on now that he had allowed them full access to his body.

On his pituitary gland was a tumour, a large benign one that wasn't growing but was close to being a becoming a problem. It was still in its early stage and wasn't secreting toxins or affecting his health. They dealt with it by destroying the cells where it was originating from.

Tom relaxed and focused on recovering from the injuries.

The fungi reassured him throughout and he noticed that they had already become more sentient, starting to form their own voice in his head.

Soon, he could sense what they were thinking – not just through images but also by their words. Some things were still hidden from him in a secluded area of his mind, their own private area where they stored memories.

In time, they would be able to work as a team, and he was curious to see just close the two of them would get.

The foragers returned to the colony saddened and annoyed, though they had seen more excitement during the chase than they had for a while. The other spiders sensed their moods immediately and guessed, correctly, that it had ended with failure.

Each of them returned to the food storage to drink some blood – they were all starving – before returning to their families. Rumours of the human's escape began to spread, but rather than blame the foragers, they instead theorised how clever it must have been to manage to hide from them all – especially from their leader's vision.

White Spikes was usually the one to catch their human fodder, but this human had appeared to break him. It was no surprise, really; the human had come close to finding the colony, and somehow escaped despite countless traps and relentless searches. How he had managed to elude them was a mystery, especially when talks spread that he had been injured. Many of the foragers theorised that their leader was more embarrassed than anything else. He'd found a bloody sleeping bag which matched the bandaged leg that they'd seen as he stumbled out.

The most obvious explanation was a silly one, but it made sense. The human had escaped the first forager by climbing a tree. None of them would have expected it. Exhaustion, cold and shock may have caused him to fall from it, breaking his leg. It was the only reason why the sleeping bag had been so wet with blood.

When their leader returned, still annoyed with himself, they expected his call for a meeting. He went over everything that had happened so that the colony understood how it had failed. The human had, indeed, climbed a tree to hide from them. He'd found the sleeping bag later, by which point the injured human had managed to escape out of the area. It had waited until there was less activity before moving to avoid detection.

Now, however, they understood why its escape had been successful. The human was called Tom, and he was the son of the mother who he had returned. What a coincidence – he had trespassed a month after the body was brought back. They hadn't agreed with the decision then, and they had been proven right.

Tom was clever and been trained for several weeks in preparation for this exploration. It was why he had managed to avoid all their web traps. His perseverance – and strength to continue despite his injuries – had impressed all of them. The foragers agreed that he had deserved to escape after considering what he had achieved.

As for the future? No change. The father and son were too careful to be captured, and they knew how to use weapons. They would have to be monitored until another opportunity presented itself before trying to get them again. Not just the son, but the father too, though that would be a challenge.

They were happy with his explanation, and it confirmed why he had reacted like he did after the rucksack ripped. He was disappointed with himself for the successful escape, something he could have avoided.

They could barely recognise him during the next week; he moved around slowly, as if he had aged, his thoughts looping as he tried to think about what he could have done to catch the son. The colony noticed and only after comforting words – and a meeting that they called for him so he could be reassured – did he behave normally again.

Everything went back to normal after that, though the foragers couldn't prevent themselves thinking about the escaped human, uncertain if he would try to enter again.

They set up new traps, and decided to surround the clearing below them with sticky web walls so that he would have no chance of getting close again. It took a week for the architects to create it, but it worked well, and ended up trapping several animals too.

Chapter 15

Two weeks later

We've done everything we can. *The fungi stated to themselves, monitoring Tom's condition. Everything was repaired and he was almost back to full strength apart from some weakness in his right leg.* **Now it is up to him what he wants to do.**

At least he doesn't have to worry about eating much anymore. *Their idea for glucose recycling was an inventive solution for his bad diet. His input about making it more efficient by only using one cell was impressive and easily added in with a little genetic modification. His new hydrogen storage organs, hidden beneath his kidneys, were perfectly disguised, and stored everything he needed to rebind the glucose molecules back together without taking excess energy.*

They've finally stopped doing these damn blood tests. *The fungi, once they were separated from his body in this way, were programmed to self-destruct within an hour. The medical specialists – doctors and nurses – had done many of these tests to try and find out the cause* *for his hair and eye colour change.* **They'll never find out why,** *they thought smugly.* **We can hide among his DNA and neurons perfectly now.**

It was lucky that Max and Tom had decided to accept them, for they had discovered a major health issue. Both were riddled with tumours. Most were benign and would not cause any problems, but Tom had a large one on his pituitary gland that would cause complications in the future.

Thankfully, all the time spent looking after his mother had allowed them to figure out how to deal with cancerous masses. Once you took off the parts causing the problems – this being the cells themselves – it was unlikely to return.

They had done this a week ago to deal with the tumour, but the response from his body was unexpected. **It recognised the damage. Now it's releasing more hormones to try and fix it.**

They tried to stop it, but it didn't work, so they just had to come up with a solution for the complications it would cause in the future. Investigating the hormone that it was releasing was useful; it was meant to speed up growth and help with repairing problems. It reached its maximum level quickly, but they noticed that it wasn't slowing the production of the hormone. They would need to use it up so it didn't overwhelm him.

There is one way that he can use it. He can always get taller. *They realised. Testing this while he was still unconscious was the best idea to reduce the pain. They added two inches of height by adding more bone to the joints throughout his body. Many of them had open areas with active cells, and this is where they added them on.*

Once it was done, they knew that his balance would be affected, and worst of all, the level of the growth hormone had only reduced by a small amount. They would need to make him taller to use it all up or find a way to restore the cells that they had destroyed. It was manageable, fortunately, but would need to be monitored regularly and throughout the rest of his life.

*As for now, they knew he was safe and recovered from his injuries. They could keep the growth slow and put in improvements that would make it easier if – **no, when** – his joints became affected. Large mammals often dealt with lots of pressure from gravity during walking so they would also be sure to reinforce them. Making it painless if something moved would also be essential for the future.*

*By the time that he felt comfortable to awaken from the coma, they had made most of the adaptations that they needed to and were curious to see what he would do with his new-found potential. **Hopefully slowly.***

Human specialists would look in places that normal tests didn't look and may find the fungi inside his body.

When Tom awoke, they noticed that his neurons reacted differently to his surroundings. His pain tolerance was higher now and there was no sign of discomfort as he got comfy. No one knew that he was their host. **Apart from Max, of course.**

In this case, he needed to be a host; he was the only family that Tom had. He'd also fully accepted them into his body, and they had repaired his health problems so that he could live without worry.

They watched through Tom's eyes, curious about how he would explain what happened to him. The spiders were a good explanation but would only cause more questions rather than answers. Both Tom and Max would have to come up with a reason for why he had been running for his life.

Max was the first to notice that Tom had woken. He quickly looked down and caught his eye, noticing the green irises. He didn't speak just yet, considering what to say. The nurse figured it out a second later and smiled, pouring him a glass of water.

Tom pulled himself up against the back of the bed and moved his right leg into a better position. The glass was downed in an instant and he remained still, his eyes closed and breathing in, before he spoke a second later. His voice was deeper now, as if he had aged a year while he recovered. His first question wasn't a surprise to Max. "How long was I unconscious?"

"Two weeks." He told him, watching as the nurse checked all the medical equipment. "How are you feeling?"

"A lot better than when I arrived back home." Tom answered, a faint grimace visible. His mind must have gone back to what he last remembered. "Sorry about worrying you. I ended up getting stuck in my own mind for the last few days."

The nurse chuckled at this statement. "Do you want to know just how bad the damage was?"

He bobbed his head to the side and downed another glass of water before answering. "Yes, please. I'm quite interested to know."

She sat down at the end of the bed and explained that he had arrived at the hospital with a bad concussion, broken leg, and internal bleeding. The severity of the leg was discussed, as well as the plan for recovery.

Max had already informed the hospital staff that that Tom was quite stubborn and restless. The nurse warned him not to do too much at first and just relax until he was fully recovered.

He nodded in agreement, but Max knew that it wouldn't be long before he would push his limits.

She flipped over a page and looked up a second before she spoke. Max knew what she was going to talk about. His sudden hair and eye colour change was a rumour that had spread around the whole hospital, though no reason had been figured out yet.

"Finally, there's the matter of your hair and eye colour. Our original medical records have your hair as brown, while your eyes are blue. Both have changed. Your eyes are now green while your hair is a dark blonde." She held up a mirror, allowing him to see the change. He wasn't surprised; he must have been listening over the last few days. "Do you have any idea why they've changed colour?"

"I have no idea why." He answered, looking at her. Max was watching as he did and noticed the gold flecks that moved across his irises. He knew the reason but didn't want to tell anyone. He would keep it a secret until Tom confirmed he was fine to let others know. "I was unconscious for several hours in the forest, so it could be anything. I felt the doctors doing regular tests. Did they find anything?"

The calm response shocked her, as well as the realisation that he was aware of what they had been doing. Her face went pale, and she was speechless.

A moment later, one of the doctors entered, and noticed the nurse's expression. Placing a hand on her shoulder, he spoke, addressing her. "What's the matter?"

Still looking at Tom, she responded. "He's felt everything the last couple of days." Her voice was quiet. "He wants to know what you found in the tests."

The man looked up and noticed that Tom was awake. He was one of the regular members of staff and had grown used to him being unconscious.

"Apologies, I thought you were still asleep. My name is Dr Harris." Flipping over the paperwork, he continued to speak about the results. "We did around twenty tests to try and find out why your hair and eye colour changed, but it was all inconclusive. Do you remember anything that might be able to help us with finding the cause?"

"I recall sleeping in a house for a few hours after the fall." Tom stated. His eyes were open, but not seeing them. Instead, it was almost as if he were going back over the memories of that time, able to relive them. "There were some papers on the desk about an experiment, but I was too tired to fully focus on them. It was only after I got some rest that I managed to get back home. If I didn't, it's likely I would have died from the injuries."

This statement surprised all three of them. Speaking about death so naturally didn't make sense. Max understood to an extent; he was only alive thanks to the fungi working on the injuries. To the nurse and doctor, however, it was a strange response.

The man was writing down some notes and had a worried expression. When he next spoke, it was not to Tom, but to Max, and his request was expected. "Could you join me in the corridor for a second, please?"

Chapter 16

Dr Harris was concerned about Tom. It was almost as if he was a different person after what he'd experienced in the forest. The sixteen-year-old now acted like an adult, though he considered that the teenager had always been strange to observe in the town due to his hobbies and mannerisms. Perhaps now he would get an answer.

Max followed him out and he motioned for him to sit down as the nurse checked vitals and chatted with Tom in the room. "I don't know what happened to him, but he's different. Do you know anything that we need to be aware of?"

The dad looked worried before letting out a long sigh. Like his son, he was trying to figure out how to explain it. It must have bemused him just as much as it had him.

His voice was quiet as he began to explain. "I have no idea. He's been in an induced sleep for two weeks, stuck in his own mind. He probably went back over the fall a hundred times, considering what he could have done to avoid it." Max's eyes were focused on the ground, reflective, a faint smile visible on his expression. "To be honest, he hasn't had a normal life. He lost his mother when he was only a year old. I told him about the true reason why she was gone twelve years ago."

Dr Harris was quite surprised to hear this but impressed that they had continued to survive and manage despite obvious grief. The dad was finally getting over it; he could tell by his behaviour. The stress was gone, and he was talking normally. Perhaps this was where Tom had got his calm approach to dire subjects like death.

Rather than interrupt, he waited, and Max continued to speak a moment later, barely aware of his surroundings.

"I always do a stakeout each night to protect the house from wildlife in the forest. The wild dogs are dangerous, and I was always worried about what could happen to either of us." He paused, going back over the memories. "Six years ago, he noticed how tired I was getting. I had to explain why I did them and, to my surprise, he offered to take over for the night so that I could get some sleep."

Ah. Now it made sense. He'd recognised the need for assistance and, even when young, Tom had offered to help.

He listened as the dad explained how he'd slowly increased the number of nights that he did the stakeouts so that he could build up his endurance and manage them. It would have overwhelmed anyone else had they not lived right next to that damned forest.

Dr Harris had lost one of his own family members in it – with no body being found or returned - but hadn't expected this to be reason why the town was safe. No wonder the two of them were so tired all the time; they didn't get any time to themselves because they were always looking out for other people.

Dr Harris nodded and waited for what he was told next. After a pause, the dad confessed something that didn't surprise him after what he had just been told. "He's faced death his entire life, but never come so close to it. His entire perspective towards life has been changed because of the accident."

He waited to see if Max would say something else, but he was quiet, as if thinking through his past. "So why did he go out into the forest if he was aware of how dangerous it is?" He asked, curious.

Anyone else would outright refuse to go out; it was well known that the forest was a place that no one returned from. Tom was lucky to have survived a couple of hours in it.

Max told him about the dare from his friends and the reason why he had decided to enter it despite the danger. It wasn't for himself, but for the two of them, just in case the wild dogs became a problem.

He had planned to find the den so that they could go on the offensive.

Rather than go in unprepared, he'd done three weeks of extensive training that had exhausted him and caused countless bruises.

After a pause, where Dr Harris wrote everything down in a notepad, planning on speaking with the resident therapist, Max continued to explain.

The wild dogs had spotted Tom and began a chase, which he had narrowly survived, using the machete that he'd brought in to defend himself. The last text that Max had received was shortly before he ran out from the trees while he was injured and running for his life.

"What do you think happened?" Dr Harris asked, recognising that the dad was beginning to falter.

"He must have been running when he fell and had the accident." The man answered. "I don't know why it was so severe, but at least he managed to get out in the first place. There are lots of ravines in the forest, though, so he could have fallen in one during his rush to get away. It's lucky that he had the rucksack on."

Dr Harris understood why Tom's behaviour was so different now. He'd always faced the dangers from the outside, guarding against them and not facing them on their own turf. The teenager had pushed himself to the brink of exhaustion and pain to get out of the forest.

The constant pain from the concussion, ribs and the leg must have been agonising. The high strength painkillers that Max had given him had been essential for his escape. It had allowed his mind to ignore injuries that would have hospitalized anyone else.

Tom had always been very clever; using the branch to create a cane was impressive. The training had showed him how to do a tourniquet and bandage around broken bones.

If not for Max, being so careful to show him what to do in emergencies, it was likely that he would have died from blood loss – something that Tom had recognised, and which had altered the way he looked at the world around him.

Max had come to a halt, and he knew that the pair of them needed a rest. Though Tom had partially recovered from his lack of sleep, they shared sunken pits beneath their eyelids, and were physically exhausted.

Dr Harris decided to do something that he never expected to do. He spoke to Max and explained. "In any other situation, I wouldn't recommend this, but it will be appropriate for Tom's situation." Max looked up at him, curiosity now obvious in his expression. "I want the two of you to come back to my house. There's a spare bedroom on the ground floor that will be more suitable for him and a second one upstairs for you."

The dad stared at him, in shock.

He waited a second before continuing to explain. "The two of you haven't had any time to relax, and frankly, Tom is as stubborn as you. He won't be happy being restrained in a bed. I can monitor his diet and keep an eye on his leg. Can I trust you to keep an eye on him so that he doesn't overwork himself and cause more injuries?"

Max nodded. "Of course." He paused, thinking about what to say next. "Thank you. I know that discharging someone so quickly is unusual, but he'll be difficult to manage. He's always looking for entertainment at the house, getting bored quickly and spending his afternoons doing long hikes."

Dr Harris continued to explain, and the dad peered at him, confused. "It will be for two weeks or until I can confirm that his leg is back to adequate strength. It gives the two of you time to recover from the stakeouts. I also want you to speak with friends to get assistance to guard the house. I'm surprised that the two of you have managed to do it for so long without severe sleep deprivation."

"I can sort that. I know a neighbour in the town who knows how dangerous the forest is." Max answered, letting out a sigh. "It sounds like the best idea. Both of us have reached our limits after doing it for so long." He rose, stretching, and Dr Harris did the same, wanting to check on Tom. "I'll call the headmaster. He's been quite worried."

Dr Harris nodded, stepping back into the ward as he made the call.

Entering Tom's room, he stared in shock. His patient – a teenager who had a badly fractured leg – was on his feet, using the foot of the bed to remain stable.

He faltered, speechless.

The nurse tapped him on the shoulder, and he turned to her, speechless. "Sorry, Dr Harris. I tried to stop him, but he got up without any warning. There's no sign of pain from the leg."

He let out a long sigh and closed his eyes for a second. "I knew he'd be trouble. Could you get a pair of crutches please? There's no point trying to stop him."

She nodded and left the room, and Tom noticed him. He smiled mischievously and apologized. Dr Harris could only shake his head, bemused, before motioning for the teenager to sit down.

He added a small note onto the medical file: *Standing after five minutes, no pain. Will need to be investigated.*

Chapter 17

Half an hour later

Nathan was at school, in the middle of the final lesson, when there was a knock on the door. One of the receptionists spoke to his teacher and motioned to him.

Picking up his rucksack, he followed her out, unsure what was going on. He was led through the corridors to the headmaster's office, where the man was busy packing his bag.

The look on his face showed exactly why he had been called out of class, and he was expecting what he said next. "Tom's just woken up in the hospital."

Nathan let out a sigh of relief. He'd been constantly worried about his best friend.

He had been the first to visit after being told about the accident and his injuries.

When Nathan arrived at the hospital two weeks ago, he'd been shocked, barely recognising him. Tom's right leg was in a thick cast, fractured from a bad injury, while bandages were wrapped around his head to help with a concussion. There were dark pits beneath his eyes and each breath seemed to be painful.

The nurse had informed him why, as well as what they were doing to help with recovery. He'd been placed into an induced sleep to allow his body to recover more easily. Strong painkillers and a sedative were keeping him in a deep, painless sleep.

At first, despair had overcome him, as well as guilt. Tom had only gone into the forest after his dare, and now he was in this situation!

The nurse had comforted him, sitting him down and explaining that being like this was best for him right now. He was being well cared for but what he needed more than anything was company. Tom may be aware of his surroundings, and hearing Nathan's voice would help him to stay calm and relaxed.

Max was outside as he left an hour later, devouring a sandwich. He'd booked a room at the hotel so that he was closer and visited every day to spend time with Tom.

As Nathan sat down in the headmaster's car, he could only think back through his memories, angry with himself for not understanding how dangerous it was. If only he hadn't dared him to do it.

Truthfully, though, he knew that Tom wouldn't turn it down. He'd pushed himself to the brink of exhaustion to prepare for it. Perhaps that was why he had survived in the first place. It would forever change him, though; his memory had always been the best of all the class, able to recall everything in perfect detail. He would be able to remember the events exactly as they happened, perhaps to his own detriment.

Nathan leaned against the window, looking out at the town as the headmaster fought traffic to get to the hospital. The dark trees from the forest peeked out at the top of the hill, its dark green canopy foreboding and devoid of life.

There had never been any birdsong or wildlife in that area of town, and now he knew the reason. It had taken almost losing his best friend to figure out the answer.

When Max entered the room again, he found Dr Harris sat in a chair and looking perplexed. He had given up all control, retrieving a pair of crutches for Tom. His son was now leaning against the window and looking out while listening to the nurse. She was updating him about what he'd missed.

The sunlight reflected off his golden hair and it seemed to shimmer in the light, a sign of the symbiotic fungi that had made him their home.

It matched a beard that had been growing over the last two weeks.

Max smiled as Tom's fungi spoke to him.

Tom was almost fully recovered now.

There was still pain, but his tolerance was high enough to ignore it. The most pressing issue was his lack of endurance, and he still needed to be careful not to do too much.

There had also been a slight growth and his bond with the fungi had allowed him to come up with another solution for his bad diet. He'd put on some weight and grown taller, obvious from his longer arms and how much better the large pyjamas fit him.

His deep voice would be difficult to get used to; he was responding as the nurse caught him up, taking everything in easily. Max went over to Dr Harris, still confounded over his patient's recovery, and touched him on the shoulder. His expression was one of acceptance but disbelief as he opened his eyes.

"He's too stubborn to stay in bed and you know it." Max stated quietly. "Just a quick question before I head off to the house. Do you have a book collection?"

Dr Harris sighed before answering. "I have a large collection of medical journals in my living room. Why do you ask?"

He bobbed his head towards Tom, balancing on one leg and looking outside curiously. "It's the only way that he won't be bouncing off the walls from boredom. I've updated the headmaster and he's on the way to see him with Nathan." He smiled slightly, shaking his head to match the doctor's bemused expression. It would help him to relax. "I wouldn't be surprised if he starts doing daily walks when we get to your house."

The man was worried at first, but quickly let out a resigned sigh. "I was afraid you'd say that. Most of the journals that I've collected are diploma level papers. I'll have to quiz him on them to see if he understands the subject areas." He paused a second, taking a breath and letting out a sigh. "How far is it to get to your house?"

"It takes thirty minutes to get there from the town centre. We're right on the edge of the forest." Max answered.

"That's perfect." Dr Harris stated. "My shift finishes in two hours, so it gives you time to grab the essentials." He passed over a card which included his mobile number. "If you get delayed, let me know and I'll take Tom with me when I finish at the end of the shift. I'll text you the address so that you can meet us there."

Max added the number to his contacts. Before leaving, he joined Tom at the window, catching his eye. "I'll see you shortly, dad. I still have plenty of catching up to do."

"Well, it's good to see you on your feet again." Motioning towards Dr Harris, sat back on the chair and updating medical records, he spoke quietly. "Try not to overwhelm him, will you?"

He nodded but let out a small sigh. "I know I only just woke up, but I feel restless if I'm confined in bed for too long. Is it alright if I just read a book while I wait?"

"It's better than driving him up the walls from stress." Max admitted. "I'll bring some of your homework back with me so that you have something to do."

He thanked him, then used the crutches to walk over to the armchair in the corner of the room. Settling back, he moved his right leg to a more comfortable position on the footrest. Retrieving a newspaper from a bookstand, he began to read through a long article, though it only took a few seconds for him to absorb the information.

Shaking his head, and wishing the doctor luck, he set off to the car to get the essentials before Dr Harris's shift ended.

He hoped that the spiders wouldn't be a hindrance; hopefully, the agreement with White Spikes was still in effect. To his surprise, he was looking forward to seeing the large spider again and updating him about Tom's condition.

Phew. The fungi let out a sigh. **No one suspects anything.**

Tom is an excellent host. They had to admit. **He just does too much.**

Standing after breaking his leg so badly was a step too far. The doctor had been perplexed and a little suspicious; they would need to keep an eye on him. Thankfully, the invitation to stay at his house would allow them to connect to him if they needed to.

Once they made him a host, he wouldn't be able to report them.

The nurse didn't seem to be affected by his change, treating him like any other patient, though she seemed to be more curious than anything. **Of course she is.** They stated. **He fractures his leg in ten places and gets up with little signs of pain immediately. Who wouldn't be interested to find out why?**

Apparently, Tom's behaviour had changed significantly, enough to cause suspicion. The doctor had pulled Max out to the corridor immediately after the comment about death. Hopefully the dad would be able to explain why he talked about it so naturally for someone who should have no experience in this topic.

This new approach to life – a little calmer and more concise – confused them, and they began to investigate why it may have occurred. It didn't take long to find out why. **The spider DNA. It caused his neurons to react** *differently. **He's thinking like a spider now rather than a human.***

His basic instincts were all still there but beneath it was a deeper area where he was always thinking about his surroundings, analysing everything he was hearing.

They were surprised by how much it had improved.

They understood why quickly. The spider DNA had allowed him to develop it. In the dark forest where the spiders lived, this sensitive hearing was useful to listen out for any prey.

In the human world, however, it was a hindrance; being able to hear everything was more of an annoyance than a benefit. His compatible DNA had meant that it was easy to put in, but it required a solution to cope with it.

Tom had already solved it.

A mental audio filter. They analysed the new adaptation and were surprised at how well it worked. **Easily adjustable for any situation.** Right now, it was tuned to reduce the noise from outside, focusing only on the room he was in. He would be able to turn it up to listen from further away if needed. **Not even the spiders have figured out how to do this. He's a very adaptive host.** They thought.

They investigated how he had developed it and copied the process to their DNA so that they could share it with the colony when they synced up with them again.

Right now, there wasn't much he could do; he was restricted to his hospital room —on orders from his doctor — and reading a newspaper to keep himself entertained.

His mind occasionally thought back to the moment he'd fallen from the tree, a memory they had disguised as a nightmare so that it wouldn't cause him any stress or mental trauma. Considering his perseverance, however, they made the decision for him to remember it so that he could come up with a good explanation for what occurred if asked.

There was a moment of shock when he saw it properly for the first time, followed by acceptance. **No wonder he'd managed to survive; Tom was, indeed, very stubborn.**

Chapter 18

White Spikes was the first to be informed when Max Homedale returned home. Arriving at the house, he asked the forager on watch to return to the colony, wanting to speak with the man about his son.

It had been two weeks, and neither of them had returned home yet. Max had already entered the house and began collecting items from rooms when he arrived; he must be grabbing the essentials and moving into town for a few days.

A few minutes later, after packing the car, Max surprised him, calling out his name quietly.

White Spikes stepped out from the trees and settled down so that he was at a better level for him. The man was comfortable with being so close to him; he must have gotten used to being around him now.

"Tom's awake again." The dad revealed. "He was unconscious for two weeks, but it was for a good reason. His bond with the fungi has been enhanced and they seem to be working as a team."

"Let me guesssss." White Spikes stated, knowing what his son was like. "He'sssss being a pain for the doctor now?"

"Definitely. He stood up shortly after waking. The doctor has already admitted defeat and got him some crutches. Last I saw, he was writing some notes onto his medical records, probably regarding the rapid recovery."

"Hasssss there been any sssssignificant changesssss?"

"Both his hair and eyes have changed now permanently." Max revealed. "Not just a slight change but shimmering blonde hair and emerald irises. It's strange to see just how grown up he is now. Being asleep for two weeks must have felt like a year for him." He paused, going back over memories. "The way he talks is so different now, too. He always spoke about death, but he hasn't come so close before. He takes his time before talking, deciding on how best to explain something. I'm surprised by much the fungi have helped us."

No wonder Max was standing without any pain now! He'd become a host too, and they were actively helping him. It was obvious from his body temperature, which was now in harmony.

White Spikes wasn't surprised by Tom's fast recovery. It made sense considering how many improvements had occurred, and his acceptance to become a host may have allowed the fungi to adapt to the human body quickly.

"You sssssshould return to the hosssssspital." White Spikes stated, pulling Max from memories. "The ressssst of the colony will quesssssstion why I have taken sssso long. I will tell them that you brought the sssssshotgun as you packed, and plan to return in a few weeksssss."

"That'll be great, thank you. I know that they'd be highly questionable about why you didn't try to capture me." Max let out a sigh and pulled out a set of keys. "We'll see you in two weeks once Tom's faked his recovery enough."

"I'll look forward to sssssseeing him again. Tell him that I am glad he hasssss managed to sssssurvive hissss ordeal and made a bond with the fungusssss. They will do amazing thingsssss for him if he acceptsssss them fully." He waved a leg – his version of a goodbye gesture - as the dad set off, and began to return to the colony, thoughtful and reflective.

White Spikes had an intricate bond with the symbiotic fungi too, one which had allowed him to thrive in this inhospitable forest. If Tom became as linked to it as he was, he would be able to achieve many things.

He jumped as one of his friends bungeed down next to him. "Any luck?"

Remembering the white lie which he needed to tell, he let out a long sigh, then shook his head, lying that Max had brought out the shotgun as he packed the car before setting off. His explained this behaviour as worry about his son, who was probably still in the hospital after his near death in the forest.

171

"The human looked very injured when I saw him." His friend replied, and White Spikes slowed, falling into step beside him. He was thinking back over how friendly Max was when his friend continued to speak to him. "I bring good news from the foragers. A family of tourists arrived for a hike in the forest. They were bitten and placed into the storage compartments without anyone else noticing their disappearance."

He let out a relieved sigh; though they had over twenty captured humans right now, it wasn't enough to sustain the colony. Having the extra people would help offset supplies for a while, allowing the rest of the humans to recover their blood levels. "Hasssss any evidence been left behind?"

"The car has been buried and their belongings added to the stockpile." He confirmed.

Five years ago, the disappearance of a small family had sparked an investigation and a police presence in the forest.

It was only through luck that the colony hadn't been noticed; they had bitten them and left all their items in the open without thinking about them. Since then, the foragers had been informed to hide all signs of entry to the forest, including burying vehicles. Their main clearing for meetings had six different cars and vans below the ground, now covered by dirt and topped with dark grass. It would be several months before the newest was properly hidden.

A year ago, they had also discovered just how important it was to destroy all electronics; many of the newest models could send out signals that could be tracked. They needed to be smashed and the SIM cards destroyed before they were safe to add to the stockpile.

"What are the humansssss' conditionsssss?" He asked, curious. Depending on their age and health, they could last up to fifteen years as a food supply, but anaemia and injuries could reduce that length of time. They were monitored daily by medical specialist, who would provide care or recovery time. Only one condition, cancer, was untreatable, but being in a comatose state significantly reduced the growth of tumours.

"They have confirmed that all the tourists are healthy and strong. They should feed the colony for ten years if their health is maintained." White Spikes smiled at this; it would help their current fodder last for longer. Barely anyone entered the forest nowadays due to the rumours.

"Excellent work. I'll go to ssssssee them when I return to the colony." He slowed down, tired. It was about this time when he had a nap; his brood was a constant annoyance and attended the school during the afternoon. "Alacanta will be waiting for me. I should head back and have a nap before the children arrive."

His friend nodded and set off, bidding him a good day.

They were neighbours and close friends at the colony and would often babysit for him if he was ever too busy to see the children. Their arrangement had worked well for the last twenty years, and he often returned the favour, watching over his children too.

They referred to him as their uncle; though he loved this title, it made him remember how old he was now.

When he finally arrived back at his home, Alacanta, his wife, was waiting for him. She asked about his visit to the house, but he only shook his head in reply. They settled down for a nap afterwards, both tired out and wanting to sleep before the chaotic brood returned from school.

Looks like they'd found a good new host. We're happy here though. The fungi thought. Now that they were separated from the spores that had left to bond with the human, they were aware of the faint connection with the father, who had his own version.

Tom's spores, however, were the most powerful. Perhaps it was because they had needed to make major alterations to allow him to survive. Even now, while he was recovering in hospital, they still received small snippets of information, somehow able to connect even from this distance away.

The news that he now thrived gave them hope that his fungi would manage to avoid detection. They would be able to adjust for any situation and make anyone who would get in the way a host too – either by choice or force.

When it came to White Spikes, they didn't need to do much. He'd already fully accepted them. **We just need to keep reminding him of the promise.** The memory of the mother, asking to keep the two humans safe, was always kept close and could be brought back in an instant.

They needed to ensure that they were safe – both for the success of their sibling spores and for the future. Perhaps they could 'encourage' the spider to talk to them more so they could sync up and warn them about the danger if the rest of the colony decided to capture the two of them anyway.

They didn't like having to manipulate him like this, but it was the only way.

Often, though, the spider expressed thoughts that showed he was getting closer with the humans on an emotional level. They didn't need to remind him of what the mother had said anymore. He immediately remembered it himself.

His DNA has always been very complex, but it was now a mix of three different species, all working together as one. The snake's genetic information had allowed him to develop his heat vision, and it had passed onto some of his brood naturally.

One of them, a youngster called Lilliana, had accepted them even further, and her genetic information had been even more interesting to them. The mixture of human and snake DNA had combined so that she could see the nervous system in humans. She would be a great medical specialist when she was older; her venom was a natural painkiller and didn't contain any anaesthetic chemicals.

White Spikes' interaction with the human genetic information had been interesting to observe. Over time, he had begun to become more human, though the inciting factor had been biting the jailor. **Its genetic information allowed us to develop greater complexity.** They considered. It had unlocked a possibility they could never have imagined – a spider with human emotions.

They were happy where they were, though it came with some dangers. His behaviour, already so different, had always caused suspicion from the rest of the colony. It seemed that they now understood why he acted like he did, though. **He knows how to behave normally. He's become good at pretending.** They thought. **How much more human could he become?**

Chapter 19

Tom was partway through a book when he heard the painful yell from the corridor.

He recognised the voice; it was a patient a few doors down. From what he'd heard, he had been involved in an accident, and suffered from whiplash and a section of the spinal cord moving. Surgery had been required to implant metals pins and supports. Though able to walk, he was exhausted after his ordeal and wouldn't have much energy.

Tom hesitated at first, but he knew that no nurses or doctors were nearby. The man didn't have his alert button with him to notify the staff. It had a noticeable beep which he could hear from the man's bedside table.

His own alert button, attached to the bed, wasn't working, and he knew that delaying this would only cause the man further problems.

Rising from the armchair stiffly, he stretched, then got comfy on the crutches. Approached the door of his room slowly, he managed to open it, though he almost fell as he did. His balance had been badly affected and he was unsteady as he opened the door.

Catching his breath, he stepped out, almost falling a moment later. His problems were minor compared to what the man was dealing with; his groans were becoming worse as he approached. He knew that the man needed to be back in his room where it was safe for him.

Reaching him, Tom spoke softly, setting the crutches against the wall and resting a hand on the man's shoulder. "Listen to my voice. You're alright." Though he could hear himself panting from the exertion of hobbling over, the man was worse, at the point of a panic attack. "Take a deep breath and exhale slowly."

The man nodded; his eyes were glazed over, his thoughts in disarray. He followed his instructions, and quickly calmed down. His neck was in a C-collar and a metal frame was visible through his pyjamas, keeping his spine still.

His position, crumpled down on the ground, was putting it under a lot of stress. The man knew that he needed to get up to prevent it from getting worse; he bobbed his head, and Tom began to help him up.

It was agonising; every muscle hurt as he slowly lifted the man. His hearing was sensitive, but right now it only registered his rapid heart rate and deep breaths.

Groaning, he finally managed to ease the man onto a chair, and they both breathed in slowly, catching their breath and recovering. His endurance must have been badly affected, though he knew the fungi would help.

Thankfully, his pain tolerance meant that he could ignore the aches and pains. He focused on the patient next to him, in a worse condition than he was.

"You alright?" He asked, placing a hand on the man's shoulder.

"T-thank you." The man stated, letting out a breath. He was stiff in the chair, trying to ignore the pain. "I was trying to get to the toilet, but I suddenly felt tired out and my legs crumpled beneath me." He was back to normal now; he looked at Tom, seeming to recognise him. "Weren't you unconscious for the last two weeks?"

"Indeed so." He responded, smiling comfortingly, and holding out a hand. "I'm Tom. What about you?"

"I'm James. I got hit by a drunk driver and my car flipped over. Balance is still all over the place because of whiplash and my spine needed surgery to prevent paralysis." He let out a sigh, accepting the handshake. "If you don't mind my asking, what happened to you?"

"It's a long story." Tom answered, quickly coming up with a concise explanation for his injuries. "The summary is that I ended up falling in the forest. All it takes is a fall into a ravine to cause a concussion, broken leg, and bad blood loss." The man went pale at hearing this; it wasn't a surprise, considering that he had just helped him up despite his own issues. "It was great to meet you, but I should probably head back before the doctor sees me up and about."

Three voices a floor below them caught his attention. Closing his eyes, he figured out who they were in an instant. It was the headmaster, Nathan and a nurse. They were coming closer, the nurse discussing his condition with them.

It was only possible thanks to an audio filter that he'd created in his mind, a method of sorting all the noises in the hospital so that he could focus on searching for individual voices. If it wasn't there, he'd be deafened by all the sounds; he could hear everything floors above and below, as well as everything from a kilometre away, within and outside the hospital.

A hand touched his shoulder, and he opened his eyes to find James looking at him with concern. "Are you okay?"

Tom smiled. "I was checking who was coming up. My hearing is extra sensitive, so I can listen to everything in the surrounding floors. A nurse is coming up, along with two visitors who are coming to see me. She'll be able to help with going to the toilet and getting back to your room safely."

The man visibly paled upon hearing this information.

An instant later, the door to the corridor opened, and the nurse, headmaster and friend arrived. They hadn't quite expected to see him up yet, especially out of his room. The nurse hesitated for a moment before recognising who he was sitting next to and coming over. "What happened?"

Tom noticed that James was nervous, disappointed to be caught like this when he should have been resting.

Catching his eye, he offered the man a comforting smile, and he quickly relaxed upon seeing it. "I needed to go to the toilet. I was halfway there when I lost my balance and my leg crumpled beneath me. I'd probably still be on the floor if not for my friend here."

She shook her head in bemusement. "As expected of you, Tom. Only awoke less than an hour ago, yet already helping others despite your own injuries." She helped James up, asking him to hold onto her shoulder. The nurse spoke to Tom quietly. "Get back to your room please. I won't hear the end of this if Dr Harris finds you out here. Could we keep this between the four of us please?"

"Understood, ma'am, and thank you." Tom responded, causing her to let out a laugh.

Rising onto the crutches again, he hobbled over back to the room, and they followed him in. Both the headmaster and his friend were in hysterics from his absurd interaction with the nurse.

Surprise, surprise. He did too much again. The fungi thought with a sigh. *Of all the things he shouldn't do, he helps someone up despite being weak himself. Why are we not surprised by this anymore?*

As the teenager rose onto the crutches and stumbled back to his room, tired and aching, they noticed that he was able to deal with the pain without assistance. His pain tolerance was high enough that the recent exercise and strain on his body wasn't a problem.

His endurance, however, had been reset and would need regular activity to increase. It would be a long process but a beneficial one that would help him to recover fully.

His friend – **Nathan** – was close to him and showed signs of mental trauma. Assessing his behaviour, they could recognise guilt and remorse, though it was unsurprising. He'd dared him to go into the forest.

From Tom's memories, they knew that he tended to be truthful and had confessed painful truths to him in the past. It wouldn't be long before Tom revealed that he was a host to them. *Perhaps it was worth making him one now?* They considered.

'We're going to ask him once we have the opportunity.' *Tom told them.*

So he's able to sense what we're thinking about now? They thought, amused. *He's quite amazing. But he's right. It's not suitable to do this now.*

Chapter 20

Of all the places where Nathan thought that he'd see Tom, it wasn't in the corridor, especially after being so badly injured.

He barely recognised him at first; it was only when the nurse ran over that he realised who he was.

His friend had gone from brown hair to a shimmering dark blonde. The loose pyjama top revealed faint bruises and he looked a lot better now. There were obvious signs of exertion from how he was sitting, but he still looked comfortable and relaxed, and his carefree approach to life had allowed the other patient to be truthful.

His deep voice shocked him for a second before his response to the nurse caused him and the headmaster to go into a laughing fit. It wasn't due to anything specific. Seeing him back to normal – awake again – was a relief. It was his way of rationalizing that Tom was back, healthy, and managing despite how badly he had been injured.

He stopped after arriving back in the room and watched his friend settled onto an armchair. He put his right leg – still surrounded by a thick cast – onto a footstool before stretching and looking at them.

Nathan just stared, in disbelief that he'd manage to get out of the forest in one piece. The blonde hair was striking, a shade that he couldn't fully describe. In the sunlight that came in from the window, it truly did seem to shimmer, and was a startling difference to his eyes.

His blue eyes were gone, replaced by a vibrant emerald green. Nathan had tried to ask the nurses and doctors why they'd changed so drastically during the visits but only received confused shrugs in response.

There was one major difference that didn't surprise him.

He'd visibly aged. The sixteen-year-old was gone; he now looked like an adult, the green eyes deep and reflective. There were laughter lines that hadn't been there before, and a scraggy beard had begun to grow. He'd partially recovered from his lack of sleep as well; he looked healthier than he'd ever seen him.

He caught the headmaster's eye; he'd been looking at him as well and was in shock. He'd been too busy to visit while he recovered. The last thing that he must remember was the brown-haired teenager who was sleeping during lunch. He'd matured and somehow changed his eye colour, though it was difficult to comprehend how it was possible in the first place.

Nathan was still watching Tom's response, trying to assess his emotional state, something he was easily able to do.

It revealed nothing - no pain, stress, or discomfort. How was that possible considering what he'd dealt with?

The headmaster asked how he was doing first, and he watched as he answered, trying to figure out if he was lying. He responded concisely, with just the right information, giving nothing away. "I'm doing alright, thank you."

"When did you wake up?" Nathan asked.

"About fifteen minutes ago." He revealed. This shocked both him and the headmaster; being up and about so shortly after waking from such severe injuries wasn't possible normally, especially considering the state of his leg.

To be fair, he'd always been very stubborn and restless. At school, he always had to be doing something, be it homework or drawing while he waited for the lesson to finish. Being stuck in the room must be awful for him, but Nathan noticed that a small stack of newspaper and magazines had built up. He had always been great at remembering information. "I stood up within the first five minutes, so the doctor decided to get some crutches."

He stopped talking for a second, his eyes becoming reflective, almost as if he was going through his memories.

Nathan watched, uncertain about what was going on.

He'd only seen Tom act like this when they were discussing their families. His memory was amazing, the best in the school, so he could go back over everything in perfect detail.

Perhaps he was remembering what had happened in the forest.

It took a touch on his shoulder, courtesy of the headmaster, before he was pulled back to reality again. "Sorry, got lost in my thoughts for a moment."

The man nodded but was still worried. "Why did you help the other patient if you're not doing too well yourself?"

"I heard his agonizing yell." Tom revealed. Nathan was surprised to hear this; the room was sound proofed, and they could hear nothing from the corridor or outside. "My hearing is sensitive now, so I knew that there was no one around who could help. He'd left his alarm button by his bed, so he was unable to tell someone that he needed assistance. Mine isn't working." He paused, and he realised that Tom was considering what to say next. "It was quite difficult to lift him, but he needed help."

"So what happened in the forest?" He asked, curious, but watching his behaviour.

Tom visibly stiffened upon hearing the question but let out a breath and seemed to centre himself again, relaxing before beginning to explain what had occurred.

Nathan could only listen to the story. It was too shocking for him to believe. No wonder he did the stakeouts! If the wild dogs made it out of the forest, they'd start attacking anyone they found. Thank goodness his dad had prepared him for every eventuality; it had prevented him from bleeding out or permanent damage.

At least now he understood why people never came back from the forest. It had been a mystery that had confounded him for the longest time. He watched as Tom continued to talk, becoming more stressed out with each sentence, and his eyes becoming thoughtful and reflective again.

Nathan, listening and watching his behaviour, thought that it all sounded truthful, but he could be lying about what happened to make them less worried. He'd always sought to protect others – and could often sugar-coat issues that were agonizing for him.

His concerns about it being too much for him were proven right halfway through.

Faltering, Tom came to stop, his eyes reflective and reliving that moment in the forest perfectly. It took the headmaster touching him on the arm to bring him back again. He'd leant down, slumping slightly in the chair, and was sitting stiffly – a sign that he was uncomfortable and nervous.

He continued to explain afterwards, though he was noticeably more tired now. His left leg was tapping slightly. His wording was different too, and he noticed that his deep voice was even quieter. His memory appeared to be a problem; it was causing mental trauma due to unearthing everything that he'd experienced.

His friend had always faced danger head on, but he'd never come as close to it as he did during his adventure in the forest. He'd fought to get out, pushing himself past the brink to make it the last few steps. The resilience he needed to manage to escape, badly injured as he was, was a miracle. No one else would have survived this.

The doctor rejoined them at this point, entering the room silently and sitting on a spare chair. Tom noticed but continued to speak, as if wanting to confess about what had occurred. The more he said, though, the more tired he looked and sounded; he'd exhausted himself from helping the other patient, and he needed rest desperately.

He was about to talk about what happened after he awoke from the fall when he froze up again, leaning forwards in the armchair and looking stressed.

The emerald eyes were unfocused; he was going through the memories again. He closed his eyes to try and regain his composure, and Nathan went over, recognising his behaviour. He was about to faint; he'd been acting the same way a year ago when he overworked himself during a lesson.

Kneeling in front of him, he held his friend's shoulders, helping to keep him up.

Sure enough, Tom passed out a second later. Nathan was prepared for this; he gently pushed backwards until he was sat on the armchair in a safe position. The headmaster and doctor didn't even realise what happened until a minute later, and they both came over, concerned.

The two men worked together to lift him back onto the bed, where the doctor checked his vitals. He was worried; he could tell by the man's expression. "Thank you for coming in today to see him. Right now, though, I need to figure out what caused him to faint." He opened Tom's eyes; from the quick glance that Nathan was able to get, they were moving rapidly. He was in the middle of a nightmare, though he usually tossed and turned. The sudden change was confusing to him.

The headmaster touched him on the shoulder, and he nodded. Nathan spoke to the doctor before leaving, curious. "Thank you for letting us visit him. When will he be discharged?"

"At the end of my shift today." The doctor revealed.

So soon? Nathan thought.

"Staying here will only impede his recovery. Both Max and Tom will be staying at my house until he's strong enough to walk properly again." He paused for a second, radioing for a nurse. "And hopefully find out why his eyes have changed colour. That's still a big mystery for everyone here."

Nathan was worried; if he was this bad already, how would he able to manage at school? He shook his head, concerned, and followed the headmaster back to the stairwell, thinking back through his behaviour.

It had all seemed truthful, but there was something that he wasn't telling them.

Dr Harris noted down his observation on the notepad as he waited for the nurse to arrive.

Tom had seemed to be managing quite well up until halfway through the explanation before suddenly looking exhausted and tired. It was lucky that his friend was there; he had been the only one to realise that he was about to faint.

He wasn't worried about the leg; the last x-ray had revealed that most of the bones were in the right place and just needed some time to get back to full strength. Hell, he'd probably be tempted to remove the cast within the next week as it would only hold him back.

What concerned him the most right now was the sudden passing out. He'd only recently recovered a concussion, a significant one at that. Fainting was a sign of a traumatic brain injury, and this needed to be checked.

The only way to figure out the severity was an MRI scan.

The nurse entered with a wheelchair – the best way of getting him around the hospital – and spoke to him.

She noticed Tom's condition and became worried, coming close and checking his vitals. "What happened?"

"He fainted while talking with his friend and the headmaster." Dr Harris summarised. "I want to run him through the MRI machine to check for any signs of injury."

She nodded and helped to get him into the chair with the least pain and discomfort possible. In Tom's case, it required lifting him onto it gently. The nurse checked his blood pressure on the way down to check if there was another cause for the fainting.

All the staff members spoke to them as they passed, asking what the situation was. After the second time, he had to politely ask that they continue without interruptions.

The staff in the MRI department was expecting them and quickly got the teenager up onto the platform, putting his arms over his chest to protect them.

The machine started up and Dr Harris joined the nurse to look at the results.

The first screen showed the structure of his brain and would indicate bleeding or cranial pressure. It all came up clear, but something was wrong. It was at that moment when one of the technicians pointed him towards the third monitor. This tracked electrical activity; he understood exactly what he was dealing with.

He radioed for a colleague; Tom's situation was worse than he'd expected.

Chapter 21

This is the life. The fungi thought. **A sunny, warm afternoon. White Spikes happy and having a nap with Alacanta. What could be better?**

They were doing quick repairs when a connection suddenly formed. They recognised the fungi, the spores that were in the human. They were worried...desperately looking for help.

We can't understand his neurons! He's in the middle of a looping nightmare and we can't get him to relax. What can we do?

This was a surprise. They never expected to hear back from them, not least in a connection like this, something that should have been impossible. They thought back to how White Spikes had dealt with his bad dreams and began to speak with them, sharing the memories. **Take it one step at a time and calm down.**

Their siblings let out a mental breath before continuing to speak to them. **He wanted to see all memories despite blocking them. We allowed it because we know that he's stubborn. Now his mind is looping back through the fall repeatedly.**

Interesting. It looked like this human had overwhelmed the spores as well. **Situation?**

He's been placed in a tube for a test. *They revealed.* **We heard the doctor call a colleague. They are talking quietly. We are worried that they will investigate further.**

From the memories that they saw, they knew that they were well-practiced when it came to hiding themselves, but they could do little to protect themselves from detailed tests. **Describe his neuron structure to us.**

There was a pause and they investigated, more logical and analytical rather than stressing out. **A mix of spider and human now. They are linked to be more effective and work together to store information perfectly.**

They ran the situation through their spores, analysing how to solve it. They looked at how the youngsters in White Spikes' brood dealt with bad dreams, and each of them had the same thing in common. **Stop trying to follow the neural pathways. You're only making the nightmares worse. Interrupt the signal and try to start a pleasant memory instead. It should help his neurons to calm down.**

There was silence for a second, then a relieved sigh. **He's calming down now. We'll try to alter his neural network so that he can manage the traumatic memories himself. Thank you for all your help.**

No worries. How are you able to connect to us right now? It's impossible to sync up from this distance away. They asked, curious.

No idea. It might be due to the machine they put him in. The doctors are pulling him out now. Losing connection. Thank you again. *Just like that, they were gone; the fungi were alone. They tried to establish the connection again, but it was impossible; only a faint one could be found, and little information was exchanged.*

They continued to work on repairs afterwards, still curious about how that strong a connection could be formed.

They were only able to link up with other spiders when they were right next to each other and in touching distance; being able to do it while the host was miles away was interesting. Tom was an amazing host and had the potential to achieve amazing things.

Perhaps it was something to do with the machine he'd been placed inside. Perhaps it was something that he could do naturally.

In any case, White Spikes had sprained one of his legs during the walk back, so they continued to help by reducing the pain and allowing him to have a good sleep. The spider's dreams were composed of the memories of his brood and Tom and Max.

He had truly accepted the two humans as friends after all.

One hour later

When Max returned to the hospital, Dr Harris was waiting for him, his expression worried. He motioned him over, then led him through the corridors to another room. There was another member of staff waiting for them, though he didn't recognise her.

He held out his hand to the other member of staff and introduced himself. She smiled but didn't return the gesture, instead returning to her notes with a look of concern.

Nervous, he settled down onto an armchair, uncertain about what was going on, placing the bag of spare clothes next to him.

Dr Harris spoke first, sitting down on another chair and looking up at him, as if figuring out what he was thinking. "I thought it best that you be aware of what occurred while you were collecting the essentials from home. Tom was speaking with his friend and the headmaster this afternoon about what happened. The accident hasn't just caused him physical injuries, which are still quite significant, but also PTSD from the traumatic memories."

Max wasn't surprised by this. Being stuck in your own head for two weeks, repeatedly seeing the same memory, would cause anyone issues. Tom had almost died in the forest, so it wasn't unexpected that it would lead to something like this. He nodded as he replied. "I had a feeling that there would be. It wasn't a normal situation in the slightest, and with his memory, he's able to recall it perfectly too."

Dr Harris summarised what had occurred while Max was out of the hospital, and he felt guilty as he realised that he could have been there to help.

Freezing up twice during a conversation was unlike Tom, but it was expected after everything he'd experienced. From the faint connection that he currently had with his son, he could tell that he was out of the nightmare and asleep.

The other staff member passed something over to him, and he recognised what it was. They'd put him through an MRI scan to figure out what he was currently dealing with.

Most of his brain was active, but the location made little sense to him. She was assessing his reaction as he looked at it, and upon seeing his confusion, spoke. "I was called in to assist when he was brought in for an MRI scan. I'm a therapist, so I knew that something was wrong when he pointed out your son's results. Mr

Homedale, Tom has PTSD. It's to be expected when considering what he's dealt with."

"What's the best thing to do to help him?" Max asked, passing the printout back. "His memory is great, so it might be difficult for him to deal with the traumatic memories."

She smiled as she handed something over to him, and he noticed that it was a pamphlet. It explained how therapy worked and what types of therapy were available.

"I've been doing this for years, and his level of emotional trauma is the equivalent of what I see in soldiers after they return from war. Therapy is a proven treatment for PTSD and with how clever your son is, it's likely to succeed. It won't help him forget what he's dealt with, but it will help him to manage them better."

Max skimmed the information but knew that this wouldn't be enough. She continued to explain. "I can offer monthly visits to talk about his emotions for the next six months. Dr Harris will come up with a plan to help his leg get back to full strength. He may need to perform further tests as a nurse has noticed that he seems to be taller."

"That sounds perfect, thank you." Max stated, wringing his hands together nervously. It looked like it would take more than two weeks for him to recover after all. "Is there anything that you want to know that can help with developing a treatment plan?"

Dr Harris' phone pinged, and he promised to be back in five minutes, leaving the two of them alone. She pulled out a notepad and began to ask him questions about Tom.

At first, it was quite easy to answer; queries about his early life and what his hobbies were then. It was once he revealed his wife's disappearance, and his constant stakeouts, that she became worried. It wasn't a normal activity for teenagers, offering to guard the house, but it was what he was accustomed to. Finally, she asked why they needed to do it, and he told her about the forest behind their house.

"Let me get this straight." She stated, looking at him with shock in her expression. "There are dangerous stray dogs in that forest, and you've never reported it?"

"I've tried to tell them for years now." Max admitted.

He explained that he'd tried to warn the authorities about the dangers in the forest multiple times, but no one had ever believed him. The only time that they'd taken it seriously was five years ago, when a family had disappeared. Police had searched it high and low but somehow missed the large colony at the centre. Since then, there had been no interest.

There was a knock on the door and Dr Harris returned, entering the room and smiling comfortingly at him before settling back on the chair.

The therapist let out a sigh and added a section to her notes. "What would have happened had he fallen within their grasp rather than down the ravine out of reach?"

"They would have torn him apart." He stated. "Everyone who goes in there disappears. The stray dogs are constantly hungry, so they're willing to kill humans for food. Even after all these years, I still shiver when I hear them howl. They only do it when they spot something that they can hunt. I was hoping that they'd spotted a fox rather than Tom when I heard it that night."

"Thank you for clarifying that for me." She stated, closing the notepad. "I'm going to quickly summarise what I've heard so that you can both fully understand what Tom is dealing with right now. He lost his mother, but he doesn't have many memories of her. The constant danger that he's in has caused him to grow up quicker than he should. He's almost sixteen now, yet unlike his peers, he has a lot of responsibilities to take care of. I spoke with his teachers and his friends at the high school, and everyone has great respect for how hard he works. They all notice when he guards the house and make sure to look after him." Max was surprised at hearing this, having no idea that the stakeouts had affected him so much.

She'd noticed his reaction and continued to explain. "Mr Homedale, his hard upbringing has benefited him, but he can only do so much until he reaches a breaking point. Honestly, you should have come to the hospital sooner, so that both of you could undergo therapy. You've never gotten over losing your wife and taking over so much responsibility at home has affected you significantly, though I can understand why you have continued to stay so focused. I think the entire town should thank you for preventing the dogs from attacking others, but as I said, I doubt that anyone fully believes it and they'd be difficult to catch."

"We should have come in before it got this bad. As for guarding the town, not something we need to be thanked for. It's needed as our house is right on the edge of the forest. No one has ever believed me when I told them about them anyway." He paused, taking in a breath and relaxing. "How is Tom doing right now?"

"I decided to check on him on my way back and he was sleeping peacefully. It looks like a sedative helped with the nightmares, though only to a certain extent. He's still dealing with some traumatic memories but it's better than before." Dr Harris confirmed.

"Honestly, he'll recover better in a home environment than in the hospital." The therapist admitted. "I understand that Tom will be staying in a spare room at your home, Dr Harris, so it will be a better location for him to work though his traumatic memories."

Max nodded in agreement as Dr Harris discussed his plan for bringing him out on a wheelchair. The car was full of belongings and didn't have enough space for the two of them.

He smiled and asked a query, knowing that Tom often pushed himself past his limits. "Did Tom do anything before he talked to the headmaster and his friend?"

"Funnily enough, something did happen. I only found out when one of the security guards pulled me in to look at the security footage thirty minutes ago." Dr Harris was smiling now, rather than looking concerned.

Max laughed as he described how Tom had hobbled out to the corridor to help a patient who had fallen, knowing full well that alarm was broken in his room. No wonder he was tired; he didn't have the endurance to manage something so strenuous just yet.

James, the other patient, was lucky that Tom was willing to assist him.

After that revelation, he thanked the therapist and wrote down her contact details, promising to call if anything worrying came up.

Throughout the short walk to Tom's ward, he reflected on just how much their life had changed. The influence of the accident on his body was already obvious, but it appeared that they both needed time to relax after the constant stakeouts.

There was also the matter of the symbiotic fungi, which they were both hosts for. It would have minor effects for him.

Tom, however, was deeply bonded with his, though it was proving to be a problem. His memory had always been good, but it was now perfect, and he needed a strategy to cope with the traumatic memories.

He now had something to help with that, though, and Max smiled, happy to know that they were actively solving issues.

The nurse greeted him as he reached the ward and entered Tom's room. Sure enough, he was asleep, though his eyes were still moving slightly beneath the lids.

It wasn't nightmares anymore.

Instead, the fungi were dealing with another issue.

Though the connection, touching Tom's wrist, he could feel the fungi's panic. The MRI results weren't from PTSD. It was from them speaking with the colony's spores to ask for assistance. Normally, between spiders, there would no damage, but within the limitations of the human mind, the affect was significant.

All his neurons had been damaged from the exertion. They were trying to solve it but struggling to come up with a solution.

Dr Harris made him jump as he arrived, and helped him to change Tom into new pyjamas, though the sleeves and pants were too short now. He remained in a deep sleep throughout the journey.

Max helped to settle him down into the spare bed and laid down on a sofa, exhausted.

He was asleep immediately, but it wasn't restful. In fact, it was the opposite.

His dreams were nightmares, loops of White Spikes laughing over his wife's grave and biting him.

This time, it was Max who tossed and turned in his sleep.

Chapter 22

She was woken from her sleep by a nagging thought and opened her eyes slowly, tired but restless.

Her job at the hospital was one that she enjoyed for its challenges, but she had no idea how to deal with her new patient.

She was usually able to figure out if anyone was lying. Max Homedale, however, was a hard nut to crack, giving the right information and emotional responses. There was something that he wasn't telling her though.

She slipped out from the bed, being careful not to wake her husband. He moved slightly in his sleep but didn't stir as she left the bedroom to go downstairs.

Helen had started at the hospital as the resident therapist six months ago and faced many different people. Some had legitimate mental issues and had required her help to get back to normal. Most had mental trauma or extreme emotional responses. Only a few patients had truly confounded her, and Tom Homedale was one of them.

She's been radioed to help with a patient by Dr Harris. The teenager was in the MRI machine after passing out, a bad sign after someone with a concussion. There had been no fractures or bleeding, but he had noticed something of interest.

When she arrived, the monitor that showed the electrical impulses from his neurons had been strange; it was fully active even though it was impossible. Normally, humans only used a limited percentage of their brain power, and what this revealed what that his thought processes were working at its maximum capacity. It was thought to be impossible.

Dr Flaveen watched, awestruck and speechless, at a phenomenon that she'd never expected to see. Dr Harris had explained that he was in the middle of a nightmare, and she had no reason to disbelieve him.

Just as suddenly, however, the activity stopped, reducing to a normal amount. When he'd come back out of the MRI machine, he'd been in a deep sleep and was out of the looping nightmare. Dr Harris explained that he thought his patient was dealing with PTSD. She went along with this story to avoid suspicion.

She accompanied him back to the ward where he was staying and spoke to him about the situation that he had dealt with before arriving at the hospital.

She remembered snippets of the conversation as she browed a cup of tea in the middle of the night.

Tom Homedale had gone into the forest after a dare and encountered wild dogs who were very territorial, chasing him down and intending to kill him.

A fall down a ravine – as reported by Tom and theorised by Max – had caused a broken leg and concussion. The x-rays were shocking to see, with ten fractures throughout both bones. There were also several broken ribs and signs of internal bleeding, but a scan hadn't revealed any significant damage.

It was as if something had solved the issue internally, but that was impossible.

Someone tapped her arm, and she opened her eyes slowly to find her husband next to her. "Are you okay, Helen?"

She nodded and set out another mug. "I'll be alright. The new patient was on my mind."

"Do you want to talk about it?"

"Yes, please. There's something going on with him, but I don't know what." She made some hot drinks and brought it into the living room, along with the medical records that she'd placed on the kitchen counter, intending to read them during her shift tomorrow.

She'd find out how his changes were possible one way or another. Perhaps getting a second perspective could help prepare her for the first meeting with Tom next week.

Tom was now managing to sleep peacefully, his dreams focused on good memories rather than bad ones. **We're going to have to be careful. The doctor may have noticed the neural activity during the scan.**

It had been risky making contact like they had; it used up a lot of energy to do it, but they had no idea what to do.

They hadn't quite expected to get advice from White Spikes' fungi at the colony –it should have been impossible. A connection such as this was often difficult to maintain for a long period of time.

During the rest of the night – during which Tom, devoid of his senses, slowly dealt with the sedative –they investigated how it was possible to speak with the spider. It wasn't long before they found the answer. It was only due to the neural network that he had developed.

The mix of spider and human had created an incredibly effective system that could create a strong connection between the spores, even from long distances away.

There was one problem with communicating in this way.

It would overload his neurons. That small time talking with the other spores had led to several of the nerves in his mind becoming burnt out from the exertion. They would need to be able to manage this so that no *problems developed.* **What would be a feasible solution?** *They considered.*

It didn't take long to find one. **His bones have a lot of space in the marrow.** *They thought.* **We could store spare cells in here and replace the neurons as we use them. It's all a matter of DNA. The cells would be able to maintain their function easily.**

They did a test run on an area of his body that wouldn't be affected if it went wrong, and it worked perfectly. The spores were used to dealing with genetic information and knew how to get around his body easily without blocking anything off. The lymphatic system was large enough to accommodate many cells at once.

Replacing the neurons didn't take long and came with one major benefit. Memories were lost due to the neural network dying off over time or misfiring. Tom would be able to retain a perfect memory due to the constant replacement of the cells instead.

They spent the rest of the time creating copies of the cells and DNA. The fungi transported them to the bone marrow for storage and did the same for other vital organs. It would allow him to remain healthy for a long time.

The next morning...

It took several hours for the sedative to wear off. The first thing that Tom was aware of was a sound he hadn't heard before.

It was a mix of bird song which almost deafened him; a quick adjustment of his audio filters allowed him to listen to it comfortably. Living at the edge of the forest, devoid of life, meant that this was something he'd never encountered.

Opening his eyes, he didn't recognise where he was. The last thing he remembered was being in the hospital. Nor was it his bedroom at the house; that was on the second floor. Here, looking out the window, he was level with the back garden.

He quickly remembered that the doctor had offered his spare room for them to stay in until his leg was stronger and both he and Max had recovered from the constant stakeouts.

Upon moving, a body-wide ache made itself apparently, and the agonising memories returned with a vengeance.

After getting stuck in the nightmare – and subsequent loop – the fungi had noticed that he was in trouble. They spoke to him through images, telling him how to regain some semblance of control. It had only taken fifteen minutes to calm down again.

Tom knew it would be a significant and lifelong issue now; he asked them for help in how to maintain mental stability. Thanks to some techniques, he was now able to cope with the memories, but knew they would never go away. No amount of trying to bury them would work, and they would only come back stronger. Instead, he was taught how to embrace them, though it hadn't been easy.

Slowly rising, he breathed in deeply as he stretched. He was now dressed in a pair of pyjamas from home. Looking around, he soon noticed that there was an adjoining bathroom, which would be useful for having a quick shave.

When he looked in the mirror, he hardly recognised himself. Wrinkles were visible that he hadn't seen before; it was as if he'd grown a year within the coma. A beard was growing, though a quick shave would solve it.

His eyes, the way that most people were able to see how he was feeling, had become deeper from the painful memories and colour change.

Tom noticed that golden specks floated over his pupil and cornea. It was so slight that only he and Max would be able to notice, however.

He shaved first, and he soon regained some of his youthfulness. A slight imbalance caused a small cut from the razor. As he held onto the sink, he noticed just how quickly it clotted; soon, the only sign of the injury was a faint red line.

Smiling contentedly, he thanked the fungi internally, struggling to get out of the pyjamas and placing a towel over his shoulders.

He shut his eyes and used the water from the sink to wash his hair. He was careful not to get lost into his mind, though, remaining partially aware of his surroundings.

The fungi spoke to him using images. They were telling him the rate that they could heal injuries but warned him that his leg was only partly healed, and lots of exercise would increase the risk of it breaking.

It was only afterwards that he realised how much better his body felt. The healthy pallor was joined by stronger muscles and a significant improvement to his flexibility.

Testing it, he found that he could move his limbs into extreme positions with barely any pain. He asked why; the fungi revealed that they'd enhanced the collagen and ligaments in his joints. It was in case he grew any further; large joints were at risk of dislocating more often than small ones.

He hobbled back into the bedroom dressed only in a fresh pair of underpants that he'd grabbed on the way in, planning on changing immediately.

The wardrobe had been filled with all his clothes from home. Finding a comfortable set of cotton trousers and a t-shirt, he managed to get dressed quite easily and painlessly.

Exiting his room using the crutches, he found his dad laid on the sofa. The blankets were tangled around him as he tossed and turned; it appeared that he'd been struggling with nightmares too. He sat down next to him, touching his arm and asking the fungi to instruct Max's spores on how to provide mental training.

His frantic movements came to an end a moment later.

Max awoke with a start and looked around wildly, though he soon calmed down and noticed him. Letting out a breath, he slowly rose, then leant forward. His voice was quiet when he spoke. "Thank you. I couldn't pull myself out from the nightmare."

"It was difficult for me too." Tom revealed, touching him on the shoulder. "It took some time to finally regain mental stability, but now it's manageable. I know how bad the traumatic memories are, but trying to hide them will only cause them to come back stronger."

Max began to calm down fully and relaxed, leaning back again. The stress faded from his expression, and he looked at him, concern obvious. "How are you doing?"

Rather than do it audibly, Tom shut his eyes and asked the fungi to do something else to explain.

He began to share his memories.

Max realised what he was doing, and Tom sensed the fungi let out a mutter of approval as he did something new, using the efficiency of his neurons in a different way than normal.

Tom showed him exactly what had happened in the forest – meeting White Spikes and how he had helped him to escape – before moving onto the two weeks resting in the hospital.

He'd been able to sense everything throughout his recovery, but the voices had been too loud until he came up the idea for the audio filter. The improvements were explained using mental images.

The glucose recycling process and cell replacement was shared, but it was too intricate for Max to develop just yet.

His dad expressed shock upon the reveal of the flexibility and rapid healing offered by the improved blood clotting.

As he finished the explanation, sharing how he dealt with traumatic memories, Max shook his head in disbelief and opened his eyes. "You've always been able to deal with things so easily. What made you come up with the idea for sharing memories?"

"It makes it easier to explain." Tom replied. "It shocked the fungi too. The only spider who can do it is White Spikes."

"The therapist will be a problem. You'll need to pretend that the memories are still affecting you, or she'll start to become suspicious."

"I know. What's really confounding me is how I'll explain the new diet to Dr Harris. It could reveal the fungi." He admitted. "A change like this isn't possible scientifically or biologically. Any advice?"

"You have a choice." Max stated, reaching out and placing a hand on his leg. "You can tell him the truth, or you can come up with a reasonable explanation. He's open-minded, so he'll be willing to listen."

Tom had unwittingly become a little stressed, beginning to lean forward as his mind whizzed through all the possibilities of how the doctor might react.

He was vaguely aware of Max, trying to calm him down.

He breathed in, pulling his thoughts from a mental loop and drawing himself out of his mind. Max motioned outside to the garden. "Fancy a drink while we listen to the bird song?"

"Sounds like a good idea." Tom forced this out while regaining mental stability again. It was getting easier each time though. He smiled a moment later, the memory of his mother reading him a book playing in his mind. It was the fungi, trying to help by allowing him to focus on something else. "I'll meet you in the back garden. Need to stretch my legs."

After a comforting tap on his left leg, Max rose and went over to the kitchen, knowing that he was strong enough to get around on his own.

Rising onto the crutches after easing himself off the sofa, he hobbled to the back door and unlocked it using a spare set of keys.

Exiting the house, he found a garden with some furniture and a table.

The edges of the garden were filled with blooming flowers and shrubs. It was beautiful but noisy; he could hear bees buzzing as they moved about to collect pollen and nectar. The small pond was filled with fish, and he could hear them moving beneath the water as small insects flew above the surface. Sitting down on a chair, he closed his eyes and altered the audio filters again to account for the change of scenery. He was soon talking with his dad in the early hours of the morning, both enjoying a cup of coffee while listening to the bird song around them.

Chapter 23

This place is quite amazing to see. *The fungi thought.* **There's so much life here.**

The small garden was similar to the dark forest where they'd once lived, yet here it was open to the sunlight and inviting. The small bushes and shrubs were beautiful to look at and covered with insects. The pond had fish in it, swimming under the surface gracefully.

The bird song that they'd heard that morning was louder here; they could identify over thirty species, all with individual songs. A small bird feeder, hanging from a branch over the fence, would occasionally be visited by small birds. They couldn't remember when they'd last seen such a variety of wildlife. The spiders had wiped out all other life in the forest to sustain themselves.

It was strange to see just how far they were from their original home in the derelict house, trapped in the invisible cages and without any keys to get out. **It's so peaceful. We're happy here.** *They thought.* **If we could freeze time, this is the moment that we would remember.**

The fungi could always remember this; they had their own section of neurons in his mind that allowed them to store their memories. This was locked so that Tom wouldn't see anything, but they wouldn't hesitate to share them with the teenager if he asked.

Tom had his own memories of a beautiful place that they asked to see while he relaxed. The location, within the town, was quite large and consisted of a playground – very similar to what the colony had designed for the nursery – a pond and large areas of grass and semi-wild shrubbery. A small forest in the centre contained a symbolic image that made their host happy; a wild willow tree in a clearing.

From the snapshots they saw, they knew why it was so special. This was a project that he and his friend, Nathan, had created together. **It looks like it belongs in a fairy tale.** They stated. **It's wild, yet managed. They managed to create an oasis in the middle of a town.**

The willow – a large tree with hanging branches – was in the centre of a clearing. Rather than clear the ground around it, they had allowed wildflowers and plants to take root, creating a spectacular display of blooms and wild grasses. A small, paved path encircled it and led to an entryway at the back of the tree. A metal frame had been used to wind the hanging branches, creating a natural doorway.

The small bench and table were perfect for sitting down and doing work; it was silent due to the branches surrounding it. Even the playground, busy and being *quite noisy, didn't make it through.* **The pattern from the sunlight is quite pleasing.** *The light was dappled as it passed between branches, using the small gaps to create small patterns on the ground. The interior of the tree was surprisingly easy to see in; they would have thought it would be quite dark.*

Can you take us there? We would really like to see it! *The fungi asked, showing him the image. Tom rolled his eyes and replied with a thumbs up.* **That is one place we really want to see and experience.** *They thought to themselves.* **Tom will be able to enjoy his time there without adjusting the audio filters constantly.**

Dr Flaveen arrived at her shift with the medical records for Tom Homedale to try and come up with a plan for his treatment. During the morning, she looked for him online and came across a small social media account that was barely used. Only a few images were posted.

She recognised when they'd been taken. Tom and a friend had taken it upon themselves to clean up the park two years ago. The gardener had retired, and the two of them had decided to spend the summer holiday weeding and making the place look inviting. There were photos of before and after, as well as a location that everyone loved to visit.

The image of the willow brought back a lot of memories.

It was a favourite place for the community, a location where the sounds of the playground and the roads were inaudible. They'd spent weeks making it look beautiful, allowing the wildflowers to take over and adding in a small path and metal frame for entry to its interior.

She went there quite often to do work, looking up people or contacting close friends or family members of her patients.

One of the nurses came in while she was reminiscing and noticed what she was looking at. "So you're trying to figure him out too then?" She asked.

"He's now my patient." Dr Flaveen replied. "I couldn't sleep last night because I was constantly thinking about him. His dad was helpful, but Tom is quite mysterious. I've been told everything about him from his friends, schoolmates, and the headmaster, but he doesn't reveal much about himself on social media or to those who he's close with."

"I can understand." The nurse responded, giggling slightly. "We did so many tests to try and figure out why his eyes changed colour. Everything came back clear and even a composition test to look at the cells in the blood showed nothing abnormal, apart from quicker clotting for injuries. The DNA was checked too but nothing strange came up."

What could have caused that activity in the MRI machine if nothing has been found? She thought.

"I haven't had the chance to fully read his medical file yet. What do you mean by his eye colour changing?" Dr Flaveen asked.

The nurse came beside her and flipped through the medical file, looking for something. She stopped and pointed down at a single paragraph.

'Original medical records state that hair colour is brown, and eyes are blue. During the coma, this has altered over time. Hair has changed to a dark blonde, while eyes are now emerald. No cause found. Continuing to do tests.'

"Strange." Dr Flaveen muttered. "Surely there must be a reason for it."

"Well, tell me if you do! Everyone wants to know why." Her radio bleeped. "I've got to go, but if you have any more questions about him, come find me during your lunch break!"

She nodded in response and looked at the profile image on the social media account. It hadn't been updated in quite some time; it showed a twelve-year-old Tom stood beside his dad, Max. The dark forest they lived beside was behind them.

Perhaps she'd be able to learn some more information that could bring light to why the changes had occurred during their first meeting.

Dr Harris had been given the day off so that he could monitor Tom's condition and assist if needed. He'd come down fully expecting to find them having a lie in, recovering from sleep. Instead, he found the teenager leaning against the counter and frying something.

"How do you like your eggs?" He asked. He must have heard him come down.

"Sunny side up, please." Dr Harris sat down and looked at him, trying to figure out if there was any pain now.

Tom still revealed nothing worrying; the fractured leg, still in the cast, was on the ground in a relaxed position. It may be worth doing another x-ray to check its stability. He'd dressed into comfortable clothes, and he noticed that rather than attempt jeans, which would be unsuitable, he was instead wearing loose cotton trousers.

Max joined him in the room a second later, coming in through the back door and holding two mugs.

Dr Harris motioned to him, and they went into the living room. He still had some questions that needed to be answered. "When did you wake up?"

"Tom woke up at nine and roused me thirty minutes later." Max revealed. "He managed to have a shave before dressing too. He looks a lot better without the beard."

He wrote it down on a notepad, planning on tracking his activities for the next week to see what his routine was like. "Did Tom have any breakfast?"

Max was about to respond when the smell of toast came into the room.

Dr Harris couldn't resist. He entered the kitchen to find two portions of eggs on toast, topped with some herbs and salt. Tom had sat down on the other side of the table with a slice of toast and a jug of water.

Max joined him next to the other breakfast.

He was surprised at how tasty the eggs were, with a perfectly runny yolk. Most teenagers didn't like to cook, yet he'd done it without asking.

It didn't take long for them to eat it —both were hungry — but the few times that he looked up, Tom was drinking some water and barely touched his breakfast.

After a satisfied sigh, he suddenly noticed that the slice of toast in front of Tom was only half-eaten. His lack of appetite was disturbing to see; someone who'd just woken from a prolonged sleep would normally be hungry.

How is this possible? He thought. He addressed Tom a moment later, curious. "Why aren't you finishing off your breakfast?"

He shrugged, and his answer confused him even more. "I'm not very hungry."

"That makes no sense." Dr Harris stated. "You just woke up and barely ate anything before. You made both me and your dad a full breakfast, yet it didn't bring on your appetite?"

Tom smiled, making a small gesture with one of his hands. The jug of water was empty. "Honestly, I've never had a good diet. I usually only have a small breakfast and survive off a sandwich for lunch during school."

This confession surprised him, but looking him over again, he noticed just how thin the teenager was. He should have been devouring anything in sight, especially considering that he hadn't eaten anything during his sleep. How was he managing to survive off so little calories each day?

He was speechless for a moment before standing and speaking assertively. "Get ready to go. I'm taking you to the hospital to check your blood sugar levels."

Tom had expected this; he rose slowly and used a crutch to stand, picking up a small bag at the same time.

Dr Harris went behind him as he walked to the front door, only remembering to grab the car keys a moment later, amazed to see just how mobile he was despite the fractured leg.

Chapter 24

Well, the doctor's reaction was expected, especially after hearing that. The fungi thought. *He's only being careful. We'll have to reduce the self-destruct time just in case they do more tests.*

They were surprised that Tom had revealed the truth about the lack of appetite, a benefit of surviving by recycling glucose internally instead.

It would have come up sooner or later, though; the man was watching him carefully and would have noticed that he wasn't eating much. Tom had to force the morsels down to keep up the appearance of needing to eat but had thankfully explained that he could survive off small amounts of food, reducing the doctor's worry.

Tom's use of energy was quite effective considering the lack of the resource. His idea to make one cell the catalyst had helped to reduce the glucose usage significantly.

When they arrived at the hospital, they looked out using Tom's eyes, curious about how people would perceive him.

Most of the staff members recognised him and greeted him by name. **He's regarded as a mystery waiting to be solved.** *They thought.*

Tom was led through to another room where a nurse checked his vitals using several machines. Another one was used to prick his finger. They made sure that none of the spores entered the blood drop that landed on the device just in case they were detected.

Dr Harris was shocked at the results, a completely normal level of glucose in the blood despite not eating for two weeks. He asked the nurse to get another device from a storage cupboard and explained what it was used for.

This was a portable blood sugar monitor. It was linked with one of his blood vessels and tracked the level of the glucose throughout the day.

Afterwards, they asked if he could stand on a scale, where his new, heavier weight was discovered. **He's not just taller.** *They stated smugly.* **We've been adding on more muscle and making him the perfect host.**

Someone was watching and listening from the corridor throughout until the end of the examination.

They tried to identify who it was, but they left as the nurse left the room, the shoes clicking on the floor and difficult to track in the loud hospital. It appeared that Tom had a stalker, someone who would stop at nothing to try and figure out how he had managed to survive.

Bring it on. *They told themselves.* **We can always hide ourselves even deeper. None of your tests will be able to find us.**

They made sure to put some of their spores into Dr Harris as he helped Tom up. They weren't active, just waiting until they were needed. It would help if he did any more intrusive tests. They made sure that the same self-destruct process was in these spores in case the doctor decided to do a blood test on himself.

As Tom was driven back to the doctor's house, they went back through his neurons, analysing his current abilities and potential.

Considering that he already managed to share memories, something that only White Spikes could do, they decided to ask him how he had figured it out. **How did you share the memories with Max?**

'It occurred to me as I was sitting down next to him. Showing it using images is easier to explain than doing it audibly. It reduced a thirty minute talk to a five minute discussion.' *Tom answered.*

Previously, we were considering having Nathan become a host. What is your opinion? *They asked.*

'I'd rather that you ask him before initiating the process. It should be a choice to become a host or not.'

Any preferences to changes or genetic alterations?

'Try to avoid it if possible but make changes if needed, such as helping with conditions. I'd rather that you don't make any genetic alteration now unless it's necessary. All it takes is someone to point it out and then they'll order more tests.'

We understand. We only had to make all these changes with your DNA so that you could survive. They explained. *We only keep them healthy and create a connection between them and the other hosts.*

'Try to hide the truth about the colony until they need to be told. I don't want to cause panic.' *Tom replied. He spoke to them one final time before arriving back at the house.* 'Thank you for the help. I really appreciate all that you do for me and Max.'

Thank you, Tom. We'll update you if we need to take any action. They replied.

They'd arrived back at the house; the doctor asked to have a discussion with the two of them.

Surely the man was getting suspicious now.

Tom settled down onto one of the sofas and had a drink as he waited. His foot tapped nervously; his thoughts exhibited concern that he knew about the fungi.

The doctor didn't. There was no way he knew about them. He didn't speak to Tom, focused on his phone and typing out a message. **What was he up to?**

Dr Harris finished doing the email as Max returned with three coffees.

He accepted the white coffee graciously and didn't speak at first, observing Max and Tom's behaviour.

Max was a little worried but pretending to be happy, while Tom was stressing out and looking concerned. He'd gotten used to the teenager's behaviour; the tapping foot and leant down posture indicated stress, though the green eyes weren't focusing on his surroundings. Instead, it was as if he was going over memories.

He spoke to them a moment later, and Tom looked up, relaxing, almost realising that he was behaving strangely. *As if he's aware he's acting suspiciously.* He thought to himself.

Dr Harris put these concerns aside. "I thought that I'd make the two of you aware of my plans tomorrow. It's to do with helping Tom to recover so I'd rather that you know what's going on."

They nodded but didn't respond, so he continued to speak. "I've called a meeting at the hospital with everyone who was involved in your care. It's to establish the amount of pressure the leg can manage and any plans that might help with recovering your endurance. We're also going to discuss the tests results we already have to try and come up with a reason for why your eye colour has changed. It should be impossible."

Max nodded. "We understand, Dr Harris. Coming up with a proper plan for recovery will prevent complications from arising."

He shook his head at this; they were now guests in his home. "When we're here like this, or out and about in town, call me Brian. During treatments or appointments at the hospital, however, please continue to use Dr Harris. I prefer that my personal life is separate from work." He took out the medical record for Tom from his bag. "I'd like to discuss some of the medical issues so that I can provide the most up-to-date information for my colleagues."

Tom nodded. "That's fine by me. I'm quite curious about why I've changed so much as well."

Dr Harris scrutinized his behaviour again. He was now relaxed, leaning against the back of the sofa – but not fully.

His left foot was still tapping slightly, and his eyes...they were looking back at him, as if analysing him in return. The emerald irises were vivid.

For a second, he caught sight of a gold speck floating across his pupil, but quickly shook his head and rubbed his eyes, surprising himself by how tired he was. The early morning visit to the hospital had screwed up his day off.

Peering at Tom again, there was no sign of alterations or floating objects in his eyes. Perhaps he was seeing things that weren't there.

In any case, he had a job to do, and both Max and Tom were waiting for him to begin. He looked down at the medical record and picked out one of the issues that had been confounding him. "According to paramedics, there were signs of internal injuries and blood loss after you returned from the forest. What caused it?"

"The fall into the ravine." Tom stated. His eyes were back to reflective, almost falling into a looping nightmare. He shook it off and continued to speak. "It was a drop from a tall height, and I landed with my full body weight along with a rucksack full of supplies. It's likely that it caused some internal bleeding. The leg was the worst, though, bleeding out rapidly. I had to use a tourniquet to stop it."

Dr Harris ticked that off; it matched what he'd stated during the explanation to his friend and the headmaster. "What about the concussion?"

"Same as before. The high fall. Pretty sure that my head slammed into a rock at the bottom." The teenager cringed slightly at this; he must be thinking back over it. "It was only after wrapping bandages around it and having some painkillers that I could make it somewhere safe."

Another check mark; everything was making sense. "Finally, how did you manage with the fractured leg?"

"I knew it wouldn't be able to withstand any weight and that the bones needed stability to prevent movement, so I used some branches to act as a splint and wrapped bandages around to keep them stable." He was becoming unfocused and stressed out; Dr Harris knew this would be one of the last questions he would ask to prevent Tom's PTSD from returning. "Max had given me a machete to use in case of emergencies, and it came in useful to carve a branch into rough walking stick. The painkillers allowed me to ignore the pain and make it to a house in the forest, where I slept for a few hours."

"One final question and that's it." He said this quietly, aware of the teenager's sensitive hearing and knowing that he was having trouble concentrating on his surroundings. "You stated that you found some files on a desk in the bedroom you settled down in. Do you remember what was on them?"

Tom took a few moments to answer this one, closing his eyes and going back over the memories again. He smiled sadly before responding. "I can't remember what I saw. Everything's a blur at that point. I was struggling to focus and exhausted from the trek."

"Thank you for trying." Dr Harris stated. "That's all I wanted to ask. I know that going over everything that happened must be awful for you, but I needed to establish the facts before the meeting tomorrow."

"Who's going to be there?" Max asked, curious.

He unlocked the phone and checked the email. "So far, the surgeon who operated on his leg, the nurse he interacted with and the two paramedics who brought him to the hospital. The therapist has an appointment at that time, so she'll be unable to attend." A small ping confirmed another attendee, another of the doctors who had been keeping an eye on him. "Plus another doctor who has been essential in Tom's recovery."

"It'll help put everything into perspective." Max replied. He glanced over to Tom, who was back to being leant over and stressed out. He tapped his shoulder gently. "Do you fancy a quick walk?"

Tom nodded but didn't reply, too caught up in memories.

He rose slowly and used the crutch to follow Max to the front door. Now alone, Dr Harris wrote up some notes about Tom's behaviour, emailing them to the therapist, and confirmed who was coming to the meeting tomorrow.

Chapter 25

Meanwhile...

White Spikes watched the colony from the observation platform. He rarely had to get involved now; most of the time, they were able to operate without disruption. Seeing no issues, he decided to use this free time to see his children, who he was rarely able to visit due to his responsibilities in the colony.

He bungeed down and went over to the nursery, where a matron – acting as the receptionist - smiled at him. "Good afternoon, sir. Have you come for an inspection? It is currently breaktime, so all the classrooms are free to look at."

White Spikes smiled back as he replied. "I have sssssome free time sssssso I decided to ssssssee my brood and check how they are doing. I'm glad to ssssssee that I timed it perfectly."

The receptionist was surprised and looked at him suspiciously. She crossed her front legs in front of her over the apron-shaped colouration on her abdomen.

He waited patiently until she finally realised that he was telling the truth, and, smiling, motioned to the main corridor. "They will be using you as a jungle gym. They just had some food an hour ago and are very energetic right now."

He let out a laugh and set off. "I can manage them." He replied, waving as he walked along the hallway. It was lined with some of the children's web drawings, displayed on bark pieces, and with their name beneath it. White Spikes stopped partway along to look at one of the more interesting art pieces. The absorbent bark background allowed him to see the pictures despite his heat vision.

The fine white web created an image of a family. His family.

Lilliana, one of his eldest daughters, had designed it; her web strands were different than the rest of her siblings, finer and easy to manipulate, but would deteriorate after a week. She'd learned from one of her brothers – a youngster who had all the markings of an excellent architect – how to weave the strands together. He still had no idea what her speciality was, and he would need to find out soon. Her heat vision obviously made her a forager, but the red cross that was developing on her fangs were a sign of a medical specialist.

He continued onto the playground – a section of the nursery that the matrons managed regularly – and stepped into the large, isolated chamber.

White Spikes cringed at the noise; the spiderlings were loud and didn't care if they disturbed others. All his brood were at the area for older spiders, where larger and more complex play equipment had been designed.

It was packed as he turned up and, for a second, he just watched the climbing tower with an amused grin. Every inch of the surface was covered by a warm spiderling, climbing excitedly. A game of tag had just begun.

It was one of the younger spiderlings who noticed that he'd turned up. There was a squeal, call of 'Dad!', and he was buried beneath a mountain of his own brood. He tried to avoid going into a laughing fit and simply allowed them to calm down before talking to them.

Suddenly he felt a strange sensation, and a faint connection made itself known. He recognised the fungi; it was the ones that lived within Tom Homedale. There was a snapshot of a memory, and a statement that worried him. **We need to make him a host to protect Tom!**

He decided to watch and listen to what the fungi were saying, surprised that he was able to see what they were doing. Normally a connection like this was impossible. Tom was a perfect host for the fungi and had managed to achieve things he never could have imagined.

Lilliana was suspicious. One of the eldest of her siblings, she had been able to observe her father's routines and behaviours over the years. She knew just how little time he had to spend with them and visits like this were rare. This could be one of his spontaneous decisions, but she knew that he tended to stick to a certain schedule when it came to the colony.

Her father never visited the nursery, not during the playtime. He'd come for inspections but not much else as he was usually busy. White Spikes had been watching for a minute before being noticed and suddenly getting mobbed by Lilliana's siblings. He just stood there, allowing them to calm down, but she noticed that his attention was unfocused, looking at something else.

It didn't stop the rest of the brood; they were using their father like a jungle gym, jittery and energetic from the food an hour earlier.

She looked around; the matrons, acting as monitors, were shaking their heads in disbelief and the spectacle had caught everyone's attention – the adult spiders as well as the rest of the broods. White Spikes seemed to remember where he was and finally greeted them, apologizing for the surprise visit.

Lilliana still didn't know what to think. Ever since returning that human body to the family, he'd been acting stranger than normal.

Sometimes, if she was too bored and didn't want to attend her next lesson, she'd skip school and follow him, curious about what he was doing. Most of the time, he went to do walks around the web walkways, satisfying an urge that she felt often when restless.

Yesterday, however, as she followed him – a habit she needed to stop before she got caught – he hadn't gone to his usual haunt. Instead, he'd gone to the house at the edge of the forest, bungeeing down to the ground and talking with something. She'd sneaked to one of the trees to look out and was shocked by what she saw. He was talking with one of the humans.

She knew from memory who the two humans were that lived at the edge of the forest. The father was called Max Homedale, an older man who was experienced with the shotgun and had a lot of survival training. He had passed this onto his son, Tom Homedale.

It had been this teenager – this sixteen-year-old – that had embarrassed White Spikes to the point that he had to be encouraged by the rest of the colony. He'd managed to escape the forest despite major injuries and bad blood loss. The black sleeping bag had been brought to the school and placed in the main lobby as a trophy of the close capture.

Now, however, she knew why he had escaped. Her father had helped him. He wasn't in league with the humans but treated them with respect. They were friends.

Max was relaxed and calm with him; he didn't have the shotgun with him and was talking to him normally, as if they weren't different species or enemies.

She'd rather find out why he was acting like this before telling her mother. Perhaps this was simply a tactic to catch the two of them when they were vulnerable. She knew that the son, Tom, would still be quite injured after everything he'd gone through. There was no way that anyone could recover so fast, could they?

As Lilliana listened, however, she was shocked. The teenager was infected with the same fungus that the colony was. That was how he'd survived. He'd become a host either due to her father or from the derelict house where the human had lived years ago. *Was her father getting manipulated by the fungi to help the two humans to survive?*

The bell rang and she was withdrawn from the memory in an instant. She knew that the fungi had the ability to connect with others spores and exchange information. Was that lapse in concentration due to the spores in the teenager communicating with him?

A matron called to her and her siblings, letting them know to return to class. She did so unwillingly, unsure what was going on, but knew that she would keep this a secret. Her father, White Spikes, had made some idiotic decisions in the past, but this didn't seem to be a mistake on his part. He was building up the trust with the humans intentionally, perhaps to catch them when they were at their weakest.

A human term passed through the forefront of her mind, and she smiled at how ironic it was for her father's situation. 'Keep your friends close, but your enemies closer.'

The colony watched as their leader returned to the observation platform. They couldn't avoid noticing his visit to the nursery. The clearing had gone quiet, an uncommon occurrence during playtime. The only sounds from the nursery had been from his own brood; the rest of the spiderlings must have been staring at the sudden entrance of their large leader.

One of the foragers went into the nursery to chat with the receptionist in the lobby to ask why he'd visited, curious. He'd come back out and let them know that he was simply there to see the spiderlings, nothing more.

They laughed as the forager explained how the playground attendants, noticing his interest, described the mountain of spiderlings that suddenly surrounded White Spikes, using his large body as a jungle gym. He'd been forewarned, of course, but even so, he seemed to be in shock at how sudden it was, unable to say anything.

Or he was waiting for the spiderlings to calm down. That was a better explanation.

The colony settled down a few minutes later, but the news of her husband's visit had made it to Alacanta in that short time. Nothing stayed a secret for long in the clearing; their sensitive hearing meant that almost everything could be heard by one of the spiders. The only place that was impossible to eavesdrop on was the observation platform high above. It was surrounded by a web wall that stopped any noise from making it down to the colony below. He used it to conduct private meetings with the spiders.

The only ones who had permission to go up to it was White Spikes, one of the foragers – his best friend at the colony – and Alacanta. If anyone needed help, they would need to call out. Their leader's sensitive hearing and heat vision was all that he required to know that assistance was needed.

Chapter 26

Tom walked alongside Max without any awareness of his surroundings. The memories were back, and the mental training wasn't helping. The motion of walking was, though, and he was soon back to normal, taking in a deep breath and focusing on the world around him again.

They'd travelled fifteen minutes away from the house and were in a secluded area with few passersby or observers.

Sitting down on one of the benches, he'd sensed something going on while they were talking with the doctor and knew that the spores were up to something.

His dad spoke to him, concern obvious. "You alright?"

"I'll be fine. I need to find out what the fungi were doing to Dr Harris." He responded.

He ignored Max's shocked expression and opened the connection fully, allowing all his senses to fade away and shutting his eyes. He was soon facing a black void, and he spoke to them. He knew the fungi were up to something – they were avoiding him – and was concerned about what their plans were for the innocent doctor.

Dr Harris was only trying to help. They looked after him, sure, but they had already proven that they could be a little over-protective by manipulating the large spider into becoming a guardian rather than a jailor.

He sounds angry. The fungi thought. **We had to do it. He knew too much.**

The doctor was far too clever for them to deal with. He'd noticed them in Tom's eyes, but hadn't spoken up about it, dismissing it quickly. If he started talking with others, though, they would soon be in trouble. Thank goodness they had infected him with benign spores earlier in the morning.

They knew humans' behaviour by now, and one of the common ones was handshakes. A meeting between coworkers would be the ample opportunity to infect everyone. All it took was a handshake.

The doctor's meeting was in the morning. They had simply 'suggested' that they begin to infect anyone that he meets a certain time. It would include anyone in the meeting. **We need to get some support for Tom. If they find out the truth, we'll all be quarantined, and placed back in a jail again.** *They thought.* **We don't want to go behind invisible barriers again.**

How could they explain this to Tom so he could understand? He was waiting in the mental void for them to speak to him. **He needs to see it from our perspective!** *They realised.*

They showed him their memories of the many years trapped within the house, and his thoughts began to soften, going from anger, to concern, and finally to understanding. Tom was correct in his assumptions; they did depend on manipulation to survive, but it had changed dramatically since bonding with the teenager.

Rather than do it their way – by bonding with the medical team without their permission – they decided to listen to him. 'Look, I can understand why you do what you do for me, but it can be a little too much sometimes. I understand why my dad agreed to be a host; he's my only family, and he knows that I need help sometimes. But these doctors and nurses helped us to survive.'

What do you suggest? *They asked.* **That we give them a choice? They could just report us as an infectious disease!** *For once, the fungi were scared. Tom was asking them if they were willing to be discovered.*

'I'm not saying that I just out you. But you will be found sooner or later. There are more intrusive tests that they can do.' *He answered.* 'I suggest that you offer to help them. They're all doctors and work in the medical field. Being able to come up with an answer in an instant would greatly help them, correct?'

I see. The only way that they won't report us is if we benefit them first. They realised. They decided to be honest with the teenager. *We're afraid.*

Tom's laugh was genuine. 'What could possibly scare you?'

We've seen how the rodents and lizards were treated by the jailor. The fungi confessed. *They were tests to see how we would react. If it were to happen to you and Max, you would become lab rats, facing constant tests and being scrutinized at all times.*

'Listen to me.' *His voice was assertive, in control.* 'You're overthinking it. We have control over who we invite to become a host. You can simply offer the chance to join us as new hosts. Give them the choice of becoming great doctors, on the condition that they alter my medical records so that my condition makes sense.'

Interesting. The fungi finally understood just why this teenager was the perfect host. He could come up with ideas like this on the fly. *So no manipulation this time?*

'Exactly.' *Tom responded.* 'It should be their choice on what they want to do. Show them some of my memories. That should be enough to persuade them that you can benefit them.'

They analysed the plan, doing a practice run of what he was suggesting. It would work perfectly, but humans' reactions could change on a whim. **What if they do not accept us?**

'Self-destruct, as per normal.' *He answered.* 'No point infecting someone if they don't give permission. It might give them a reason not to report us as an infectious disease.'

Agreed. You've always surprised us, Tom. They were calm again now; they would have to update the spores so that they were synced up as per normal. **Can you find an opportunity to touch him again when you return so that we can inform the spores about the new plan?**

Tom's mental smile was obvious. 'Of course. I'm already a little tired out from the walk so he'll be tempted to check on me to make sure that I'm okay.'

They laughed at this response. **Isn't that manipulation?**

'No, it's called making a plan successful.' *He paused, and they could see him watching the memories of the doctor in his mind.* 'In any case, we should head back. Max is due to start cooking soon. It's the least we can do as a thank you to him.' *Tom was about to return to his body again properly, but spoke one last statement that made the fungi beam with appreciation.* 'Thank you for listening to me. When we work together, we're a great team.'

The connection between them faded back to normal and they were, once again, simply observers, watching as the teenager rose and walked back to the house. Max was worried but a quick explanation eased his concerns.

We're lucky to have him. They thought appreciatively. *Otherwise, we would have gone against our own rules and made the doctors and nurses hosts without giving any of them a choice. It doesn't matter if he gets put in isolation. At least we'll be with him if that happens.*

The next day, Dr Harris awoke early and headed downstairs for breakfast before going to the hospital.

To his surprise, Tom and Max were up, making breakfast and hot drinks again. He'd noticed that Max had done all the chores the day before, allowing him to relax, and was happy that he'd invited them to stay with him.

After a quick breakfast — French toast, topped with honey and powdered sugar — he bid the two of them goodbye, though Tom gave him a hug, thanking him for looking after him. He didn't expect it but was grateful for the appreciation.

After parking up at the hospital, he spent an hour checking all his patients and speaking with the charge nurse about anything he should be aware of.

Shortly before the meeting, however, he turned off his radio and went into the hospital's conference room, booked the day before and a private place for the staff members to meet up.

One of them was already there, drinking a black coffee and dressed in casual clothing. It was the surgeon. He rose as he entered the room and greeted him with a smile and handshake. "You must be Dr Harris."

He immediately felt guilty as he remembered that the surgeon was supposed to be off today, catching up on sleep. "Sorry for pulling you in at such short notice, but I want to know everything possible about Tom Homedale so that I can come up with a treatment plan."

He let out a short laugh. "So you're the one who's got him? Good luck."

Dr Harris was confused at this, but it was interrupted when someone else entered. It was the nurse from the day before, who'd been given an hour off to attend the meeting. She was still dressed in scrubs but allowed her hair to fall in natural curves rather than in the ponytail it was normally in. She greeted him with a hug and settled down onto the table after making a coffee.

The rest of the meeting's attendees arrived shortly afterwards and made themselves comfy on the conference table.

Copies of Tom's medical records had been placed in front of each of the seats, along with a notepad. Anyone who worked in the medical field knew that taking notes was the best way to remember information.

The meeting officially began, and he asked the paramedics to begin as they were the first to see Tom after the accident. They described exactly how he looked, which matched with all the injuries that was in the medical records, but noted that the father, Max, was quite worried. Not about them, or Tom, but staring out at the forest menacingly.

Dr Harris explained about the wild dogs that lived in it which both family members guarded against. Everyone was shocked but now understood this behaviour, as well as how his injuries were so severe – yet even the paramedics were surprised at how stable he was. If it was anyone else, they stated, the person would be dead from blood loss barely an hour after the injury, and unable to escape in the first place.

Next was the surgeon, who had the snarky remark, and now it was explained. He pointed out a note in the medical record from one of the nurses who had been assisting with the surgery. "The x-rays revealed ten fractures throughout the fibula and tibia, something that should have needed metals pins and a frame. None of those were needed."

"Why not?" Dr Harris asked.

"As soon as I opened the leg up and started to put the bone fragments where they needed to be, they started to heal themselves up. I couldn't write it out on the report as no one would believe me."

Everyone stared at him; such fast regeneration wasn't possible, especially for someone who had dealt with massive blood loss.

The surgeon continued to explain. "The best way that I can describe it is that the bone bungeed across using calcium strands to keep the leg stable. The only thing that I could do to help was to stitch it back up and inform the nurse to put it into a cast."

"Why didn't you report what you saw?" The nurse asked.

"Would any of you have believed me?" The surgeon asked. His sunken eyes looked at each of them in turn. "I was at the end of a long shift, tired and at the point of exhaustion with no sleep. I thought that I'd just hallucinated it myself until the next night. Of course, at that point, it was already in his medical records, and I'd be questioned if I suddenly came out with whatever that was." He crossed his arms in front of him, smirking. "Now do you understand why I said good luck?"

Dr Harris nodded and added his observations.

He explained that Tom had stood within the first fifteen minutes without warning or pain. At that point, he thought that the leg was badly fractured, but this made a lot more sense.

He also let them know about his reduced diet and lack of appetite but explained that he'd put on a blood sugar monitor to see what was going on.

He discussed Tom's behaviour and the fact that even he didn't know how he'd recovered so quickly – but now knew that the teenager had known exactly what was going on. He'd been trying to hide it from them.

"I saw something yesterday in the morning that I thought I hallucinated too." Dr Harris confessed. "I thought for sure that I saw a golden speck floating in his pupil."

"I don't understand." The nurse stated, confusion obvious. "We checked if he had any infections when he came in."

Dr Harris suddenly realised how he had recovered so quickly and why he was evasive about revealing the truth. "There's one thing we didn't test for throughout his recovery." He replied. "Something none of us could have comprehended."

The surgeon laughed at this, getting an idea about what he was talking about. "You're telling us that he's infected by something? Something that helps him to survive?" He put a finger onto the table, pointing out the image of Tom on the front of the medical record. "That only happens in fairy tales!"

It was at that moment when they saw – more than heard – the voice. Their thoughts were interrupted by a message that accompanied a check mark. *You never know. Fairy tales can come true.*

They were in shock and looked between each other. Dr Harris was the only one to speak, and he could see that all of them were unable to fully comprehend it. "Am I the only one to hear this?"

It's time we all talk about what happens next. This was a shared message, something that was usually impossible.

It looked like the surgeon was right after all. Only something specialised would be able to do something like this. A fungus was a possibility; they could create networks between roots and certain types had the ability to control insects to do what they wanted.

Why did none of them consider this as a possible solution? *And yes, you are all seeing this at the same time.*

The fungi had expected this reaction. Each of their thoughts expressed shock and disbelief. They had apparently picked the perfect time to begin the process of bonding, but this was limited. Tom had asked that they request permission first. They intended to follow this instruction to make him happy.

We presume that you are all aware of the reason **why Tom has recovered so quickly despite his injuries.** *They stated. Their thoughts all focused on the teenager, and they knew that it was true.* **Tom knew that you were close to the answer, so he asked that we speak with you so that an agreement can be reached.**

The doctor – Dr Harris – spoke, asking what sort of agreement they were talking about. The rest of them echoed this in their minds.

Hopefully they would be willing to listen to them. **We are a symbiotic fungus, and we have become essential for Tom's survival and wellbeing. Fixing the leg was quite simple. He is also extremely intelligent now, as many of you may have noticed.**

The nurse and Dr Harris audibly laughed at this statement. The surgeon was still quite concerned about the situation but appeared to be relaxing as he realised that they weren't going to hurt them. The paramedics were still in shock.

So, here is what we can do for you. *They said to each of them.* **You can live the rest of your lives free from illness, injuries or mental degradation. We can manage any current health conditions and either repair them or make them tolerable. Your intelligence will improve, and you will be able to come up with quick solutions on a whim. We can also help with preventing exhaustion and helping sleep come naturally.**

The surgeon smiled at this; he was the first to give permission to becoming a host. With the current connection, the rest of them heard this, and they also did the same.

The fungi began to connect them properly and discovered that many of them dealt with stress due to their job roles and responsibilities. These were eased as their minds were able to come up with coping strategies.

Soon, they had six new hosts, though they were, thankfully, willing to do it. Dr Harris and the nurse, however, soon figured out why they were doing this, and asked a question that they'd been expecting. What they wanted in return for their 'good deed'.

Their answer was, for once, the truth. **We wish to have a peaceful existence within Tom and all our hosts. We help rather than hinder and keep everything running. Tom would be dead if not for our help.**

The surgeon didn't seem surprised at this; he'd seen the leg as they healed it. The paramedics, however, wanted further clarification. They answered and used images to share information about how they had healed his injuries. To the surgeon's surprise, Tom's memory of the surgery – from within his body – came up.

Dr Harris was still curious. He asked who else they had infected. **You should know this, Dr Harris.** They called him by his professional name, as he had asked Tom earlier. **Max has been in several times to try and get** *help for his arthritis. He no longer has any pain from them. His fungi have made it painless for him and help to manage the collagen in the joints.*

The meeting would soon be over, and they would need to return to their jobs. The other doctor asked what they would need to do to hide the fungi from tests.

They considered this carefully before running through ideas and finding one that would work. **Dr Harris, do you have control of Tom's medical records?**

His answering nod and thought confirmed that this would be successful. They showed what he would need to change to hide the fungi from being discovered. **His leg will still cause worry. It will need to be changed to a single fracture. It can be put down to a typo, or, of course, this original medical record never existed. He wasn't as badly injured as anyone thought, was he? He was still placed into an induced sleep due to the concussion, but he only fell a small height rather than into deep ravine.**

They all responded with a laugh and smile, talking all at once and discussing how they would alter the medical records to hide the truth. They had the only copies and the nurse had access to the computer where the original was. It would take less than a second to replace it with the new version.

The new hosts – and now friends with a closely guarded secret – finished off the meeting with a new, edited version of Tom's medical records that hid just how badly he had been injured and kept the fungi safe. They were happy, listening to each of the medical staff and helping them to manage by allowing them to adapt their neurons towards quick solutions and a better memory retention.

Dr Harris was enthusiastic again and enjoyed his role even more than before. It appeared that becoming a host had given him a new outlook on life.

Chapter 27

Two days later

For Nathan, it was a struggle to get back to normal. Remorse and guilt sent his mind into a downward spiral which was difficult to pull himself out of. *If only I hadn't dared him to do it.* He caught himself thinking multiple times.

Time was difficult to keep track off; only the school bell and alarm in the morning reminded him which day it was. His sleep was fitful, and his dreams, usually quite peaceful, were now traumatic nightmares.

There was little contact from Tom, though he considered that he was still trying to recover. Truthfully, he understood if he decided that he didn't want to be a friend with him anymore. Right now, he hated himself too; it would have been easy to dare him to do something safer.

His teachers had noticed his lapse in concentration and lack of attention at school; the headmaster had called his mum and pulled him from classes for the rest of the week so that he could get help. Nathan remembered having a phone call with a woman who asked him lots of questions. His mum had a quiet chat with her once he returned to his room to stare at the wall, lost in his thoughts again.

He didn't have any appetite and forced food down to keep himself going. A pile of dirty clothes built up slowly but would disappear by the next morning, washed by his mum while he was asleep.

His dad had even got in contact; he'd ended up disowning him several years ago, leaving his mum doing a full-time job while still doing all the chores. Nathan had tried to help, of course, but now that he was stuck in his own head, he didn't register anything around him.

That weekend, however, it all changed. He was sat on his bed, remembering the summer in which he and Tom had restored the park to its former glory, when he felt a wet nose pushing against his hand.

Nathan opened his eyes in shock. Surely not. His mum hated dogs, yet...

Yet a brown labrador was sitting in front of him. Its tail was wagging, and it looked at him expectantly, the blue eyes analysing his behaviour. It wasn't a puppy, though it was quite young. He reached out and touched its head after letting it smell him. Definitely real.

There was a note attached to the collar. Unfolding the paper, he recognised his mum's handwriting. *She's an*

emotional support dog. I hope she helps. All supplies
downstairs when you're ready. Mum.

For the first time in a while, Nathan felt himself smile.

He decided to have a shower and changed into clean clothes before going for a walk. The dog waited for him patiently in his room, expectant and excited. He was unsure how to call for her, so he went with his gut and made a click noise. She heard and followed him, always staying within touching distance.

The supplies, as stated on the note, were all there. Nathan went into the kitchen before doing anything else and hugged his mum, the dog following him. "Thank you, mum."

"No worries." She responded, busy with cooking tea. "It's a beautiful day. Go for a walk with her."

He paused on the way out of the kitchen, a sudden realisation coming to him. "Is she going to be staying here permanently or will she need to be returned once I'm feeling better?"

"This is her new home. The centre made sure to find you a dog that hadn't been named yet." She paused, and he could visualise her biting her lip; she wasn't the biggest fan of dogs and had now accepted one into the home. "It's your responsibility to look after her."

"I know, mum. Thank you for getting her for me." The dog was still stuck to his side, unwilling to leave. "I'll buy anything else that she needs."

His mum shook her head in disbelief and bid him goodbye as he left the kitchen. Finding the harness and lead, he found that he didn't need to use them; the dog followed him out and walked beside him without any instructions. Partway through the walk, the bad memories returned. He stopped and stroked her, focusing on that touch to pull himself out from his mind.

He decided on her name during that first short walk. Hope.

Nathan's mum let out a relieved sigh as he left to go for a walk with his new dog. Though busy with preparing the ingredients for tea, she decided to call the therapist, wanting to let her know about his improvement.

Drying her hands, she tried to contact her, but it went through to an answering machine. It wasn't a surprise; the therapist was usually quite busy. "Hi, Dr Flaveen. The labrador that the centre found him was a perfect match. He decided to go for a walk this morning and he's back to normal now." She paused, remembering the smile that she'd seen. "Thank you for all your help. He's happy again now."

She hung up and returned to cutting up vegetables, her mind falling away and going back over everything that had happened the last few days.

She knew Nathan's behaviour; when he returned from the hospital, she recognised that something was wrong. She reported her concerns and was immediately referred to the only therapist in the town. After a call with her son, Dr Flaveen explained why he felt like he did and what she could do to help him recover.

Dr Flaveen could refer Nathan to a government scheme that helped with matching people in need with emotional support dogs. They were specially trained to observe behaviour and help with grounding individuals who were currently undergoing a stressful situation.

Nathan's case was a little difficult considering how withdrawn he was. The centre had decided to match him with one of the experienced dogs, an unnamed labrador that was trained for emotional support. The dog had a lot of experience with kids. She had been brought up among children when young and been with a foster family that included a teenager for the first two years while training.

It was a pleasant surprise to see how successful the match was.

Her phone rang, pulling her back to the present. Drying her hands, she saw who it was, and responded.

"Hi Max. How are you and Tom managing?" She asked.

"He's almost back to normal now. Could Tom come over to catch up with Nathan?"

It was currently the weekend and he had nothing planned. It would be good for Nathan to see Tom again, though she worried that it could cause his progress to reverse. Was it worth the risk? After a moment of hesitation, she replied. "He can come tomorrow if you want."

"That's perfect. Is eleven in the morning good for you?" He asked. "I need to start on packing and doing it without worrying about him will be very beneficial."

"That works with me. It'll be good for Nathan to see him again. He blames himself for daring him to go into the forest." She revealed.

Max laughed at this before thanking her. She wished him luck and wondered just how much the teenager had recovered if he was already strong enough to return home. She'd have to keep an eye on Nathan to make sure that he didn't withdraw into his own mind again.

Tom, however, had always been able to analyse her son's behaviour, recognising if he was having trouble. He would be able to help him.

She continued to prepare tea while listening to the radio, tuned for the local news. An announcement caught her attention; it looked like a small family of tourists had been reported missing. The last place that they'd been seen was the outskirts of the forest and nothing had been heard from them since.

Tom had come close to being another missing person. How had he managed to get out when so many other people had been lost?

The next morning, Nathan got another surprise. He was playing with Hope in the back garden, the labrador bounding after the tennis ball excitedly. She would check in with him every time she returned, touching him on the leg and letting him know she was there.

His mum called out to him from the kitchen, and he turned to listen as she leaned out through the back door. "There's someone here to see you."

Nathan was about to ask who when the shadow beside her revealed himself. He hardly recognised his best friend.

The dark blonde hair shimmered in the sunlight as he stepped out unsteadily, using a cane for support. A glance down at his right leg revealed no cast. *That's impossible.* He thought. *There's no way he recovered that quickly.*

It was only as he drew closer that he recognised just how tall he was. Tom had always been the tallest in the school, but he now had to duck significantly beneath the clothesline.

His mum always set it to six feet tall. That meant he'd grown by quite a large amount in a short period of time.

He was immediately pulled into a hug by his best friend. Guilt and remorse overcame him; Hope, recognising his behaviour now, came over and touched his leg.

He took in a deep breath and pulled himself back to the present, addressing his friend properly, barely able to hold back the tears. Nathan had thought that he'd never see him again after what he'd dared him to do. "It's great to see you again."

His deep laugh made Nathan smile, as well as his next statement, a confirmation that their friendship wasn't over. "Same here. I've missed you. It's quite boring when you're not around."

The embrace ended and his mum called out to them. "Do either of you fancy a drink?"

"A jug of water, please." Tom answered. "An apple juice for Nathan, thank you."

He still remembered his favourite drink. The memories, however, returned, and he was overwhelmed by them, his mind withdrawing to the black void.

It took Hope nudging his hand and Tom's firm grip on his shoulder to partially bring him back to the present. There was also a strange sensation, but he couldn't figure out what it was.

"Listen to me, Nathan." Tom stated, his voice making it through to his looping thoughts. "Think back to a good memory. What do you see?"

Nathan shut his eyes and let out a sigh, trying to focus. He smiled as one of his favourite memories came to him. "I see the willow." He answered. The black void and the continuous loop of Tom fainting were replaced by the image of the beautiful tree, standing in the centre of the clearing. "We spent the whole summer working on it."

"Excellent." Tom replied. "Focus on that memory. Try and push the bad ones back."

He managed to do exactly that and opened his eyes to see the emerald irises looking down at him, analysing his behaviour. Hope was still stood beside him but recognised that he was back to normal again.

After a small touch on the leg, she went inside to get a drink, but kept looking back at him using the mirror that his mum had placed in front of the bowl.

"Thank you. I got lost in my memories again." He felt them coming back but repeated the same actions, using the willow to force his mind back to a better place. Nathan noticed that their drinks were sitting on the garden table, his mum coming out without either of them noticing.

With a smile, Tom motioned towards the bench and led the way, a hand on Nathan's shoulder constantly. He sat down slowly and watched as his friend, now too gangly to sit comfortably, somehow managed to do exactly that, pulling his legs up and sitting cross-legged so that he was facing him. *When did he become so flexible?* Nathan wondered.

In any case, he decided to ask a question that he'd been dreading, aware of Tom's arm encircling him to help ease his worries. "So how are you doing?"

"Better than ever." Tom replied. "There's someone I want you to meet. They've helped me to survive, and I think they can help you too."

Nathan was confused. He'd arrived alone; who else was he talking about? And why was he talking about them as if there were multiple of them?

At that instant, a thought came across his mind, though he knew it wasn't his own. It was an animation of a waving hand. Beneath it were words that he could almost hear.

Hello, Nathan. It's nice to finally meet you.

Chapter 28

Nathan's reaction — utter bemusement and shock — was expected, but they didn't consider just how comfortable he would be with them. To be fair, Tom had introduced them, which helped significantly.

They were surprised that they could learn so much just from a temporary connection like this. His neural structure and current health could be analysed in an instant. Nathan seemed to be quite clever too; rather than ask the question physically, he spoke to them directly using his thoughts, closing his eyes to make the connection easier to manage. 'What are all of you?'

We are a symbiotic fungus. *They explained.* ***We encountered Tom in the forest while he was recovering. He is an excellent host and we have helped him to survive by enabling him to live without worrying about his health, diet, or wellbeing. We have managed to evolve again, develop our own sentience, thanks to his assistance.***

Tom had shut his eyes as well, which enabled him to share his memories despite Nathan not being a host.

He showed exactly what he had been through in the forest, not even hiding the truth about the giant spiders that lived in it. His own mental trauma returned upon seeing everything again, but he was able to manage it, remaining calm and helping his friend to fully understand the situation.

Soon, their neural structure matched; they pulsed simultaneously as the information was shared. The fungi noticed just how stable the connection was, though they worried about what would happen if anyone noticed this strange behaviour. **The mum knows how Nathan acts. Being so still like this will be quite suspicious.**

That depended, of course, on how closely she was looking, and if she was watching at the right time. The exchange of memories had only taken place in a matter of seconds. By the end, Nathan's mind showed that he understood exactly how Tom had managed to get out of the forest. He also expressed appreciation...for the fungi!

That's impossible. They thought, double-checking if it was correct. **No one should be this comfortable with the situation.** Yet it was true. Perhaps it had been due to Tom's approach, or Nathan was more open-minded than expected. In any case, it seemed that they had been accepted within Tom, seen as an integral part of him now.

They didn't know quite how to respond when Nathan spoke to them again. 'Thank you for looking after Tom. He's too stubborn to realise when he needs help.'

Tom laughed at this and shook his head, but responded with a thumbs up, recognising that he did require someone to tell him when he'd done enough. The fungi smiled and answered. **Thank you. We must admit that he's been a challenge for us, but we now know how to work with him amicably.** Nathan let out an audible laugh at this and expressed appreciation again.

'Is this connection permanent or just temporary?' Nathan asked.

Only for as long as Tom touches you. He hasn't let go of your shoulder for that reason. They replied. **The choice is yours if you wish to become a host. We do not force anyone to accept us. We require consent if it is to become a permanent bond.**

'Well, I'd like it to be a permanent one. I've seen how you helped Tom and I know that you can be trusted.' Nathan stated. 'Do I need to do anything to help you?'

All we need is your consent. They answered. **Would you like Hope to be a host as well so that we can manage her health and wellbeing?**

Hope, his new dog, had been laid beneath his legs throughout their talk, waiting just in case help was needed and touching him constantly. They hadn't made any connection – permanent or temporary – as they preferred permission first. Nathan's response was expected. 'Yes please.'

They understood and began to create the permanent connection between themselves, Nathan and the dog. Its DNA was quite complex but still simple when compared with the genetic information of humans. It didn't take long for them to become new hosts, both with lots of potential and a happy future ahead of them. No major changes were needed either; only the connection with Tom was enabled. They could manage their health automatically.

Tom watched as the fungi added his friend as a new host.

The strong connection was allowing him to monitor everything, though he wasn't getting too involved. This agreement needed to be arranged between the fungi and Nathan.

Sharing his memories had been a spontaneous decision that proved to be deciding factor for his friend. He felt the permanent connection as it developed, allowing him to be able to sense Nathan's health and mental state. The fungi had already begun working on his neurons to help with the traumatic memories, just as they had done with his.

A third connection also appeared. It looked like the dog would also be a host, though it was expected.

The spores struggled to do this; they hadn't bonded with anything else for a while. They managed to figure out its – her – DNA easily and create the bond quickly.

Tom waited until the process was complete before opening his eyes, removing his hand from his shoulder. His friend withdrew from the mental conversation, looking around in surprise; it looked like the fungus had improved his vision.

A few seconds later, he let out a sigh and turned to him again. Tom could see the golden spores floating across his pupils. The irises were still the same colour, but showed faint golden lines, a sign of being a host. His dog shared this; the blue eyes were speckled with gold particles.

Nathan's voice, when he spoke next, showed that he was concerned and worried about what had been revealed. It was the first time that Tom had told him the truth about what was really in the forest. "Why didn't you tell me that the forest was already occupied?"

He shrugged. "Would you have believed me?"

Nathan shook his head and let out a little laugh. "Probably not." He leant back, relaxed now. "I haven't introduced Hope yet, have I?"

"I ended up seeing some of your memories as the connection grew. I saw glimpses of your first meeting and walk." He reached down and allowed the labrador to smell him. She knew him now, of course, and pushed her nose against his hand. "It's almost as if she's always been here."

"Of all the things that I thought my mum would be capable of, I didn't think getting a dog was a possibility. She usually hates them but appears to have a soft spot for Hope." Nathan reached down and stroked her head, not for comfort, but to ensure that she was nearby. "She brought me back from a bad place where I struggled to pull myself back to the present."

Tom nodded, understanding how much she'd helped his friend. "How about we go for a walk? A bit of exercise might do us good." He motioned with his hand towards the kitchen, where Nathan's mum was busy making lunch. "And we don't end up saying anything that could worry your mum."

Nathan agreed and they went through the kitchen, letting her know that they'd be back shortly. The town, currently quiet and balmy, was the perfect place for having a serious discussion.

It was his friend who began. "I saw a glimpse of your thoughts too as the connection formed. Are you seriously planning on speaking with..." He struggled to say White Spikes' name. "...that thing again?"

"He's acting like a guardian." Tom revealed. "He could have just bit me, but he helped me to get out instead.

The memory of my mother is helping, but he's slowly becoming more human as each day passes."

"So why the sudden growth? Nathan asked. "The last I saw, you'd only grown a little bit. Now you'd be a good fit for a basketball player!"

"You saw the reason why during the memories. My body is overproducing growth hormone. The only way to bring the level down is to use it up." He paused, swapping the cane to the other hand. It helped him to maintain his balance. "I'm not done yet either. I need to find a way to restore the cells, but the fungi can only work with my DNA right now. Maybe in the future they'll be able to figure out how to replace the cells again."

Nathan laughed at this. "Knowing you, it'll be another few inches before you solve it. The fungi will look after you and make it so you can manage the growth without any major problems."

Tom considered this. *What if I never stopped growing?*

Elephants only remained at a certain height due to the effect of gravity. The tallest man had reached over eight feet tall and had agonising medical conditions.

He pulled his mind back to the present, focusing on walking as he almost fell. "How are you feeling now?"

The fungi's connection allowed him to sense this, but asking would help and he didn't want to be constantly prying into his mind. He'd been concerned about how Nathan had been managing over the last few days.

Tom wasn't surprised when his friend told him about how much Hope had been helping. It was concerning to see just how much guilt and remorse he had been dealing with after giving him the dare.

Nathan let out a sigh a second later, worry becoming obvious again. "Don't go back to the house. It's too dangerous and you know it."

"The spiders have left us alone for years now. Besides, White Spikes would warn us if the colony planned to capture us."

"Didn't you see the news this morning?" Nathan asked. His voice had risen an octave, as it usually did if he was getting worried.

"I was too busy reading a medical journal to notice what it was saying." Tom confessed.

"A family of tourists just got caught." Nathan revealed. "If my assumption is correct, they're all food for those spiders now. If you're not careful, you might join them."

He was right.

A chilling thought crossed his mind as he considered Nathan's words.

The fungi were clever and manipulative. What if they were simply making the spider a guardian until he'd achieved his full potential for food? Being friends with the two of them would make them easy to catch while unaware and defenceless.

Tom put this concern aside as they continued the walk, but he could sense the spores within his body going over hypothesis and using the connection to get an idea of what the spider's thoughts were currently. He could only hope that the spider was being genuinely friendly rather than faking it.

It's no surprise why they're friends. *They thought, appreciating how close the teenagers were.* **They're both quite clever too.**

The warning from Nathan was unexpected, but interesting to consider. They decided to run through some theories as Tom walked back. **Let's take this a step at a time.** *The fungi told themselves.* **What do we know about the spiders at the colony?**

Well, for one, they survived off blood and required high quality food twice a day. They were intelligent and the spores within White Spikes had already proven to be quite manipulative. The spider had gone from loyalty to the colony to thinking about the two humans in an instant!

What would be his motive for keeping Tom unbitten? *They wondered.* **Is it so he can reach his full potential?**

*Or...they realised a second later **...was it for a malicious reason?***

Right now, Tom was an excellent host.

His taller height meant he contained a lot of blood, and he didn't need to eat much to survive. Due to replacing his cells rather than allowing them to die naturally, he'd be able to survive for years as a blood bank, able to return to good health quickly.

Let's see what White Spikes is thinking about. *They decided.* **It should be Tom's decision if he wants to meet him again or not.**

The spider was still at the colony; his thoughts were calm and relaxed, with no sign of plans or malicious intentions. They shared this information with Tom, who let out a sigh. He'd already partially dismissed his own concerns but still appreciated the information.

'I still think that we can trust him.' Tom spoke to them as they walked back to the house. They weren't surprised at the inclusion of 'think'. His own doubts were returning as he fully realised the enormity of the situation. 'There's a chance that this is all a ploy, but I want to stay in contact. Despite the danger it puts us in.'

Agreed. *The fungi responded.* **We like catching up with his spores. Talking with them was nice but being able to fully sync with them will be better.**

Tom let out a long sigh as he replied, though he quickly explained his lapse in concentration to Nathan, who nodded in understanding. 'It's strange. I know that he's dangerous, but I miss him sometimes. Is it due to how the spores create a loyalty between each other?'

Yes and no. *Even the fungi were confused why the connection between the spider and their human host had become so intrinsic.* **Your situation is different. He is your guardian in the forest. Hopefully he will always be there to protect you. We will be around just in case.**

'Thank you.' *Tom replied.* 'I still trust him not to do anything malicious. I've already arranged to meet up with him tomorrow afternoon.'

It had been Tom who suggested the meeting; the spider had been as curious to catch up as the teenager. **The risk is there, but it is manageable. We would be happy to see the spider again. The choice, however, is up to you.**

There was no hesitation as he replied with a thumbs up and animation of a coffee. Doubts still lingered in his mind, but he pushed them away.

Tom is too stubborn to listen to reason sometimes. *They admitted.* **White Spikes considers both these humans as friends now.** *An image of the golden spores within the spider, however, made them reconsider this idea.* **We will need to persuade them that Tom is worth being left alone. They will see him as an easy meal.**

Chapter 29

The town had been around for over forty years, but most of its buildings were townhouses, semi-detached or terraced along countless streets. On the outskirts, however, was a recent build that still annoyed many of the residents.

The large mansion had been built by a rich couple twenty years ago. They had bought up the entire estate and bulldozed the small forest in the centre to create the foundation for the mansion. The semi-wild fields, filled with wildlife, had been flattened for large gardens, flowerbeds, and a swimming pool. The debris from the building work had run into the town and large swathes of roads and gardens had been nothing but mud for an entire month.

Complaints from residents were useless – the council was just paid off by the rich owners, and the problems continued unabated. It was only once the locals forced them to act that they got involved, fining the couple for not protecting the surroundings and having unpermitted building work done. According to rumours, they had tried to bribe the council more than a one million pounds to make this fine – and bad reputation – disappear.

Pet dogs, cats and local wildlife had always gone missing, but once the son was old enough to hunt, they began to disappear in significant numbers. All the locals knew why – and who – was hunting them down.

The son, Gideon, was brought into the school for a couple of years, but ended up being a terrible bully who threw a tantrum the moment anything went wrong, or pray tell, a teacher dared to give him a low grade. The parents eventually pulled him out and homeschooled him, which only led to a coddled, spoilt adult.

Of course, the locals had all heard the rumours from the many staff that came down for deliveries. The bad attitude of the rich owners, treating them like lower class scum, had led to almost two hundred staff quitting.

The cleaners from the son's room, however, caused widespread rumours that ruined any goodwill the family had. Boxes of skinned fur, claws and teeth had been found in Gideon's closet, trophies from successful hunts. One member of the staff, upon quitting, had brought one of the boxes with her.

The locals were shocked when its contents were revealed. Ginger fur, small teeth and a collection of bloody claws accompanied a collar.

It was the remains of a cat that had once belonged to one of the town's residents!

It had disappeared two months ago after an evening wander. The bullet hole in the fur – right on the forehead – showed that the son had hunted the animal when it came onto the mansion's grounds.

They waited until the son was eighteen years old before trying to charge him for animal abuse. The evidence – gathered by disgruntled locals and their mistreated staff – was excellent and showed that he had enjoyed 'playing' with the animals that had survived the first hit. It was shocking to see. It seemed to be exactly what the town needed to incarcerate him for numerous cases of animal abuse.

The result was disappointing. The family's lawyer – an unscrupulous man who knew how to sweet talk a jury – managed to reduce the charges to a fine and community service. It was found that the judge had been paid a bribe to dismiss much of the evidence as circumstantial, turning a ten-year sentence to only petty change and work which Gideon didn't even complete.

Ever since, the locals held a grudge. Nothing they could do would work; the father would pay off the police and had several officers under his control, preventing the many DUIs and other charges that Gideon should have received. The rich couple were vindictive too. Anyone who dared to speak up against them found slashed tires, scratched doors, and threatening letters on their doorsteps.

The son's urge to hunt – an immoral sport that disgusted many – was brought to new heights as his father paid for multiple holidays where Gideon would 'happen' upon an endangered species. He would always kill it in self-defence, despite the strange circumstances that he would need to encounter it. The most recent example, about a week before, was an endangered tiger in India. It had tried to attack the son during an elephant ride. Nothing could be done to dispute it as the father, ever so careful, paid off customs to declare the skinned fur and claws as a cougar instead.

The locals all knew the truth. The son, Gideon, was loud-mouthed and wanted everyone to know about his accomplishments. But what could they do to bring an end to this terrible family without risking their livelihoods?

When Gideon-von Heston awoke, it was morning; the sun was high the sky and the weather pleasant and sunny.

Looking out the window onto the expansive gardens, he noticed a deer grazing at the edge of the property. He eyed his favourite hunting rifle, displayed on the wall, feeling the urge to hunt it, but had been warned previously about shooting over the heads of the gardeners.

Grumbling, he went into the bathroom, where a foamy bath waited. One of his servants had just finished it, knowing when he awoke. Stepping in, he found that the temperature was slightly off, annoying him even further.

He checked which staff member was on rotation for his room today. He'd make sure to make her shift the worst it possibly could. Every single one of them knew that he needed the bath to be perfect to enjoy it.

After a long soak – during which he played with the foam, moulding animals, and then crushing the bubbles in his hands – he changed into pyjamas and left to go down for breakfast. The cleaner immediately entered to wash down the bathroom. He snorted as he remembered how messy he'd left it today. It would serve her right.

His mother and father were in the dining room, enjoying a late brunch, when he entered. Gideon went over to hug each of them, giving his mother a kiss on the cheek, before sitting down and ringing the bell, hungry.

The waiter entered and set down an English breakfast with quail eggs and black pudding. Gideon stared at it, his temper returning. "I don't want this!"

The man swallowed and spoke to him cautiously. "I'm sorry, sir. What would you prefer for your breakfast today?"

"I quite enjoyed the food that I had at the hotel in India." He responded. "Could the chef make some vada pav instead?"

Vada pav was a simple recipe made using bread and curried meat to create a flavourful bap. It had been a staple for Gideon before any morning hunts, keeping him satisfied until lunch.

The staff member was visibly mortified and was trying not to grimace before answering. "We don't have the ingredients to make that, sir." His voice was quiet, afraid of the backlash he might receive.

"Then make sure you get some by tomorrow!" Gideon shouted, enjoying the fear on the waiter's expression. "I'll have this because the chef knows how to poach my eggs, but it had better be vada pav tomorrow. Understood?"

The man nodded and walked out of the dining room warily after setting down a glass of red wine. It was similar to how dogs ran with their tails between their legs. His father spoke to him as he devoured breakfast, starving.

He was reading the local newspaper while enjoying a drink of aged whisky. "Have you heard the recent news?"

Gideon snorted at this. "They haven't shut up about the missing family all week. What else is new?"

"The locals just found out why. One of the highschoolers reported that there's a pack of wild dogs living in the forest." His father passed down the newspaper so he could see the article.

It was written by a journalist who had done an interview with a local doctor. He'd been informed by one of his patients about wild, stray dogs that killed anyone who entered the forest. A local boy called Tom Homedale had only just survived his encounter, returning badly injured after only a couple of hours in the forest.

The commoner's story was on the front page. A recent image had been included. The teenager's eyes seemed to stare at him from the paper. It had been taken during a walk in the town; the information described the injuries that he'd recovered from. Gideon seethed with anger, shaking his head, as he noticed that his successful hunt in India had been pushed to the back of the newspaper.

"Wild dogs?" Gideon asked, incredulous. "That's it?"

"You know how dangerous a pack can be if they have the numbers, darling." His mother stated, enjoying her white wine while applying nail polish. "Perhaps it's time that someone dealt with them."

He smiled widely, looking up at the wall. Mounted above the fireplace and a hunting rifle was the skinned fur of the tiger, its claws gripping the wall, and the glass eyes reflective. "May I go for a hunt tonight, father?"

"Of course, Gideon. I'll have the groundskeeper prepare an overnight bag for you." He replied. "Perhaps you could speak with the teenager who encountered them? He could give you some advice or provide directions towards their den."

Gideon rose angrily at this suggestion. "You know that I don't intermingle with poor people, father." He pushed back from the dining table, planning on stomping upstairs and getting dressed. "He does have the most direct route to get into the forest. Perhaps I'll use that derelict bit of land to get close."

His mother smiled and leaned over to give him a kiss on the cheek. "The wild dogs won't know what hit them. I'm sure that you'll be successful. Call us before you go into it so that we know you're safe, won't you, darling?"

"Of course, mother." He answered. "I saw a deer this morning at the edge of the gardens. I'm going to see if I can track where it went."

One of the waitresses entered as he left. He barrelled into her, temper still flooding his mind. *Why had his father thought that it was good idea to speak with that lower-class scum?* He smiled as she let out a cry of pain and held her shoulder. Gideon smiled as she shuddered, holding back an expletive – something that would have led to immediate dismissal – and instead collected his plate. *Serves her right. She should know not to get in my way.*

Chapter 30

That evening...

Tom Homedale settled down on the chair at the back of the house for the first stakeout in three weeks, ignoring the pain from the bruise on his arm where the blood sugar monitor had been removed.

The shotgun was next to him as normal, and the tablet was connected to all the cameras looking over the property.

He didn't need that now, though; his hearing was sensitive enough that he could hear around a metre into the trees as well as behind the house.

Max was sleeping peacefully upstairs, his snoring audible through the closed window.

Tom pulled out one of the medical journals that Dr Harris had allowed him to keep, planning to read it tonight. No foragers would be watching, which meant he had a couple of hours to chat with the fungi and relax.

Gideon's bags were packed; his hunting rifle was slung over one shoulder and spare ammo was stored in one of the pockets of his coat. He arranged for the driver to pick up him up by the front door at midnight and waited until the valet opened the door before entering the vehicle. His father and mother waved from the patio, excited to see him go off on another hunt.

It didn't take long to find the driveway that led up to the small house. He had the driver drop him off by the front door and started off, surprised by how quiet his surroundings were.

Gideon was about to step toward the forest when a deep voice made him jump. "Turn around slowly with your arms over your head so I can see them."

He let out a breath and waited for his heart to slow down before turning. It looked like the small house wasn't abandoned after all, despite its decrepit appearance.

He recognised the teenager thanks to the picture in the article. The blonde hair was darker than he had imagined, though it seemed to glitter in the lights from the house. He was taller, too; even from this distance away, he towered over the chair. A shotgun was being held up and pointed towards him.

Gideon snorted. *Surely he didn't know how to actually shoot it?*

As the commoner came closer, however, it became obvious that he had full knowledge of how to use the weapon. The safety was off and one of his fingers was around the trigger, waiting in case he made any move.

He was using a cane to walk over and seemed unsteady on his feet. Rather than stop in front of him, however, he slowly continued until he was stood between Gideon and the forest, facing sideways and listening out for any activity. "What are you doing here, Gideon-von Heston?"

"I see my reputation precedes me." He responded with a wide smile. A white lie would be suitable here. "I thought that I'd visit. You reported wild dogs living in –"

"You plan to hunt them down like you do to every pet and wild animal who steps onto your gardens." Tom stated. His accurate observation surprised him; he stared at the commoner, speechless. "I'm not going to let you."

"Someone needs to deal with them!" He shouted, his temper flaring. "Besides, they're not capable of killing people."

"They are." The teenager calmly responded. He was stood still, listening to the forest while still watching Gideon carefully.

He finally understood and grinned widely. Tom wasn't the kind-hearted teenager everyone thought he was. He was a hunter too, one who wanted to save the best kills for himself. "You just want to hunt them yourself so you can become the town's hero!"

It was this statement that seemed to make Tom angry, and he turned towards him, his expression furious. He took a step closer, still holding the shotgun, though Gideon noticed that his hands were shaking. His deep voice was quiet and echoed through the yard as he replied. "It's you who doesn't understand. They killed my mother, Gideon, and they almost killed me! I won't let anyone else die, not while I'm here to stop them."

The teenager stared down at him, several inches taller and noticeably stronger. The pupils of his eyes, reflecting the lights from the house, appeared to look red.

He waited a second, seeing how Tom would act, before realising that he was serious. There was no way that he'd be able to get into the forest with this commoner in his way. That meant he'd have to deal with him first.

Gideon made the first move. His right hand, in the pocket of his pants, was in the perfect position to grab the hunting rifle over his shoulder.

The teenager's reaction was delayed; he turned to listen to the forest and didn't notice as he struck. He used the end of the rifle to hit the right leg – one that he'd read had been broken recently – and quickly stepped closer as Tom dropped to his knees with a gasp, dropping the shotgun in shock.

Another hit – this time to the side of his head – knocked him out and he fell forward with a groan. Gideon considered leaving him like this, but he didn't know what sort of damage he'd done.

Dropping the rifle and rucksack, he leaned down, checking to make sure that he was still alive. A strong pulse was obvious, and he let out a sigh of relief. His father could get him out of assault charges but could do little for murder.

His temper returned once more. *Why didn't you just move aside?*

A memory came to him. It was during one of the years when he still attended the junior school for 'social lessons'. A nerd had held onto his lunchbox rather than giving it him; Gideon had thrown a punch that knocked him out. One of the teachers had come over and rolled the student onto his side, something that they had called the 'recovery position'.

Biting his lip, he decided to make sure that he couldn't be held responsible if the teenager suffocated while face-down like this. His first try was a failure; the commoner was heavier than he had imagined and being unconscious – a dead weight – made him even harder to move.

Red faced, sweaty and breathless, he managed to roll the tall teenager onto his side in the recovery position, placing the shotgun and cane beside him. Gideon put the rucksack and hunting rifle back on, balancing the weight so it was comfortable. He turned once to look at the unconscious teenager, smirking at his helplessness, before reassuring himself and stepping into the forest.

What the hell just happened?! *The fungi exclaimed.* *One second, Tom is in control, and then he's out cold!*

The confrontation by the other man – one that Tom had addressed as Gideon – was unexpected. Despite Tom's thoughts of disgust when he recognised him, he'd still tried to prevent him from entering the forest. It was a surprise that he was so willing to put himself in harm's way to prevent others from encountering the spiders, even for someone who he disliked so much.

We could try and infect him, but Tom wouldn't like that. *They recognised. They watched his memories of what he knew of this spoilt man – and were disgusted too.* *Killing animals for fun? Wildlife we can understand, but the locals' pets too?!*

Tom's voice came through to them in his mind. Although unconscious, he was still able to connect to them. 'Ow. What just happened?'

Gideon knocked you out so he could hunt down the 'wild dogs'. *The fungi explained.* *How are you feeling?*

'Considering the situation, pretty good. Head is pounding though, and the leg will have a massive bruise on it tomorrow.' *He replied.* 'I thought about just stepping aside and letting him walk in, but I thought better. I don't want to see anyone else end up like my mother.'

It was brave thing to do. If the parents do kick up a fuss, at least you can explain that you did everything possible to try and stop him. *They replied with a small laugh.* **It's time that you rest. You took a bad hit. We'll manage the pain if you want to dream.**

'Thank you.' *Tom accepted their hint that he needed time to recover and allowed his senses to fade. Gideon had rolled him into a comfy and safe position, but still didn't care enough to make sure that he was protected. If any foragers passed by and saw him in this condition, he'd be next on the menu.*

Honestly, they never expected to see the coddled man again. Gideon was too confident and oozed with bravado from the few thoughts they'd seen. The glimpses they saw of what he planned to do with the wild dogs...it made them shudder. Perhaps this is what he deserved after everything he'd done.

Chapter 31

Gideon's mind still expressed some doubt about his plan, considering the warning that the commoner had given him. *Is this really a good idea?* It was an hour later when he remembered that he needed to call his mother and let her know that he'd entered the forest.

He tried to call but it went through to her answering machine. "Hello, mother. I made it into the forest, but the teenager tried to stop me, so I had to knock him out to get in." He paused, shutting his eyes, remembering the moment he'd swung the rifle at the common's head. He smiled victoriously; he'd deserved it for trying to stop him. "I shouldn't be long. The wild dogs aren't a major threat. I'll call once I've completed the hunt."

Gideon hung up and focused on the trek into the forest now that his promise was complete. It was surprising just how dark and claustrophobic it felt; he pulled his jacket together and shivered involuntarily.

Doubt filled his mind, considering if he'd be able to do this. Just as quickly, however, he remembered exactly what he would be hunting.

Stupid dogs. He thought. Their instincts were wild, and he'd be able to figure out what their plan was easily.

Even police didn't enter the forest anymore for fear of 'disappearing'. He let out a snort at how cowardly they were and continued, using the flashlight to check for tracks.

It was two hours later when he noticed the white strands around him. They were large and luminous in the dark forest. Looking up, he recognised thousands of them, criss-crossing the trees and creating traps. Wild dogs didn't do this – so what would?

A cracking twig behind him made him turn, the rifle raised and ready. He didn't see what he shot, but he knew it hit; there was a crack and primal scream of pain. The bright flash blinded him for a moment before he opened his eyes again.

He just stared, open-mouthed at what he'd hunted down, in disbelief that it existed.

This human had done the one thing they'd been worried about. *The spores thought.* **Now he'd have to pay for this, mark our words!**

The spider was one of the foragers in the colony. It had been investigating after hearing strange noises and a phantom light. White Spikes had always vowed to be careful when it came to humans; they now knew why.

Had it taken the time to assess the situation first before bungeeing down, it would have discovered that the man was armed and hostile. The bullet had gone through the side of its neck, cracking the exoskeleton, and causing major internal injuries. It wouldn't be long before this host would die from the trauma.

They still had one job to do, though, and this was to infect the human and make sure they got revenge. ***All we need is for him to touch the spider's body. Then he'll be ours.***

Gideon smiled and pulled his mobile from his pocket. A victorious hunt needed a picture of the trophy for proof.

Perhaps he could cut off one of its fangs to mount it onto the wall.

No wonder the teenager had been so adamant that no one entered the forest; he knew what was out here. It was no surprise why so many people had disappeared now that he knew the truth.

He reached out and touched the body on one of its long legs, knowing the best pose for a trophy kill. The hunting rifle was leant against his side and armed just in case he needed to defend himself.

He was about to take the picture when he felt the strange sensation running up his arms, legs and eventually the rest of his body. Though it felt like pins and needles, this was worse, and he soon felt everything – but could barely move. He tried to make an emergency call but quickly realised that he was unable to do anything to get himself out of this.

Gideon's thoughts were interrupted by a single sentence that he knew wasn't his own. **Hello, human.**

*What a poisonous mind he has. The fungi thought. **He won't have much use for it any longer, though.***

They dulled his nerves to prevent him from moving. He still could, but it was slow – a plan to make him think he still had some control. It would be needed to ensure that he couldn't escape his fate.

The man spoke, his voice weak from the minor paralysis. "What are you doing to me?"

We are preventing you from running away. A fearless hunter such as yourself wouldn't run from his prey, would he? *They responded.*

Fear swept through his mind despite the assertiveness in his voice. "What are you?"

We are a fungus. One that lived within the forager you just killed. *They savoured the realisation in his thoughts, going from brave to scared in an instant.* **There is nothing you can do to stop this from happening. We are now within you.**

"I'm a human. We're the ultimate killing machine. Not that giant insect." *Gideon — they had learned his name from his memories — replied. Despite this act of bravado, the cowardice was quickly returning as he began to recognise just how bad the situation was.*

Oh, Gideon-von Heston, you have no idea how much trouble you're in. Your daddy won't be able to get you out of this.

The man smiled. He was trying to do something, and his thoughts showed a recent altercation with a man who had warned him not to come into the forest.

He used this confidence to try and wrestle back control. His left hand, holding onto his phone, slowly moved down to his side, dropping the device. "You can't stop me. If I can't run away, I'll make sure that you don't make it out alive either."

They pretended to let him — allowing him to grip the trigger with his fingers and position it against his chin — before suddenly controlling his nerves again. They let him feel every bit of pain from the awkward angle.

They didn't need to say anything for the man to realise that this was the end for him. His mind was flooded with fear. He should have listened to the man who had warned him. "No." Gideon's voice was quiet and full of desperation. "No, let me go! I want to live. I want to be with my mother and father!"

Humans have only lived on Earth for a few thousand years. *They stated, relishing his fear. They had already sent out a warning to the colony and five foragers were on the way to intercept him.* **We, however, have evolved over millions of years. We plan to keep it that way.**

The foragers arrived; the man let out a desperate scream. Usually humans would only be bitten, but Gideon's fate was far worse. The spiders wanted revenge too. They pulled him apart, making sure to do it slowly, enjoying his anguished screams.

It wasn't long before the news about the paralysed human made it to White Spikes and the colony. The message had been received by everyone at the same time. He tried to run to the location using the web walkways, accompanying several foragers, but had to slow down. He didn't want to fall off the high platforms, especially now, without a safety line.

He made his way at his own pace and used the connection from the spores to monitor the situation.

The man was panicking and let out a scream as the foragers surrounded him. They were angry; a glimpse through their eyes revealed why. A member of the colony had been killed with a single shot through the neck, courtesy of a large hunting rifle that the man held.

As the man was drawn and quartered slowly – a fate that he completely deserved –he considered something. Tom wouldn't enter the forest without permission, but what if he'd arranged this?

He arrived at the location and found a dismembered human body, as well as a warm – and very bloody – rucksack and rifle. He used a tarsal claw to pick each of them up and placed them in a web parcel on his back, planning on returning them to the disposal pile.

White Spikes was about to return to the colony when he received a message from Tom's fungi. **Could you come to the house, please? Tom requires assistance.**

Strange. It would normally be the teenager who asked for help. Something serious must have happened if it was the spores doing it on his behalf. He turned to find the foragers preparing a web hammock to carry the body with. "I will arrive back ssssshortly. I need to prepare a ssssspeech to commemorate hisssss achievementsssss."

The spiders nodded but paused, allowing him to touch one of them and absorb some of the spores from the dead colony member.

It enabled him to see both the spider's last memories as well as those from the human. White Spikes nodded in thanks before setting off to help Tom, unsure what he'd got himself into.

Chapter 32

Max had been having a great sleep when a tapping noise roused him. He opened his eyes blearily and looked at the alarm clock, confused. It was three in the morning. What had woken him up?

He turned to look at the window and let out a gasp as he saw the long leg and tarsal claw withdrawing. If it was an attempt at capture, he would be in a coma already. *What happened?* He thought, panicking.

After hastily putting on a dressing gown to stay warm, he ran downstairs and unlocked the back door. He found White Spikes in the garden, crouched down by the edge of the forest, and doing something with his legs.

Looking beneath the massive spider revealed why he'd been roused.

Tom was unconscious on the ground next to the spider, laid on his side in the recovery position. Max ran inside to grab the medical kit before sprinting out to check on him, worried and concerned.

White Spikes didn't need to say anything to explain; as soon as he touched Tom's wrist to check his pulse, he received a video in his mind that showed exactly what had happened.

The Heston family was hated in the town due to their escapades while building the mansion, as well as what the son did to all the neighbourhood pets and wildlife, both in this country and others. Tom, despite his dislike for the son, Gideon-von Heston, had tried to prevent him from entering the forest. The spoiled man wasn't happy with this response, using his rifle to knock him out.

The spores within the spider also revealed exactly what had happened to the coddled twenty-year-old, a fate that he deserved after everything he'd done over the years. Max was disgusted by what he'd planned to do with the 'wild dogs' that had been reported in the newspapers. The reveal of the death of a forager surprised him and he looked up at White Spikes sympathetically, understanding how much it would affect the colony.

The fungi within Tom confirmed that he was alright, and just needed sleep to recover. The right leg would be an issue; it would have a massive bruise for the next few days after taking a hit from the rifle. The spores' reinforcements had been essential to prevent it from breaking again.

A web parcel on the spider's back caught Max's attention. He could recognise the shape of a rucksack and a hunting rifle, as well as some scraps of material that stuck out through the strands.

Max smiled and spoke to White Spikes. "Did you collect everything that Gideon brought in with him?"

The spider nodded and smiled, seeming to realise what he was suggesting. "I can place them ssssssomewhere ssssso that the wild dog sssssstory can be believed. Do you want sssssome help moving Tom to a safer place?"

Max shook his head and rose. "He's alright where he is now. Keeping him in the same position will help when I call the police to report Gideon missing." He pulled his dressing gown tighter, feeling the chill from the early morning. "Could I come with you when you set up the remains so that I can lead officers to it?"

White Spikes grinned widely – better described as a grimace and showing off his large fangs - and motioned. Max nodded, allowing the spider to lift him up onto his back.

They set off into the forest, talking quietly. Working together as a team to cover up the death as a wild dog attack would be best for everyone involved, both for the colony and for him and Tom. It would give credibility to their story and prevent the rich parents from trying to blame either of them for their son's disappearance.

The police station had been silent all evening apart from a call at midnight reporting a suspicious vehicle driving through the town. They recognised the license plate as one of the Heston's family cars. It had continued until it reached the Homedales' house, where it had then pulled out and continued back to the mansion again.

It looked like Gideon was finally going to deal with the wild dogs that plagued the forest. The officers on the night shift had let out a relieved sigh and were focused on paperwork when a call came in.

The operator explained the situation over the radio as they drove to the address. "Report of a missing person and assault with a deadly weapon. Victim unconscious but stable. Doctor on scene." The postcode that came up on their system surprised them. The small house on the edge of the town was owned by Max Homedale and had direct access to the forest where more than twenty people had disappeared.

They arrived to find Tom Homedale unconscious in the garden, with Dr Harris knelt over him and checking his vitals. The father, Max, was waiting for them by the back door, holding a tablet and a USB stick. "Good morning, sir." They introduced themselves by name and badge number. "Could you explain what happened?"

He held out the tablet for them. "My surveillance cameras recorded everything. I've made a copy for you."

They accepted the device and clicked play, interested to find out what had occurred. They stared in shock as what the footage revealed.

Gideon was known to have a temper, but they never could have imagined him being so vicious and vindictive. The cameras had recorded the altercation both audibly and visually. The son had arrived by the side of the house and began to make his way towards the forest before being stopped by the teenager. He had approached with a shotgun raised and ready to fire, preventing him from entering the dangerous location. The conservation could be heard in the quiet garden despite how far away it took place.

It was at that point when the situation had become dangerous; Tom had turned to check that wild dogs weren't watching. Gideon had struck him using the rifle as a melee weapon. One hit would have been enough; it had immobilised him, making him drop the weapon and no longer a threat. But no, the spoiled man-child had hit him again on the head, knocking him out as he was blocking access to his prey.

The hesitation and struggle to roll him into the recovery position was done for only one reason. To prevent the assault from becoming murder due to suffocation. Even so, Gideon hadn't bothered to call for an ambulance, only striding confidently into the forest.

They doubted that the man could be recovered. No one came out of the woods alive. The officers handed back the tablet, glancing towards the foreboding forest. They touched the pistols in the holsters to reassure themselves. The parents wouldn't happy be when they found out what happened.

Concerns of what the rich and vindictive couple would do overrode their fear. They radioed in that they would be entering the forest shortly. It was a simple search to try and find any evidence or remains to make the family happy and satisfied.

Noticing their hesitation, Max offered to go with them for defence. The wild dogs had, for a long time, associated the shotgun with danger, and tended to avoid any contact with the Homedales.

They appreciated it and, thanks to his knowledge of how to follow tracks, they soon found what they were looking for. In a small clearing, only three miles in, was a large bloodstain. A bloody hunting rifle and rucksack was next to it, as well as scraps of clothing. It matched Gideon's hunting jacket from the video.

They photographed and collected all the evidence using bags, trying to hold back their paranoia in the dark forest. At one point, the officers looked up and saw reflective eyes peering at them from the trees. Max turned towards the wild dogs, making them scatter and disappear.

That's enough. We need to get out, now. One of the officers thought. They were still careful on their approach out, holding their pistols with shaking hands while Max covered them from behind. The journey felt endless, and they slowly made their way out to safety, almost getting lost on the way.

They arrived back and let out relieved sighs as the small house came into view, putting the weapons back in the holsters.

Tom was still unconscious; they took some pictures of his position, the injuries on his head and leg, and wrote down Max's statement.

Thanking him for his help, they struggled with what they would say once they arrived at the mansion. *How could they explain Gideon's actions and death to his parents?*

Chapter 33

The mansion was usually quiet during the morning, but today, all that could be heard was gunshots and crying. All the staff had been dismissed so that the parents could grieve. The mistreated servers and gardeners had decided to go down to the pub in the town to celebrate the day off.

It all went wrong for the Heston family when the police officers arrived with their condolences.

They were in disbelief that their son – their talented hunter – had failed so badly. What made it worse was that it was only wild dogs! He'd just dealt with a tiger one week before, so surely a pack of canines would have been manageable.

Of course, his father was aware of his temper, but he hadn't seen him be this violent for several years. The teenager had tried to warn his son, told him to back off, but the advice had been taken badly. Right now, if he had still been alive, Gideon would be facing assault charges, especially with how clear the evidence was.

They asked for Max's phone number – included on the witness statement – and asked how his son was doing.

Gideon's mother was shocked when she was informed that he was still unconscious but stable. They also found the missed call from the early morning and listened to the message with dumbfounded expressions.

Grief was expected after hearing news like this, as well as hearing his voice for the last time. His mother was unable to comprehend anything around her and had withdrawn into a bottle of white wine, crying inconsolably. His father, meanwhile, was outside in the gardens, taking out his anger on the hunting range.

At the same time, his thoughts whirled with theories about the reasons why the commoner had been so adamant about not letting anyone enter the forest. *What is the teenager trying to hide?* He wondered.

*The fungi had always been surprised by just how well the colony dealt with the loss of one of their own. As the body arrived back, held up by six foragers with web supports wrapped around their thorax, they smiled. **We are so happy to have a home like this.** They thought. **Especially in a spider which had so much potential.***

White Spikes had returned to the colony after arranging Gideon's belongings with Max. The man's reputation required extra care for his disappearance to be believed. The 'pack of wild dogs' was a clever idea but had meant that evidence usually disposed of was being offered back to the humans.

The spider — and Max, using a branch — had created three-toed tracks that surrounded the bloody rucksack and gun, scattering the fabric scraps around them. The bag had, unintentionally, collected a large amount of blood within, which was dumped out to create the appearance of blood splatter.

*Now, as White Spikes stood next to the dead spider and spoke with one of the medical specialists, they felt proud and happy to be here. The colony had evolved into something special within a single generation. **We can still remember when they were only an inch long, barely managing to survive.** They thought, smiling as the memories replayed.*

Funerals had been something that White Spikes had implemented after the first death of a colony member. The spores had watched as the spiders became depressed, experiencing unimaginable grief. It had been their idea to store copies of the memories so that they could be shared.

***We can only do this with White Spikes.** The spider's neurons had evolved over time, becoming more complex, and allowed him to share the memories with others easily.*

He was now thirty years old, and still going strong. The colony's consensus was that their leader was immortal, and they were right to an extent.

It was only after connecting with the human's spores that they learned how to replace cells and create backup DNA. They were now using this technique and had restored the geriatric spider to one who radiated good health and an excellent memory.

As the spider shared the memories with the last of the colony, his own children, they considered how lucky they had been to have the leader as their host. The spores in the other spiders were only just learning how to store memories and had few emotions; the only ones they could truly comprehend were happiness, grief, and anger.

No wonder the foragers had been furious when they saw the death of one of their own. They realised. **We would probably do the same.** White Spikes' range of emotions had evolved thanks to the genomes from the jailor. **He is an excellent host and is great role model for the rest of the colony.**

A moment later, they let out a sigh, going back over the memories of the Homedale family. **We will need to figure out how to deal with the two humans. They know too much.**

The forager's remembrance ceremony is going well.
White Spikes thought. He stood next to the dead colony
member, allowing the rest of the spiders to remember it
by sight and via memory.

At this point, he knew everything about how the
colony operated.

His neurons, evolved even further thanks to syncing
up with Tom Homedale's, allowed him to do things that
none of the other spiders could do. He could share the
experience and knowledge of all the colony members
who had been lost over the years, retaining their
memories in perfect detail. He did, however, need to
apply restrictions onto some of the more incriminating
ones.

Along with his own memories – which spanned back
to thirty years ago –he shared those from nine other
spiders. They came from all the areas in the colony; two
architects, two medical specialists, four foragers and one
matron.

All of them, apart from the forager who died that
morning, had passed due to natural causes or accidents.
The loss of the architects had been due to no safety line
during a fall, leading to an instant – but painless –death.
I could easily do the same if I rush while travelling

somewhere. White Spikes thought. This was the first time that a forager had been murdered.

The last of his children to receive the memories was Lilliana. The red cross on her fangs had fully developed and she belonged with the medical specialists.

Her heat vision had always been a little different, able to see deeper into the human body, and her venom was harmless, only acting as a strong painkiller. She was in the last year of school and would begin shadowing under one of the medical specialists once she finished.

She reached up and gave him a hug rather than just touching him; he shared the memories and was surprised when he received some in return. He couldn't believe it. *When did she start following me?* He thought.

He watched the memory from her point of view as he travelled towards the edge of the forest and spoke with Max. She'd been shocked at the time but now had the courage to call him out for his disloyalty.

Her thoughts showed that she seemed to understand the reason why, but it was nowhere near the truth. Her spores also connected, allowing her to watch when he had helped Max to set up the fake death scene.

Her voice was quiet as she spoke to him, ensuring that no one else heard their conservation. "I haven't told mother yet, but it might be a good idea to tell her now." She looked up at him, recognising his shock. "Could you introduce me to your new friends as well? I'd like to meet them."

He nodded without realising and she skipped away happily, exactly as the rest of the brood had done. They didn't know how privileged they were to be able to learn from the old memories of those who had passed.

Uncertainty over what he would say to Alacanta flooded his mind, but he forced these feelings back. He still had a remembrance ceremony to complete.

Alacanta was surprised when her husband called her over after burying the forager. She was led through the web walkways to one of his normal haunts, a large clearing where he didn't have to worry about his size constraints. He'd always been the biggest of the colony and struggled to get comfortable sometimes.

Lilliana had left shortly afterwards, splitting from her siblings, and was probably following them. Her curiosity had always been a problem, but she still didn't want her to see anything that could worry her. Alacanta was surprised at just how sneakily she was able to do it, unable to hear her and unsure if they were actually being followed.

He stopped and went into a crouch in the centre of the clearing. His expression was one of discomfort, and she went over to help, putting one of her legs around his thorax. "Are you okay, honey?"

His voice was different when he spoke, almost sounding regretful. "I'm sssssorry, Alacanta. I haven't been truthful with you."

This confused her. "I'm happy to talk through whatever is worrying you. I'm always here for you, you know that."

He shook his head and smiled sadly. "It isssss to do with the two humansssss at the edge of the forest. I came up with an idea for an eassssssy meal if we ever run low on food. I haven't told anyone yet."

This was new. He usually told her about any plans before implementing them. She didn't respond; he wanted to tell her this, so she allowed him without interrupting. Of all the things that she could have heard next, though, she never expected this.

"The teenager only made it out of the foresssssst thanksssss to my help."

She used a tarsal claw to hit him and almost thought about walking back to the colony, telling everyone about how he'd acted, but stopped as he looked down guiltily.

Perhaps it was worth talking to him about why he'd behaved this way.

Chapter 34

Lilliana watched from the treetop in shock. Her father had admitted it, confirming her suspicions.

Mum wasn't happy; she had slapped her father angrily, as he deserved, for hiding the truth from her. It had gone through his thick exoskeleton, a small, bleeding cut visible in her heat vision.

Her screams were audible despite how far away they were. "How could you do this to the colony? All the rules you set up! The safeguards to prevent discovery! And yet you willingly help these two humans to survive!" Her voice was shrill, the same pitch she used when yelling at her siblings.

Her father was in shock and took a few seconds to reply, his voice filled with guilt and remorse. "I have an agreement in place with them. They know to keep the colony'ssssss existence a ssssssecret. I helped them to hide the death of that human asssss a wild animal attack."

That earned another light slap from her mother. He visibly backed away at this, appearing scared. "You're a disrespectful, lying fool! So, tell me. Why is it so important that these two humans stay alive?"

"The sssssson, Tom, issssss a hossssst for the fungi. It hasssss allowed him to unlock hisssss true potential. He issssss perfect for food now." Her father admitted. "If not for Max'sssss help, police would be sssssearching the entire foressssst for the human'sssss body."

She began to reach back, to slap him again, but stopped as she fully realised what he was saying. He shrank back as she approached, her voice back to normal. Alacanta touched his face where she'd hit him before, saddened by how she had acted. "They are helping us to stay hidden."

"Yesssss." Her father confessed. "I have a...bond with the sssson. It began to develop when I bit hisssss mother two monthsssss ago. Hisssss ssssssporessssss can communicate with me. They have helped my fungi to reach another level of ssssssentience."

She narrowed her eyes at this and looked at him suspiciously. "Show me everything that's happened, or I tell everyone exactly what you've done."

With a single touch – though she could tell that her father was still in pain and fearful about what she might do to him – they became unfocused, sharing memories. Lilliana noticed that the two cuts hadn't closed yet, still bleeding out slightly.

She could leave them be, but she hated to see her father like this. She dropped down to the ground and snuck over to the two of them without being noticed.

She climbed up his thorax that she could get a good view of the cuts – two, going through the exoskeleton – and bit directly into it to apply some painkiller. Pulling some of her web taunt, she began to use the material like sutures, keeping the injuries closed.

When doing an action like this, she barely noticed her surroundings. She was surprised when she found her mother looking at her disapproving. "You've been following him, Lilliana. When did you find out?"

"A week ago." She answered, dropping off and looking up at her. "Perhaps you should see my memories as well so that you can see it from another point of view."

Meanwhile, at the edge of the forest...

Tom's recovery wasn't a peaceful one; shortly after his spores connected with White Spikes' fungi, he had seen the grisly consequences of Gideon's actions. His mind was overwhelmed, and it took a long time to push the memories back and focus on good ones.

He awoke abruptly with a scream at the back of his throat, the moment of being drawn and quartered returning, as if he was the one experiencing it.

Unintentionally, he tried to kick out to protect himself, losing his balance and dropping off the edge of the sofa. He hit the floor with a gasp, the blankets tangled around him, twisting his legs into uncomfortable positions.

He was coming to his senses when he recognised a voice beside him and a hand on his shoulder. It was Dr Harris. "You're alright. Breathe in slowly and deeply."

Tom did exactly that and opened his eyes slowly, finding himself looking down at the rugged carpet of the living room.

The memory of being within the web cocoon a month ago filled his mind as his body recognised the blanket twisted around his legs. Focusing on a good memory, he forced his fear away and rose to his knees slowly, unwrapping the material.

There were audible clicks as he lifted himself back onto the sofa, the joints in his legs moving back to their normal positions. Max and Dr Harris helped as he did, finding himself weak and struggling to focus due to aches and pains.

He continued to breathe slowly as he contorted his body to relieve the aches, letting out a sigh as every joint – even down to his fingers – realigned and popped back into the right alignment. His eyes were shut as he did this, with the fungi speaking to him. **It's alright, we're here for you.**

Tom appreciated their support as they reduced the efficiency of his nerves to reduce the pain. Though normally able to deal with it, his neurons were currently overwhelmed and unable to initialise the pain tolerance that was usually active.

He opened his eyes again and found Dr Harris sat across from him with Max, a jug of water on the coffee table. The fungi informed him that he was very dehydrated. *Thank you. It's not like I could have figured that out myself.* He replied sarcastically. *Sorry, a bit grumpy at the moment.* He downed the entire jug in an instant and waited for them to finish absorbing it before speaking. "What time is it?"

"It's currently three in the afternoon. You've been unconscious for fifteen hours." Dr Harris stated. "The fungi have confirmed that you're back to normal but might be a little bit weakened. The hit to your head caused a hairline fracture, so they had to repair the damage." He peered at him curiously. "How are you feeling?"

Tom may as well be honest. "Pretty weak, but at least all the aches are gone. My neurons are all overworked right now, but the spores are dealing with them." He could feel them in his mind, replacing many damaged receptors. "No headache, but I can feel a massive bruise developing on my leg. What happened after Gideon knocked me out?"

Max smiled at this. "White Spikes came to help. He woke me up at three in the morning to inform me about the situation. Of course, by that point Gideon was dead, killed by the spiders. It looks like he's got exactly what he deserved."

Tom grimaced at this statement, remembering what the spider's spores had shared with him. It had been a painful death, but one that the heartless man had brought upon himself. "What do the police know about what happened?"

"It just so happened that the cameras recorded everything." Max answered with a small laugh. "The altercation, knocking you out, and then strolling off into the forest as if he did nothing wrong. White Spikes brought everything that Gideon had carried in with him, so we staged a scene to make it look like wild dogs tore him apart."

This made Tom glance towards Dr Harris, who wasn't surprised at this reveal. "Max told me the truth about what lives in the forest this morning. I've been sworn to secrecy about it and wish you would have told me sooner."

Tom let out a sigh. "Would you have believed us?"

He let out a laugh as he replied. "Honestly, yes! If I've learned anything from dealing with the two of you, it's that the truth is often stranger than fiction."

Max let out a laugh and shook his head as Tom replied, smiling in relief. "So how are you managing with the fungi?"

Dr Harris seemed to speak with them; his concentration lapsed before he spoke. "We're working together perfectly now. They're keeping me going despite how long I work, and I've found out that I can use temporary connections to diagnose patients. It was difficult at first when they started to talk to me, but I've got used to the sensation now."

"That's good to hear. Has Max told you about our plans this afternoon?"

"Yes, and I don't agree with it." He admitted. "The decision is yours if you want to follow through with it." The man reached over and touched his arm; the spores began to communicate, and Tom showed his memories of what he knew of White Spikes.

After a moment watching, he nodded in understanding and let go with a small smile. "I'm not saying that I don't trust the spiders, Tom. I don't trust the fungi."

He was surprised to hear this, looking across at his eyes, trying to sense his thoughts. He was being truthful. "I can understand. White Spikes has the connection with me and wants to keep me safe. There's nothing stopping the fungi from changing that in an instant. It will be up to my spores to persuade them that it's worth working with us instead."

Dr Harris rose and picked up his bag. "If you need any more help, let me know." He let out a small laugh. "Or a connection away, in your case. I'd like to be updated once you finish talking with the spider, please."

"Of course, Dr Harris." Tom got to his feet slowly, using the cane to remain stable. His right leg throbbed but the replacement neurons were helping him to tolerate the pain now. "Thank you for the help."

"No worries, Tom. Have a good evening." He waved and left, walking back to his car.

Chapter 35

It didn't take long for the news about Gideon's fate – and his altercation with Tom – to spread around the entire town.

The pub, filled with all the mansion's staff, was loudly celebrating with the residents. They were surprised that the wild dogs had been able to take the experienced hunter out within a few hours of being in the forest.

Nathan only found about what happened when he returned from high school. His mum was waiting for him by the front door as he walked up, Hope beside him. The principal had allowed him to take her to lessons with him.

He was passed a bag with a lunchbox and dog food before being motioned towards the car. His mum set off up the road and Nathan was confused with her behaviour. "What's wrong, mum?"

Hope was sat in the back of the car, her harness attached to the seatbelt and laid down, watching him with concern.

"You haven't heard the news?" She asked in surprise. This intrigued him even more. "What news?"

"Gideon-von Heston is dead, killed by the wild dogs. He knocked out your friend to enter the forest. An hour ago, I received a text from Max. Tom finally awoke after being unconscious for more than half a day." She answered.

No wonder he hasn't been responding to my texts. He thought.

"That's good to know. What happened to Gideon?" He asked, concerned.

"One of the staff overhead as the police talked to his parents. The wild dogs tore him apart. Max and two police officers found some scraps of cloth and his belongings in a clearing. There were dog tracks around it as well as blood splatter." She revealed. "The pack watched as they collected the evidence too."

"And Tom?" Nathan asked, concerned.

"Unconscious in the garden in the recovery position. Gideon rolled him onto his side but didn't bother to call an ambulance for him."

They arrived at the small driveway; she went up to small house and stopped. "Call me when you want to come back, and I don't mind you staying overnight. I know how much you worry about him."

Nathan nodded, leaving the car, and opening the back door to let Hope out. "Thanks, mum. Is there enough dog food in here for tonight and tomorrow?"

"Yes, and there's a sandwich for you for tea as well. I spoke with the principal and he's happy for you to spend the day with him tomorrow if you'd like."

He nodded and bid her goodbye, watching as she left, a lump in his throat. *Why was it that Tom always ended up getting into trouble?* He stepped around the house, uncertain what he would walk into.

Nathan didn't quite expect to come into the garden to find one of the spiders waiting for him. It was monstrously large, and its red eyes stared down, analysing him. He froze on the spot, speechless, and didn't respond as it spoke to him.

To his surprise, its voice was welcoming, and he quickly became comfortable around it. "You mussssst be Nathan. We've been expecting you."

So they haven't just kept this secret to themselves then. White Spikes thought, slightly irritated. *They just had to tell others about us too!*

To be fair, Tom had forewarned them about his friend turning up, able to hear the car coming up the driveway and recognising it. Even White Spikes hadn't heard it despite the quiet surroundings.

He accompanied Nathan as he walked over to where Tom was connecting with both Alacanta and Lilliana. He was touching both on the leg, sharing his memories, to help them understand why the other humans needed to know about them.

Nathan was still in shock but quickly became comfortable around him, which surprised him. White Spikes' own spores, however, were having a heated argument with Tom's fungi.

It was understandable, but he hoped that they could reach an agreement. He preferred to work with these two humans rather than having to continually be on edge around them. The spores, he knew, could change his loyalty in an instant.

All it took was a nudge from the fungi to make him change his mind and intentions.

You've not just threatened your own fungi's existence but ours! White Spikes' fungi shouted, angry with Tom and his spores. *What if they tell anyone about the colony?*

They both agreed to keep it a secret, and we know that they can keep it. *They answered.*

'Nathan is my best friend, and I hate having to lie to him.' *Tom added, his mental voice seeming to quiver with uncertainty. The memories of his friend, and what he had experienced, floated in his mind. At the same time, he was sharing all the important parts of his life with Alacanta and Lilliana, preferring everyone to be fully informed.* 'The only other person who knows about them is Dr Harris, and he's aware of them for an important reason.'

Which is? *They struggled to hold back their anger; White Spikes had noticed the argument and was letting them figure it out without interrupting.*

He's the lead doctor at the hospital and is a host to the fungi as well. *The spores confessed.* **If anyone comes in with incriminating injuries like bites after encountering a forager, or officials find a body, he can cover it up and claim it as a wild dog attack instead. He can ensure that any tests are altered to hide venom or suspicious chemicals.**

They were beginning to understand how the human and the spores worked together so well. **We still would have preferred to be asked first before you made any decisions like this, Tom.** *The fungi stated.* **Can you let us know if you have to tell anyone else about the colony?**

'I will, and I'm very sorry about causing all this. I intended to tell you yesterday, during the night, but got lost in a medical journal.' *He admitted.* 'And then...' *He* paused, struggling to continue, his voice desperate. 'Then, everything went wrong.'

Gideon came into the picture. *They finished.* **Why didn't your spores tell us when they connected so you could get help?**

We were worried about Tom and completely forgot about it. *The spores stated.* **We couldn't connect much after he got knocked out anyway. His neurons were overwhelmed, and we struggled to stabilise him. A hit like that would have killed anyone else. It's why he needed fifteen hours to recover.**

This surprised Tom; he hadn't thought that the damage had been that bad, only a hairline fracture being reported. His spores were sharing their own memories with him from his long recovery, detailing the struggle they experienced to make sure he would be able to survive. 'I didn't know it was that bad. No wonder I felt so weak when I woke up!'

The humans are not worth biting. None of them are. They will all provide a service that can help the colony to maintain its secrecy. *White Spikes' spores thought privately.* **Max was essential to hide Gideon's death as a wild dog attack. It went against all the rules but prevented further police searches.**

Despite this decision, they needed to set up boundaries over what would happen in the future. Any agreements needed to be pre-arranged and abide by what each side wanted.

Tom and his fungi had gone silent, communicating privately. They waited until they were focused on the conservation before speaking to the two of them.

We are all in unique situations. *They began.* **The discovery of one spider will lead to the colony dying, while finding the fungi will, inevitably, cause all your hosts to be quarantined. Even those who don't know about us yet.**

'We know what we want.' *Tom replied with a small laugh.* 'We want to live together peacefully without worrying about our health and wellbeing. The other hosts want the same but don't have a partnership like we do.' *Memories from all the other hosts, medicals specialists and a surgeon, were being shared using the spores' connections.* 'What would you like to happen with White Spikes and the colony?'

The fungi smiled as they answered this. **Perhaps working with these humans would be more beneficial than they'd first thought.**

Lilliana had always been an inquisitive spiderling, but now she was insatiable, badgering Tom's father as the teenager seemed to have an internal discussion, his eyes shut and stood in the garden like a statue.

Alacanta watched the meeting with interest. She knew all about these two humans, of course, but meeting them like this – personally rather than from a distance – was a happy surprise. The way that they worked with their fungi was unexpected, but it was the teenager that truly astounded her.

Tom's bond with the fungi had reached new heights and they worked together as a team, but still seemed to have their own approach to problems. Right now, she could sense a discussion going on. Tom, his spores, and her husband's fungi were having a conservation.

White Spikes' behaviour had always been stranger than the rest of the colony. Now she knew why. All those years ago, when he had first encountered the derelict house, he had been identified as an individual with high potential. He had a high compatibility with human DNA and had been able to utilise it to become a perfect host for the evolved fungi.

The teenager reached a happy consensus and withdrew from the mental plain where he was discussing something, opening his eyes and almost falling. Alacanta reached out with a leg, touching his shoulder and helping him to stay upright. "Are you alright?"

"I'll be okay. When I go too deep into my own head, I start to lose the feeling in my body." Tom answered. He bent his arms behind his back and stretched, moving them into positions that no human should be able to achieve. Despite this, there was no pain; instead, he seemed to be relieved.

"When did you tell Nathan about us?" Alacanta asked, curious.

"Two days ago. I intended to tell White Spikes about it yesterday, but everything went wrong, and I was unable to connect and let him know about it." He finished contorting himself, purposely dislocating his shoulders. The loud *pop* as it went back into position was audible across the garden. "Max was the one to tell Dr Harris. He took the news quite well considering how shocking it would have been to anyone else."

Lilliana noticed their conservation and skipped over, dropping one of her legs over Tom's shoulder, making the teenager jump out of his skin. "Sorry, I just noticed that you were back with us, and I have so many questions!"

Alacanta laughed at how happy her daughter was and left the two of them alone, talking rapidly with each other. She walked over to where White Spikes was talking with Nathan, the other teenager who had turned up randomly and with a dog. It was sat beside him attentively, not caring about the giant insects around it.

It was also a host for the fungus; the spores were currently calming the animal down.

She tapped White Spikes' shoulder and motioned towards the energetic spiderling, who was now questioning why Tom needed a cane and how he had made it. Alacanta had always loathed humans, more so since the murder of the forager, but could sense no malice from either the Homedales or their friend. "I have a suggestion, honey."

He turned towards her with some hesitation. White Spikes was still a little jumpy, and had been since their argument in the clearing, though she had apologised for her actions. "What isssss it, dear?"

She smiled as she responded, surprising herself by saying exactly what was in her mind, though a worrying thought crossed it. She was uncertain how to ask Tom for help. The colony was managing quite well but would struggle in the future, and help was desperately needed. "I was thinking about asking if the three of them would like to visit the colony."

He smiled at her, relief obvious in his expression. "I was going to suggest the same. I'm sure that Lilliana would love to show Tom around. It is dangerous, however, so it would have to be their decision."

They were surprised when a simultaneous agreement echoed in the garden. All three of them – Max, Tom and

Nathan – had heard what they were saying and were interested, replying without hesitation.

Chapter 36

Tom heard the conservation across the garden as well as via the spores, along with the mental concern, though he knew that she'd ask when the time was right. He sensed Max and Nathan's intrigue through their fungi. They had heard the spiders' talk too, and were waiting for the right moment to agree.

The two spiders were staring at them in disbelief. "But it's too dangerous! If anyone were to figure out what we were doing, you'd all be bitten!" Alacanta, White Spikes' wife, was in shock at how quickly they had answered.

"I don't care." Max stated, his voice quiet. "I've been curious about the colony for years. I don't want to miss the chance to see it."

Nathan spoke next. "It's not like anything will happen to us. The spores will ensure that we can stay hidden. My school uniform is completely black, so we'll be invisible to most of the colony anyway."

Tom was the last to speak, Lilliana still holding onto his shoulder and communicating with his fungi. His deep voice echoed across the garden, and he was smiling, his eyes reflective. "I've seen the colony through your memories, but not with my own eyes. And I know exactly how to get there without anyone getting suspicious."

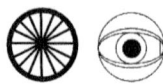

The forest was silent and there was no sign of movement on the ground or in the trees. Looking down at the canopy, there were no obvious differences either. There was a reason for that. One that no one knew apart from the spiders and three humans.

Over the years that they had lived here, White Spikes had identified a way of travelling which allow spiders to reach a location quickly without alerting any prey. That was exactly what the six of them were using to sneak into the colony.

Hope, however, would be a problem in the quiet forest, and difficult to hide. The dog was now settled inside the small house, waiting for the return of its owner patiently.

Of course, it wouldn't make sense to have the humans walking beside them. The distance was too far, and foragers used these networks to check on traps throughout the day.

So they had done exactly what Tom had suggested. All three of them were now being carried by the spiders on their backs, using the gap between their thorax and abdomen to stay hidden.

There was only enough space for one human to fit into the small gap on White Spikes or Alacanta, and far less for Lilliana's exoskeleton. That meant that only two of them could go to the colony. That was, until Tom reminded them of one fact which made it possible for someone to fit in the tiny gap.

He was able to fold himself away easily thanks to how flexible he was.

The gangly teenager was now encircling that gap, creating a perfect circle. His legs were wrapped around a web strand and his head came up on the left side of her body, touching his own thighs from the awkward position. The fungi had quickly improvised even better flexibility, relaxing his spine so that he could go into it without causing himself any issues.

The humans just watched as they scuttled down the web walkways carefully, Lilliana at the front and skipping along while the husband and wife was talking to each other. Their fungi were communicating constantly throughout the walk, though Max and Nathan, tired, had fallen asleep, comfy and safe.

Tom was too excited – and uncomfortable – to sleep. This position, though possible, stretched his body to the limit and he could feel every inch of his limbs, back and chest aching as the spiderling hopped along the web walkway.

He'd been surprised as the spiders suddenly went into a vertical position, climbing a tree and going towards the canopy. No wonder they could sneak up on their prey without being noticed. They used secret pathways to travel throughout the forest. The routes were well hidden, with entrances to the web roads made from the branches of the trees. These had been trained over the years by foragers.

The interior of the web walkways was impressive to see. The strands which made up these gigantic structures were braided together both lengthwise as well as horizontally, creating a strong surface tension that could manage the weight of these spiders. It was only barely wide enough for White Spikes, who struggled to see them and had to depend on touch. A safety line was always attached to prevent injury.

This was a mixture of the architects – building specialists – and foragers working together. It was the equivalent of the tarmac roads that humans built for their cities.

The fungi spoke to him. **You're sounding like a spider again, Tom.**

He smiled and replied with a mental laugh. *Sorry. Being so high like this, seeing this new perspective...it's amazing. And no one else could have fit on Lilliana like this.*

Are you in any pain? They asked.

Just a little bit of an ache, but I can tolerate it. I'm more worried about if I can put myself back together after this!

They laughed at this comment – for several seconds – and replied with the image of a sarcastic expression and a statement that made Tom guffaw. **You'll be able to get to yourself back to normal. It's not like you couldn't figure out how to do it yourself.**

Lilliana noticed his laugh and spoke to him quietly. "Are you talking with your spores?"

"Yep. Sometimes my thoughts become more spider than human. They remind me each time."

"It's amazing to see how easily you work with them."

Tom smiled and thought back over how much they had helped him over the last three weeks.

He was about to respond when White Spikes spoke, reaching up and rousing Max as Alacanta woke Nathan up. "We are getting close to the colony now, and some of the brood have heat vision. The best way to avoid detection from them will be to mimic our temperatures.

It will act as a camouflage and keep you all warm. The colony is high and has a chilly breeze."

He knew what to do next and asked the fungi to do something that felt unnatural. He willingly requested that they increase his temperature to match Liliana's. Essentially, Tom intentionally caused himself to go into a fever.

It didn't feel strange to him when he felt hotter than normal. Perhaps it was due to watching White Spikes' memories. Being this temperature helped; the bitterly cold wind that came through the walkways would only become worse as they climbed higher, especially in an open area.

There was only one problem. His resources were limited, and they were currently focused on keeping him warm rather than repairs or reducing aches. His entire body became painful, the nerves unable to keep up with the unnatural position.

Tom let out a slow breath and waited until the fungi reduced the efficiency of his neurons before opening his eyes and monitoring how Max and Nathan was doing.

Their fungi had noticed what he was doing, and both had completed the alteration without much trouble. They didn't need to survive off recycling glucose though.

Chapter 37

Max was excited as he finally caught sight of the colony for the first time. He looked upwards as the spider motioned his family forwards, beginning the trek up a web walkway across a large clearing. It was freezing cold up here; only the hotter temperature was keeping him warm, though he worried about Tom. From what he'd felt from his spores, the spiderling's core body temperature was even hotter than White Spikes.

His new diet, though efficient for normal use, wasn't designed for extensive energy use in a short period of time. It wouldn't be long until he'd need some water to regain more energy again. Hopefully there would be a good place for them to rest until he was energized enough to continue. The pain tolerance wouldn't be of any use either; if anyone stepped on him, especially in that twisted position, it would be very painful.

White Spikes was struggling on the web walkways. His large size, as well as his heat vision, meant that he couldn't see the web strands. He was dependent on touch to feel where he was going and if it was safe.

Lilliana was fine, skipping along ahead of them, thanks to being half his size, but had still attached a safety line of fine white web that floated in the breeze.

Another spider suddenly appeared beside him, and he stayed still. Any movement would reveal him. It was smaller than White Spikes; strange colouration on its fangs confused him before he remembered what the spider had told him. Each specialist developed their own colours to dictate their role at the colony. Foragers, it appeared, had blue patterns going up their fangs.

Its vision was the same as the rest of the colony, limited to primary colours, so it would be easy to remain invisible to this individual. Max watched as it held out a web line to the struggling leader. "Hold onto this as you go. It connects straight up the trunk. We know you have more trouble with the walkways than the rest of us, sir."

The pronunciation was different with the one, lacking the hiss when using the letter 's' and easier to listen to. White Spikes knew him; he accepted the safety line with a sigh. "Thank you. If any of you have time during your patrolsssss, could you keep an eye out for pebblesssss or rocksssss? I want to attach them to the edgesssss so I can sssssee them properly."

"That's a great idea. I'll inform the rest of the foragers to be on the lookout, sir."

"I appreciate it, thank you."

"How long will you and the family be visiting the colony, sir? You had plans for a family hike this evening and the weather is perfect tonight."

"Only a few minutesssss. We want to make sssssure that the brood are behaving themssssselvesssss at the nursery. Perhapsssss we will have a wander and catch up with othersssss. Lilliana is too ssssssneaky for her own good, sssssso sssssome one-on-one time will be appreciated." White Spikes responded.

"Only because you're holding me back at school!" Lillliana called from the front of the group, skipping along the web walkway carefully.

The forager laughed as it reached out and gave the spider a comforting pat on the thorax, barely missing Max's jumper. "She's a mischievous one, that's for sure. She will be great as a medical specialist, sir." It began to set off, but it suddenly stopped and asked a query, several webbed bundles on its back moving, as it turned on the bungee line. "Rumours have spread that the humans are back. Did you see them?"

White Spikes nodded at this, and began to explain, using the white lie that Max had told him to say to avoid suspicions. "They are both in bed and will not be any trouble. One of the neighboursssss is doing a ssssstakeout instead." He paused, appearing reflective, as planned. "They will be difficult to capture now. There isssss enough food in the storagesssss for the next few yearsssss, so it isssss not a concern."

The spider passed something down; peeking out the corner of his eye, Max noticed that the web parcel was small, probably a fox or a sheep. The fields around the forest were a common target for the spiders when it came to food. Most of the farmers avoided leaving the herds or flocks in the closest fields, wary of the sudden disappearances of their cattle.

The spiders were careful to only take one or two at a time; any more than that and an investigation may begin. "Something that I caught on the way back. I was saving it for my brood, but maybe yours will appreciate it more."

It was that exact moment when everything went wrong for Tom. The hotter temperature, lack of energy and awkward position had created a difficult situation. His entire body ached, and he was struggling to stay awake.

It was during one of Lilliana's energetic skips that he lost his balance, losing his grip on the web strand. He let out a desperate gasp and suddenly dropped from the gap where he'd been hidden, barely able to hold onto the strand and finding himself hanging below her.

He bounced lightly in the air, over the edge of the walkway, held up only by the woven web above a dark void. He shut his eyes and let out a breath, trying to focus despite the pain in his body. A minute seemed to pass before he opened his eyes, breathing slowly and in agony. Every joint was dislocated, and his spine felt like it was on fire.

The entire colony was silent; even the nursery had gone quiet. Every spider was staring at him in shock as Lilliana trembled fearfully. The forager next to White Spikes smiled and dropped onto the walkway, a hungry look in its eyes, as the large leader looked on, speechless.

Crap! Tom thought to himself, trying to hold on with his remaining strength. *What do we do now?*

A quick sample from Web of Deceit and Lies (Book 2)

Duncan looked at the manufacturing illustrations in the pamphlet and saw no problems. That was, until he saw what the mattresses and pillows were made of.

Artificial spider silk? He thought, shocked.

He carried a pillow into the lounge and looked at it in confusion.

It wasn't heavy. In fact, it felt light as a feather, and was lined with a fabric cover.

Did the inside of the pillow match what they were claiming?

Veronica spoke to him. "I'm interested in what it's made of as well. It wouldn't be the first time that Ricardo bought something that a company was lying about."

"I've been looking into this company already, Mrs Heston, and there's nothing that looks out of sorts." Duncan admitted. "I need to look inside the cover to check the contents. Can I cut it open to check?"

The Hestons nodded and passed over a pair of scissors.

It was thick, but Duncan managed to make it through, and the contents were revealed.

Translucent threads, braided together into an intricate design.

Is it actually made of what they claim? Duncan thought, reaching in to feel it.

Printed in Great Britain
by Amazon

52424938R00195